"From now on, I don't let you out of my sight, lady."

Quinn stared at her. "And if I think you've finally told me the truth I'll go to the wall for you."

There was no mistaking the unwavering conviction in Quinn McGuire's words.

"Why?" Jane whispered. "Why would you do that for me?"

"Because that's what having a bodyguard means, up to and including dying for you, if that's what it takes. But you have to be straight with me. What is it you're hiding?"

Jane gazed at the impassively silent man in front of her.

He'd just said he'd die for her. Even though she couldn't remember her past life, she knew no one had ever made such a vow to her before. And all he asked in return was her trust. She shook her head, her expression tortured. Would Quinn still go to the wall for her, when he learned her most closely guarded secret?

Dear Harlequin Intrigue Reader,

Welcome again to another action-packed month of exceptional romantic suspense. We are especially pleased to bring you the first of a trilogy of new books from Rebecca York's 43 LIGHT STREET series. You've loved this author and her stories for years...and—you ain't seen nothin' yet! The MINE TO KEEP stories kick off this month with *The Man from Texas*. Danger lurks around every corner for these heroes and heroines, but there's no threat too great when you have the one you love by your side.

The EDEN'S CHILDREN miniseries by Amanda Stevens continues with *The Tempted*. A frantic mother will fight the devil himself to find her little girl, but she'll have to face a more formidable foe first—the child's *secret* father.

Adrianne Lee contributes a terrific twin tale to the DOUBLE EXPOSURE promotion. Look for *His Only Desire* and see what happens when a stalker sees double!

Finally, Harper Allen takes you on a journey of the heart in her powerful two-book miniseries, THE AVENGERS. *Guarding Jane Doe* is a profound story about a soldier for hire and a woman in desperate need of his services. What they find together is everlasting love the likes of which is rarely—if ever—seen.

So join us once again for a fantastic reading experience.

Enjoy!

Sincerely,

Denise O'Sullivan
Associate Senior Editor
Harlequin Intrigue

GUARDING JANE DOE

HARPER ALLEN

HARLEQUIN®

TORONTO • NEW YORK • LONDON
AMSTERDAM • PARIS • SYDNEY • HAMBURG
STOCKHOLM • ATHENS • TOKYO • MILAN • MADRID
PRAGUE • WARSAW • BUDAPEST • AUCKLAND

ISBN 0-373-22628-4

GUARDING JANE DOE

Copyright © 2001 by Sandra Hill

Visit us at www.eHarlequin.com

Printed in U.S.A.

ABOUT THE AUTHOR

Harper Allen lives in the country in the middle of a hundred acres of maple trees with her husband, Wayne, six cats, four dogs—and a very nervous cockatiel at the bottom of the food chain. For excitement she and Wayne drive to the nearest village and buy jumbo bags of pet food. She believes in love at first sight because it happened to her.

Books by Harper Allen

HARLEQUIN INTRIGUE
468—THE MAN THAT GOT AWAY
547—TWICE TEMPTED
599—WOMAN MOST WANTED
628—GUARDING JANE DOE

Don't miss any of our special offers. Write to us at the following address for information on our newest releases.

Harlequin Reader Service
U.S.: 3010 Walden Ave., P.O. Box 1325, Buffalo, NY 14269
Canadian: P.O. Box 609, Fort Erie, Ont. L2A 5X3

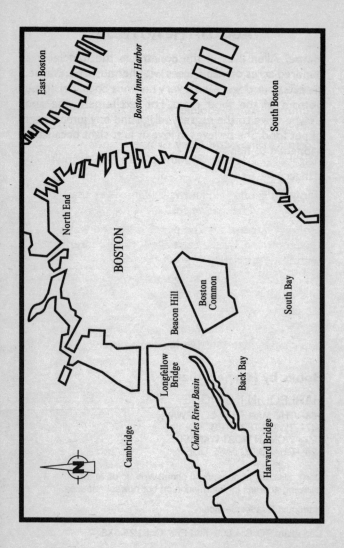

CAST OF CHARACTERS

Jane Smith—Even if a bodyguard can protect her from a murderer, she fears that no one can save her from her shadowy past.

Quinn McGuire—Soldier for hire and sometime bodyguard, he's haunted by the ghosts of his past.

Carla Kozlikov and Gary Crowe—Jane's neighbors—has their friendship with her put them in danger?

Terry Sullivan—He knows Quinn better than anyone—and he's powerless to help him.

Donny Fitzgerald—The police detective was once Quinn's friend, but he can't allow that to interfere with his investigation.

Jennifer Tarranova—Fitzgerald's partner, she's almost sure she's met Jane before…under very different circumstances.

Sister Bertille—The nun saved Quinn's life once—and it's time she called in his debt to her.

To Brian Henry.

Prologue

If he hadn't received the letter from the dead woman that day, Quinn McGuire would never have heard of Jane Smith. He'd been about to leave his apartment to make a secure phone call from the pizza joint down the street, and if the man he'd been planning to call had mentioned the right figure, Quinn would have been catching a night flight out of Boston and the country within hours. But just as he'd shrugged into his ancient leather jacket a hesitant knock sounded at his door and a quavery old voice called out his name.

"Mr. McGuire? It's Agnes Lavery from downstairs. I've got some mail for you."

Quinn knew he hadn't left anything incriminating lying about—he never did. But even as he unlocked the apartment door and slid back the heavy-duty dead bolts he'd installed himself when he'd moved in here several years ago, he scanned the room behind him with the caution that was second nature to him.

There were a few reasons why he'd stayed alive for thirty-one years, he thought wryly as he noted the innocuous china mug on the kitchen counter and the half-folded morning paper littering the surface of the table against the wall. They were simple reasons, and easy to remember.

Don't trust anything. Don't trust anyone. Watch your back.

But a seventy-two-year-old woman probably wasn't going to pull a fast one on him, he thought. He unfastened the forged-steel security chain and turned off the alarm sensor. Of course, Paddy Doyle must have been thinking something similar in the split second before that crazy rebel assassin opened the large black bag that had been part of his disguise and had pulled out a weapon big enough to blow even a tough and lucky Irishman like Paddy away for good.

Quinn blinked. For the life of him he couldn't recall what country or what war that had been. All he could remember was Paddy, his chest torn apart and the life leaking out of him on that dusty street, his blue eyes fading as Quinn held him, and that sweet smile that had driven women wild on five continents lifting the corners of his mouth one last time.

"Another wild goose, boyo," he'd whispered. Blood so dark it seemed black had welled up and mottled his lips as he gasped his last breath. "Look for me flying home with the rest of them, will you?"

And the moral of that story was that luck was a bitch, Quinn thought abruptly. Entirely. As soon as some poor bastard started depending on her, she'd be sure to shaft him. He opened the door and smiled down at the frail old lady standing there.

"You're a complete saint, Mrs. Lavery, you are." He allowed a little more brogue than usual to creep into his voice as he held out his hand for the flimsy airmail weight envelope. He shook his head. "With all the gadding about I do for the head office, it's a real favor for

you to let me use your address. That's the first thing
thieves look for—uncollected letters in a mailbox. And
how's Mr. L. today?''

She was inclined to talk, and for fifteen minutes ex-
pounded on everything from her grandchildren to the
selection of cookies she planned to bake over the next
few weeks in preparation for Thanksgiving. Quinn retained the recipe for strawberry powder jelly balls for as
long as it took him to gently disengage himself from the
garrulous old lady and to close and bolt the door behind
her. Then he wiped his mind clean of all extraneous
details. He looked down at the envelope in his hand, the
mask of affability that he'd worn for his neighbor gone,
his jaw rigid.

It was postmarked Belgium, and it had been mailed a
week ago. He already knew what it contained, since the
handwriting wasn't the one he'd grown familiar with
over the last seven years. His face expressionless, he
ripped it open and let it fall to the floor unheeded as he
held up the single sheet of lined paper it had enclosed.

''My dear Mr. McGuire...'' it began.

Despite himself a ghost of a smile passed across his
features. She'd seen him naked a score of times and still
she'd never been able to bring herself to use his first
name. He read on, the smile fading.

> You know what this is, of course. The doctors
> tell me that what time I have left should be mea-
> sured in hours, not days. I have said my goodbyes
> to everyone here so that I can prepare myself in
> peace for what is to come, and now this last good-
> bye is to you. But the real reason I am writing you
> is this: you owe me, Mr. McGuire—and it is high
> time you paid up.

Startled, Quinn stopped and reread the last line. The writing was scrawled and uneven but it was still recognizable, and he hadn't made a mistake. What he was holding in his hand was, more or less, an unpaid bill. He continued reading.

When I nursed you back to health all those years ago I expected no repayment, but you insisted that you were in my debt. Since then you have reminded me many times that I only have to name my price and you will gladly pay it. Mr. McGuire, my price is this—I want you to take on an assignment for me. I want you to use those talents and skills that you have employed in wars all over the world, but this time I want you to use them in the role of a protector. You will know when the right case presents itself, and—

Whatever she had intended to add had never been written. Except for a small splatter of ink on the page, the letter ended there. Quinn squeezed his eyes shut for a second, as if he was riding out a wave of pain. When he opened them he turned the paper over in his hand and saw that someone had added a postscript.

Mr. McGuire, Sister Bertille was unable to complete this letter to you, but before she slipped into unconsciousness for the last time she asked me to make sure that I sent it to 'her Quinn,' as she always called you. I know you held a special place in her heart, and we will all continue with our prayers for your safety and your soul, as we have done since Sister Bertille came to live with us.

It was signed by the Mother Superior of the convent in Belgium where she'd retreated when the cancer had started to spread, he noted numbly. Apparently somewhere in that tiny country was a group of nuns who knew him by his first name—she'd been pretty damn tricky with that formal "Mr. McGuire" business in her letters, Quinn thought—and who now had taken up the burden of saving his soul that Sister Bertille had obviously carried all these years. A muscle in his jaw jumped.

"So who the hell asked you, Sister?" he muttered. His fist tightened around the flimsy piece of paper, crumpling it. "And what kind of an underhanded scam is this for a nun to be running—calling in your markers and then getting up from the game before a man can negotiate the price, dammit?"

She'd been small, wiry and middle-aged when he'd first met her, with thick-lensed glasses held together by a piece of wire that he'd recognized as the discarded firing pin of some light semi-automatic pistol. She'd worn the traditional nun's black habit of scratchy coarse material, but in that hellhole of a jungle clinic, she had always seemed cool and unruffled. She'd saved his life.

And now she was dead. Quinn rubbed his arm wearily across his eyes and then walked slowly over to the kitchen table. Unclenching his fist, he tried to smooth out the creases that he'd created in the letter. He'd only known her for a few weeks, but she hadn't let a month go by since then without writing to him. Sometimes he would come back from an assignment and find four or five envelopes waiting for him, and once in a while he'd scrawled a postcard back, just to let her know he was still in the land of the living.

Jack Tanner. Paddy Doyle. The Haskins kid—the one

they'd nicknamed Hemingway, because he'd always been writing in his journal. And now Sister Bertille, who in her own way had been as much a soldier as any of them: going wherever she was sent and fighting for the cause she believed in as implacably as they had. He glanced down at the letter once more, his gaze bleak.

"When mercenaries die, Sister, their souls become wild geese. That's how the legend goes, anyway," he whispered softly. "And those of us who are left behind go out and get drunk, and sometimes we persuade ourselves that we hear our friends high up in the night sky, flying through the darkness toward home. I owe you that much, Sister. I owe you a drink or two to your memory, and I'll wish you safe journey to wherever it is that you believe we go when we die. But what you're asking of me is impossible. This is the only way of life I know."

Drunk sounded good, Quinn thought. To hell with the phone call he'd been planning on making earlier; there would always be another job. He'd go out to the nearest bar, stay just sober enough to walk out under his own power at last call, and then he'd come back here and finish off the bottle of Bushmills he kept at the back of the cupboard. Sometime during the evening he'd try to call Terry Sullivan and let him know about Sister Bertille, and if Terry hadn't grown too respectable to be seen with an ex-comrade, he might even join him in the wake of a woman they'd both known and respected.

A protector, for God's sake. She'd always told him he was a better man than he knew, he thought in irritation, staring at the still-crumpled letter. It seemed that right up to the end she'd been too damned stubborn to discard her naive belief in him.

He turned away and was halfway to the door when

his phone rang. Grabbing it up impatiently, the caller's first words froze him in his tracks.

"Mr. McGuire? Quinn McGuire? I was given your number by someone who knows you." The soft voice quavered. Then it steadied. "I—I need a bodyguard. I want to hire you to protect me."

Chapter One

The bar was smoky, the music was loud and apparently Quinn McGuire wasn't going to show. He was over an hour late already. Avoiding surreptitiously interested glances from the surrounding tables, Jane took a miniscule sip of the orange juice that she'd been nursing since she arrived. The ice-cubes in it had long since melted, but even the watered-down citrus tang did nothing to relieve the tight parched feeling in her throat. What was she doing here anyway? How had it happened that her life had spun so far out of control that she'd been reduced to waiting desperately in this raucous Irish pub for a man she'd never met?

In marked contrast to this unlikely meeting-place, earlier today the reception area of Sullivan Security and Investigations had given the impression of a professional and successfully run organization. She should have realized right from the start that the firm was well out of her price range, she told herself now with a brief flicker of embarrassment. The Irish trio on the small stage at the far end of the room launched into a new song, and all around her enthusiastic voices took up the refrain. Her temples throbbed dully, and she set her drink down on the sticky tabletop. The female operative she'd finally spoken with had been diplomatic enough not to mention an actual dollar amount, but her keen glance obviously hadn't missed the fact that Jane's outfit was working-girl attire, and that her jewelry—a pair of gold-toned studs in her ears and a leather-strapped wristwatch—was department store at best.

The woman had advised her to go back to the authorities to alert them to her most recent problems and had outlined a few basic safety precautions that she should take, a shadow of sympathy on her features. Even as Jane was leaving the reception area on her way out, the woman had come after her, a little breathless. She'd thrust a piece of paper into her hand and told her that the name and phone number written on it belonged to a personal friend of Mr. Terrence Sullivan himself, and that Mr. Sullivan had suggested she call Quinn McGuire to sound him out about the possibility of hiring him for a short while.

At the time Jane had felt as if she'd been thrown a lifeline. Even after that disconcerting phone call with Mr. McGuire, she'd still held onto the possibility that somehow he might be able to extricate her from the nightmare her life had become over the past few weeks. The man had been brusquely antagonistic, and the mention of Terrence Sullivan's name hadn't seemed to effect any positive change in his attitude. But when she'd finally apologized for taking up his time and had been about to hang up, he'd grudgingly given her the name of a pub, told her to be there at seven and said he'd meet her.

If she'd had any other options at all she would have thanked him politely and told him she'd changed her mind, she thought bleakly. But that was just it—she'd come to the end of the line and this Quinn McGuire had been her last hope. Now she was forced to face the fact that even the dubious possibility of his assistance had faded.

Gathering up her purse from the chair beside her, she started to rise. She should feel angry at the man, she told herself, but somehow during the last couple of weeks even the capacity for anger had been drained out of her, overridden by the numb and ever-present fear that seemed to be the only emotion she had room for anymore.

"Waiting for me, beautiful?"

Startled, she looked up and met a pair of bright blue eyes. With a slight grin the dark-haired man staring down at her set a glass of beer on the table.

"Mr. McGuire?" she ventured, automatically distancing herself from his familiarity. He had the same lilt to his speech that she'd heard over the phone, she thought, but without the antagonistic edge that he'd displayed earlier. For some reason a flash of confused disappointment overlaid the nervousness that was her usual reaction to men who stepped across the invisible but inviolate boundaries she tried to keep around her. He was tall and well-built, with a hint of muscle filling out the shoulders of the light wool sweater he was wearing, but she'd expected something more. *Like what?* she asked herself. *Did you think he was going to be some kind of superman?*

"I'm not McGuire, whoever the hell he is," he said easily. "But any man crazy enough to stand up a lady like you deserves to lose his chance. What are you drinking, sweetheart?"

"Screw off, boyo. Now."

It hardly seemed possible that such a big man could come up so unobtrusively, but suddenly he was there.

As Jane's accoster turned and saw who'd just spoken, he swallowed visibly. She didn't blame him.

Silvery-gray eyes stared out of an implacably expressionless face that looked as if it had been carved from teak. In stark contrast, his close-cropped hair seemed to have been bleached to pewter by the same tropical sun that had tanned him so darkly. He was wearing olive-drab chinos, and an olive-drab T-shirt strained over his massive torso. He looked about as solid and unyielding as an oak tree. Even though he hadn't raised his voice, the tables around them fell silent.

"You'd be McGuire, I'm thinking." The dark-haired man smiled weakly in a valiant attempt to retain some of his previous jaunty charm.

"You don't have to know my name. You don't have to do anything but walk away." The softly spoken words were uninflected and matter-of-fact, but at them the other man swallowed again.

"Sure. No problem, entirely." Not even meeting Jane's wide-eyed gaze, he edged hastily away, halting nervously as the other man spoke again.

"Your beer, boyo. Don't rush off without it, now." The big man handed his glass to him and, without looking to see if he'd left, sat down across from her.

"Quinn McGuire. Sorry I'm late." He crossed muscular forearms on the table and met her eyes with no hint of apology in his as he made the terse introduction. "I had some business to attend to."

Besides the slight brogue, there was the faintest hint of a slur to his speech. Jane stared at him, taking in the other signs that had escaped her notice until now. His economy of movement appeared to be an integral part of him, but there was an additional stillness about his attitude that gave the impression of a man who was trying very carefully to stay focused. Those pale silver eyes, veiled by startlingly dark lashes, seemed to be looking through her and past her. For a moment, she had the disconcerting feeling that either he or she was a ghost.

But that was stupid. It was obvious what his problem was.

"Are you *drunk,* Mr. McGuire?" she asked incredulously.

"Not enough." As he spoke, a waitress came up to their table and set a squat glass of some dark amber liquid down in front of him. He handed her a bill, waving away the change. "Don't let me run dry tonight, Molly," he said, nodding at the glass. "And it looks like the lady's drinking screwdrivers. Bring her another, would you?"

"It's plain orange juice, and I'm fine," Jane said tersely. She waited until the young woman had moved out of earshot. "Is this the business you had to attend to, Mr. McGuire? Did I take you away from an important appointment with a bottle of rye?"

He gave her a pained glance, the mild expression of disgust looking out of place on those otherwise hard features. "Rye? I'd pour it on a wound if I didn't have anything else handy, but I'd never drink the stuff. No, darlin', it was good Irish whiskey. But enough of this small talk. You said Terry gave you my name?"

"He must have made a mistake. It's obvious you're not interested." For the second time in a few minutes, she reached for her purse and stood. "I'm sorry I took you away from your more pressing engagements, Mr. McGuire."

Despite herself, her voice trembled on the last few words. It was the exhaustion, she thought. It was the fact that she hadn't had a normal night's sleep for weeks, and that for days now she'd been living on her nerves, waiting for the next incident. She had no more resources left to draw upon, no more strength. Tonight had utterly defeated her.

She'd pinned all her hopes on this encounter, and the man had shown up drunk.

"My name's Quinn. Sit down." There was a harsh edge to his tone, but she'd had enough. The look she gave him was steadily assessing and at it, something flickered at the back of those gray eyes.

For a moment she'd thought she'd seen contrition, Jane thought. More likely it had been relief.

"I'll never know you well enough to be on a first-name basis with you, Mr. McGuire. I doubt that many people are." With an effort, she fought back the telltale trembling that had started up again. "I also doubt that you care. Goodbye, Mr. Mc—"

"Stop calling me that." Like a snake striking, one large hand shot out and wrapped itself around her wrist. His grip was firm but even as she reflexively pulled away from him he let her go. His gaze met hers opaquely. "It's a bad night to be stirring up old memories. Call me Quinn. And please—sit down."

She didn't move. She wouldn't let herself look down at the wrist he'd grasped and released so swiftly, for fear of letting him see how badly he'd rattled her. "Quinn, then. But the rest still stands. I asked you here because I was told that you might be able to help me, and you seem to have slotted me in between bouts of partying." Even to her own ears her voice sounded thin and high, and she took a deep breath, willing her tone down to a more normal register. "You made it clear earlier that you weren't really interested in this meeting, so don't feel you have to go through the motions now just to oblige me. You don't owe me anything.''

She smiled tightly at him, holding on to the last of her composure, and turned to leave. Behind her she heard him speak.

''Dammit, Sister. You've got absolutely no intention of letting me go to hell in my own way, have you?'' His words were quietly bitter and Jane looked back at him, startled. She almost expected to see someone else at the table with him, his voice had been pitched so low, but it was her eyes that Quinn McGuire met. ''You're wrong, lady. I owe you, all right. I'm guessing one of my old debts just got transferred.''

''I don't understand.'' She hesitated. For the first time, he seemed to be looking at her as if he was really seeing her, and his scrutiny caught her off-balance. She flushed a little, wishing suddenly that she presented a more prepossessing sight—and that desire itself was totally unlike her.

She knew she wasn't the type to turn heads. There just wasn't anything so special about her, which made what had been happening to her that much harder to understand. Her hair was about as ordinary a brown as it could get. Her eyes were standard-issue blue. She weighed less than she had a few weeks ago, but she had an average figure for her average height. Her skin, a warm ivory tone, was her best feature, and her mouth was a little wider than she thought attractive.

Men didn't usually look twice at her. She wanted to keep it that way.

''The Star of the County Down,'' Quinn murmured, confusing her further. ''Irishmen write songs about women like you.'' The pewter eyes darkened and then cleared. "I wasn't at a party tonight. I was holding a private wake for a friend."

An explanation was the last thing she'd expected from him, and that particular explanation disarmed her completely. Jane caught her breath in swift compassion. "I'm sorry." She fumbled with the strap of her purse awkwardly, knowing how inadequate her response sounded. "I—I had no idea. You must want to be alone—"

"I want you to sit down, but I'm damned if I know how to get you to do it." Under the T-shirt the massive shoulders lifted slightly, as if he was attempting to shrug off the burden of his earlier mood. One corner of his mouth lifted wryly. "Why don't we start all over again?"

Maybe she was projecting her own feelings onto him, Jane thought slowly, but behind the easy manner she could have sworn there was an edge of desolation in that incongruously soft voice. Still holding his gaze and clutching the strap of her purse, she lowered herself cautiously back onto the chair, her posture rigid as she tried to keep as much distance between them as possible.

"I called Sullivan after I spoke with you this afternoon," Quinn said, frowning slightly. "He said you think someone's watching you. He told me there've been some incidents—and that these incidents have been escalating."

"Escalating?" A jagged little bubble of laughter escaped her. "That's one way to put it. Except when I told the police about this, they said the situation hadn't *escalated* to the point where they could justify an investigation. When they can spare the manpower they send a patrol car cruising by my apartment, but I'm still walking around alive and unharmed, which means that my case isn't high priority—yet.''

"So whoever's targeting you is still at the skirmishing stage,'' Quinn continued. "He hasn't officially declared all-out war. He must have some kind of battle plan that he intends to follow.''

Her head jerked up, her features pinched "Skirmishing? Battle plan? We're not playing soldiers here.''

He stared at her impassively, seemingly unfazed by her outburst. Smoke-filtered light from the bar beside them gleamed palely on his hair, and his eyes, silvery and reflective, betrayed no hint of his inner thoughts.

"What exactly have you been told about me?'' he asked.

"Just that you were a friend of Terrence Sullivan,'' she answered, taken aback. "I went to Sullivan Investigations to hire someone to find out why I'm being stalked—and to keep me alive in the meantime. I—I assumed that's what you did.'' Her voice trailed off. "I'm wrong, aren't I? Just what *do* you do for a living?''

"I'm a professional soldier,'' he said shortly.

She frowned. "You're in the military? Are you on leave right now?''

"I put in my time for Uncle Sam.'' In the first extraneous gesture she'd seen him make, Quinn raked back a short strand of sun-bleached hair. "Now I choose my own wars, Ms. Smith.''

"You're a—a *mercenary?*''

Dear God, she thought. She'd expected an ex-cop, or maybe a private eye who could hold his own in a physical confrontation, and instead she'd gotten some kind of hired gun. He was a soldier of fortune, for heaven's sake!

"I told you—I'm a professional soldier. It's what I

was trained for.'' He picked up his glass and drained most of it, setting it back down on the table with a little more force than necessary. ''I don't work for just anyone, and I never take on an assignment that could conflict with my loyalties as a citizen of this country. But there's always trouble somewhere in the world. Right now it appears that someone's waging war against you.''

She stared at him, her thoughts chaotic. Quinn had just voiced the feeling she'd had for weeks now. She had felt like some unknown person had declared war on her—a very private, very personal war, but war nonetheless. And from the start she'd had the conviction that her enemy wasn't interested in taking prisoners.

With Quinn McGuire on her side there was a possibility that she might be able to turn the tide of this one-sided battle, Jane thought slowly. But before they came to any definite arrangement he had to know just what she was up against.

As a soldier, he would want as much information as he could about both his enemy—and his ally. How was she supposed to tell him that her adversary wasn't the only participant in this war whom she knew nothing about?

''You said earlier that tonight was a bad night for stirring up old memories, McGuire.'' Her voice was barely above a murmur, but his eyes narrowed in response. She went on, knowing that she was picking her way through a minefield. ''You sound like a man who's got too many of them.''

''Everybody's got something they wish they could forget,'' Quinn said harshly. His eyes seemed almost silvery. ''Everyone's got a few too many memories.''

''Not me.'' Jane stared back at him, her own eyes shadowed. ''I don't know anything about my life up until the time when I came to in a hospital bed eleven weeks ago—not even what my real name is or where I come from or if I have a family.''

Her voice cracked. She fought to keep it under control. ''And the only person who can fill in the blanks for me is my stalker.''

Chapter Two

Quinn shook his head. "You can't remember a thing about your life. That's quite a trick. Could you teach me, do you think?"

His tone was tinged with admiration. She stared at him. "It's called amnesia," she said shortly. "It's not a trick, it's a medical condition. When I came to in hospital I was told I'd been hit by a car. I had head trauma."

"Head trauma, was it?" His attitude wasn't exactly mocking, but there was something off-kilter about the way he was responding. He shoved his glass to one side, his elbow on the table. "What happened next? When did you first figure out this fella was followin' you?"

His accent had thickened, and again the impulse to get up and leave crossed her mind. But even drunk, the man's very appearance would provide some protection. He was physically intimidating just sitting there, half-slumped across the table.

"It was a few days after I left the—" She drew in a sharp breath. Looking down at the strong tanned fingers that rested idly on her forearm, she forced her voice to remain even. "We're not on a date, Mr. McGuire. Please remove your hand."

"It's Quinn, as I told you before. And the hand stays. It's for your own good."

"What do you mean, for my own good?" Her jaw was so tight she could hardly get the question out.

"I keep a low profile, but who I am and what I do isn't a complete secret to those in the business," he said softly. His thumb moved up the length of her forearm in an unobtrusive stroking motion. Her fingertips curled against the smooth surface of the table. "Our conversation was beginning to look too much like what it was—a business negotiation. And there just might be a curious soul or two around who would find it interesting to question you later, to find out what new project I'm considering." He smiled. The smile didn't reach his eyes. "It's a dog-eat-dog world. Let's throw them a bone to keep them satisfied, and try to blend in with the other couples in the room."

"Pretend this isn't—this isn't business? If you think it's necessary, I'll play along, but not to this extent. Being touched—" Her gaze slid away from his. "Being touched makes me nervous. I don't like it."

"I'm not about to start groping down the front of your dress, lady." The thumb that had been stroking her forearm stilled. "We're making the barest of human contact."

"I still don't like it." Her voice was firmer this time, she noted with shaky relief. "Please let me go."

This last request was unnecessary. Already he'd released her, but although there was now a space of a few inches between her arm and his hand, her flesh still retained the heat of his touch.

"I've gotten the message—there's a no-man's-land around you and I won't be trespassing again. Let's hear your story."

His soft voice was as emotionless as if he were asking her for the time of day, and suddenly Jane knew she'd made a mistake. There'd been no need to fear any blurring of the barriers between herself and this man. Even if she'd involuntarily let her own down, they were nothing compared to the wall that she belatedly perceived around him.

For reasons she didn't understand, there was a part of her deep inside that was frozen. But Quinn McGuire was ice through and through—glacial ice. He wasn't like other men. She had nothing to fear from him in that respect.

Except it wasn't him you were afraid of a moment ago, was it? a small voice in her head asked. *It was yourself—and the way you felt when he touched you.*

She sat up straighter. "Three days after I was released from the hospital I found work with a cleaning company." Her shrug was a taut lifting of her shoulders. "It was all I could get. I was a non-person, officially at least, but the rest of the night cleaning crew were in the same situation as I was—no papers, no legal status."

"Already this doesn't make sense," he said carelessly. "Tell me this—why didn't the doctors contact the authorities when they learned you were suffering from amnesia? Why didn't they run a check with missing persons?" He lifted his glass and looked at her through the golden liquid, as if he were examining her through a microscope. "You'll have to shore up the gaps in your fairy tale, darlin'. It's still a little shaky."

"You think I'm lying? *Why,* in heaven's name? What would I have to gain?"

"Like I said, what I do for a living isn't a total secret to certain people." A corner of his mouth lifted. "A couple of years ago a woman tried to spin me a story about needing her husband eliminated. I found out she was a reporter hoping to do an exposé on murder-for-hire.''

''I'm not a reporter—'' Jane began, but he didn't let her finish.

''I've had the odd head wound myself, angel. I've seen men who've totally forgotten their names, what country they were in, what year it was. But they all regained their memories within a day or two.''

''I know it's rare.'' She pushed a stray strand of hair away from her face distractedly. ''I've gone to the library and read everything I could on it. But it happens. It happened to me, whether you believe it or not.''

''The rest of it doesn't hang together either.'' Folding his arms on the table, he lowered his voice. ''Here's how it would have happened in real life.... The police would have written up a description of you and gone back to the station to file a report. From then on it would be a matter of matching you up with someone who'd been listed as a missing person.'' He shook his head. ''What wouldn't happen is that a woman in your supposed condition could just be discharged without any question. You've lost your audience, darlin'. Go home.''

''They were going to contact the police. When I learned that I ran.'' Jane looked away. ''I didn't even know why I was running. All I knew was that I didn't want to talk to anybody about who I could be or where I might have come from. I just wanted to be left in peace. But that didn't happen.''

The broad shoulders shifted slightly, as if he was restless and getting ready to leave. ''I could ask you where a penniless woman found the change for the phone calls to prospective employers. I could ask how you got bus fare those first few days. For God's sake—I could ask what the hell you were wearing while you trudged around the city looking for work—you said you'd been in an accident, so presumably your clothes were a write-off.''

"And I'd tell you. But you don't want to hear it.'' Slowly she shook her head at him, her eyes never leaving his. "Soldiering is what you do, McGuire, so I guess I shouldn't be surprised that you seem to be at war right now. What I haven't figured out is who you're supposed to be fighting…because it can't be me. You haven't let yourself learn enough about me to count me as an enemy.''

"That's right, I haven't.'' A muscle at the side of his jaw might have moved, but it was hard to tell. The rest of his face remained immobile. "And you know just as little about me, but you keep making these off-the-cuff assessments. Why don't you finish this last one? If I'm not at war with you, who the hell is this mysterious enemy I'm supposed to be fighting?''

A moment ago she wouldn't have had an answer for him. But at the unnecessary harshness of his tone, it was suddenly clear what her only response could be.

"No mystery, Mr. McGuire,'' she said softly. "It's you. For some reason you're at war with yourself.''

"That's crazy.'' His answer was as immediate as a burst of gunfire. Then he took a deep breath. "When I take up arms, darlin', I'm facing a real foe, not some unresolved Freudian conflict with my inner child.'' His shrug was mocking. "Sorry to blow your theory out of the water, but I'm a simple man. What you see is what you get. Sure, I've made some mistakes in the past, but in my business you can't afford to lose your focus. Believe me, I don't waste a whole lot of time in soul-searching.''

"Then why did you bring up the subject of past mistakes, McGuire? I didn't say anything about that." She searched his features curiously. "I don't think what you see is what you get with you at all. I think there's a very different man underneath that hard exterior—maybe a better man than you realize. Maybe *he's* the man you're at war with."

Quinn stared at her—but not the flat, angry stare he'd directed at her earlier. With a start Jane saw raw pain film his eyes, before all expression was quickly veiled as the thick dark lashes came down. As if he had a headache, he squeezed his eyes shut for a moment.

"Dammit, Sister, if I'd known you'd turn out to be this persistent, I would have told you to let me die the first time we met. Is it an emissary you're sending me now instead of letters?"

His words had been barely audible, but she caught the gist of them. They didn't make any sense, she thought, confused. "I may not know who I am, McGuire, but one thing I'm sure of is that I'm not your sister. You've got me mistaken with someone else."

He opened his eyes, his gaze meeting hers. "That must be what I'm doing, darlin'," he said heavily. "But when you quote her almost verbatim, you can't blame a man for feeling a little beleaguered." He saw her lack of comprehension. "Just someone I knew once. She's dead."

She still didn't understand what he was talking about, but what did it matter now? she thought in defeat. She hadn't convinced him to help her, and when she left this place she'd be walking out alone into the night. He'd made up his mind about her. Nothing she'd come up with had persuaded him to change it.

Maybe only his own words could, she thought with sudden hope.

"I'm your unpaid bill, Mr. McGuire," she said, taking a shot in the dark. "I'm the debt you referred to earlier—the debt that got transferred. She saved your life, didn't she?"

Jane was just piecing together fragments of his own incomprehensible remarks, not even knowing if they would make any sense to him, but Quinn's reaction told her that one of those fragments had found its mark. His head jerked up, the pale gaze a little out of focus, and when he spoke his voice was low and strained.

"Dammit, yes—you saved my life. I never denied it, and I never tried to get out of repaying you, Sister. But now you're trying to save my soul—and to do that, you want me to turn my back on the rest of them. I'm telling you once and for all I can't *do* it!"

Jane felt as if she'd just pulled the pin on a grenade and had it blow up in her face. She scrambled to bring some semblance of normality back to this suddenly chilling conversation.

"She's dead, Quinn. Whoever she was, she's dead and gone." Needing only to assuage the naked pain that etched his features, she placed her hand lightly on his clenched fist. "I'm not her, and I'm not her emissary. And whatever debt you feel you owed her, she sounds like the kind of woman who wouldn't ask more of you than you could pay. I should go now." Her eyes sought his. "I should have gone before I reminded you of all this. I'm sorry."

Slowly his hand relaxed. He looked down at it, and at hers, pale against his own tanned skin. "I've just come off a bad assignment," he said softly. "The way things have been going lately, I'm sure the next one will be much the same. I know you're not her, darlin'. I'm not that far gone. Chalk it up to a slip of the tongue, will you?''

It hadn't been, she knew. For a moment he hadn't been seeing her in the seat opposite him, but a ghost—a ghost who, for reasons she'd never know, had some kind of loving hold over him.

"You're touching me." His low comment interrupted her thoughts. "I thought you said you didn't do that."

"I don't." With a jerk she drew her hand back, flustered. "I mean—I didn't know...I didn't realize I'd—"

"It's okay, I won't report you this time."

He was actually smiling, she saw with a slight shock. The expression took some of the harshness from his features, and all of a sudden she realized that he was a devastatingly good-looking man. Trust Quinn McGuire, she thought shakily, to keep the most dangerous weapon in his arsenal concealed until he really needed it. With an effort, she brought her attention back to what he was saying.

"The police are right. If a stalker's determined enough, sooner or later he's going to accomplish what he sets out to do—unless he loses your trail or someone puts him out of action permanently. And that's illegal. They call it murder," he added dryly. "But tell me what's been happening to you, and I'll see if I can come up with any kind of strategy."

At his words, she almost sagged with relief. She was well aware that just making that concession went against the man's ingrained wariness. They'd gotten off on the wrong foot, and he was still making no promises. But his cautious acceptance of her was a start. She had a ghost to thank for that, she thought.

"I couldn't sleep at night in the hospital. At first it

was just because of the—the pain. But my physical injuries weren't that bad, and after a few days that wasn't what was keeping me up.'' She swallowed. ''I'd lied to the doctors. I'd given them a false name, the most common one I could think of, and told them I was a street person so they wouldn't ask me too many questions. But I knew they didn't really believe me.''

''Why did you lie right from the start? If you knew your memory was a blank, wouldn't you have wanted them to investigate?'' Quinn was still playing devil's advocate, but this time with no edge to his voice.

''I don't know.'' It wasn't an adequate answer, but it was the only one she had to give him. ''I realize how crazy it sounds, but as soon as I regained consciousness and found that I couldn't remember a single thing about myself, I felt like—'' She stopped, her eyes squeezing shut for a second. Opening them, she took a deep breath and went on, feeling his gaze on her. ''I felt like I'd been given a second chance. I didn't want to know who I'd been before. I just wanted to slip into this new, empty life and start fresh.''

''That doesn't sound so crazy.'' His expression was unreadable. ''Go on.''

She looked at him. ''Anyway, at night the cleaning crew would come through the wards. One of them was an older woman—Olga Kozlikov. She would stop by my bed and talk to me sometimes, when the nurse on duty wasn't watching. She said she was Russian, and had come here to make a new life for herself.''

''So you had a common bond.'' He raised his glass and drained it. ''Two refugees, right?''

Jane was startled into an unwilling smile. ''I hadn't thought of it in that way, but you're right. One night I told her a little about my situation, and she seemed to understand how I felt. She said she'd lived for so long fearing the authorities under the old regime in Russia that she herself still didn't trust the police, even though she knew it was very different here in America. She told me she'd help me.''

''So she set you up with some clothes and some money and helped you find a job?''

She nodded. ''Three or four days after I was admitted, the doctor who'd been monitoring me suggested it might be a good thing if I talked to the police about the accident. That scared me, because there really wasn't much to tell—a dozen witnesses had given statements saying that I'd run right out into the road, and there'd been no way that the woman who'd hit me was responsible. And although no one knew that I had complete amnesia, I'd told them I had no recollection at all of the accident.''

''And that's true? You don't remember it?'' He gave her a searching look. ''Whatever you've told anyone else, it's important that you don't lie to me, do you understand? If I think you are, then this meeting's over.''

''I haven't lied to you.'' She sighed. ''I've just left something out. When I was brought into emergency, apparently I was as high as a kite. They couldn't give me any medication for twenty-four hours, because my system was full of drugs already. For the next couple of days I went through withdrawal—not as bad as if I'd been a longtime user, but bad enough.''

''What had you been on? Did the doctors tell you?''

''They rattled off some pharmaceutical names at me, but as far as I was concerned they could have been talking another language. I didn't know what they were. But since I walked out of the hospital I swear I haven't taken so much as an aspirin, Quinn. Whoever I used to be, the person I am now doesn't take drugs.''

Unwaveringly, her eyes met his, and finally he gave a curt nod. "I believe you. If you were a junkie you'd be out trying to score, not sitting here talking to me."

"And if I were an addict, then no one could help me but myself. But drugs aren't my problem, and I don't think I can handle this on my own anymore." She felt the prickle of tears behind her eyelids, and forced them to remain where they were. "The night before the police were supposed to come and talk to me, I just walked out of the hospital. Olga had arranged for me to be hired on by the same firm she worked for, with a crew that cleaned an office building downtown, and at first everything was fine. Olga's niece Carla was a nurse at the same hospital, and Olga persuaded her to help me get a small apartment in the rooming-house where she lived. I had a home, I had a job, and the new life I'd wanted was beginning to become a reality. Then he left the first sign for me to find."

"What do you mean, the first sign?" Quinn frowned.

"Just that." She clasped her hands tightly together on the table. "I was teamed up with another woman and we cleaned the same area each night. Everyone worked in teams of two or three, and the area that Martine and I cleaned was a secretarial pool. On my third night there, we walked in and all the computers were on. All the monitors displayed a single line of type, sized large enough so that I could see it from the doorway, and they all said the same thing—*I Know Who You Are.*"

"That was it?" Across from her he raised his eyebrows. "For God's sake, woman, it was probably a prank directed at someone who worked there."

"I told myself that." Stung, she glared at him. "My first reaction was that it was meant for me, because it seemed to fit my situation, but then I realized just how ridiculous that was. Martine and I cleaned the office, finished the rest of our area, and went back to the company depot with the rest of the workers like usual. I always took the same bus home every night and got off at a stop only a few steps away from my place. Except when I got off at my stop that night I saw that the bus shelter had been papered over with flyers. They were bright yellow, and in big black letters was—was—''

This time she couldn't control the shaking. Her head bent, she didn't see the waitress pause by their table, but when Quinn pushed the full glass across to her she looked up.

''Drink.'' His tone brooked no argument, but she shook her head at him anyway.

''I don't—''

''I said drink.'' His mouth was set in a grim line. ''It'll help.''

Reluctantly she raised the glass to her lips, opening her mouth just enough for a trickle of the amber liquid to pass down her throat. But even that miniscule amount was enough to distract her, at least temporarily.

''It's *awful*,'' she sputtered.

''It's not awful, you heathen, it's good Irish whiskey. Look at your hand now—steady as a damn rock.''

She *had* stopped shaking, Jane saw. But she was only at the beginning, and there was much more to come. If she took a drink each time the tremors started she'd have to be carried out by the time she finished telling him everything.

Quinn took up where she'd left off. ''The flyers had the same message as what was on the computer monitors?''

Jane nodded. ''It was raining a little, and at first I didn't look up. When I did the bus was just pulling away, and it felt like those garish yellow posters were screaming at me, each one saying the same thing. I was sure that whoever had put them there was somewhere close by, watching me, and I ran as fast as I could. I didn't stop until I was inside my apartment.'' She grimaced. ''Not very brave of me, was it?''

''Don't beat yourself up over it. That'd be enough to give anyone the heebie-jeebies.'' He pronounced his *e's* to sound more like *a's,* and despite herself she smiled faintly at hearing such a quaint turn of phrase coming from a man as tough and hard-bitten as McGuire. Her smile faded as she continued.

''That was nine weeks ago. Since then the messages have come every few days, and always in a different way.''

''Like how?'' He reached for his drink, forgotten at her elbow, and took a thoughtful sip.

''Like being whitewashed on the inside of the window of an abandoned store that I pass on Sundays. Like being written on a scrap of paper and tucked into the serviette I took from a dispenser in the coffee shop I frequent before work—I still can't figure out how he managed that one.''

''He knows your routine. He probably knows which table you usually choose to sit at, and the approximate time you'd show up, if you were going to be there at all that night. If you'd checked, you probably would have found the first half-dozen or so serviettes had been tampered with, just to make sure one of them got to you.'' Quinn rubbed his jaw. ''Of course, whoever's doing this could be a woman. What else?''

''More of the same until this week. It's getting worse—that's why I eventually went to the police.'' She looked away, her gaze fixed on nothing. ''Three nights

ago Martine and I were taking bags of garbage to the
service elevator. I was coming down the corridor and I
could see Martine at the elevator, throwing her bags in.
Then it looked as if she fell forward into the elevator,
and the doors closed.''

Her eyes closed briefly and then opened again.
''Serge, our supervisor, and another man took the regular
elevator down to the basement, because that was where
the service elevator was preset to go when the cleaning
staff was working. I stayed where I was, waiting for
them to come back. I thought Martine had had a fainting
spell or something, and I was out of my mind with worry
for her. Then I saw the indicator light above the service
elevator show that it was beginning to climb again, and
I assumed that Serge and Julio had found her and were
bringing her up in it. But when the doors opened, Martine was in there alone, and she was screaming.''

Nothing, not whiskey, not the fact that she was in a
crowded room with people all around her, not even
Quinn McGuire's reassuringly broad-shouldered presence across from her could stop the shaking now. The
coldness of remembered terror seeped through her.

''She was hysterical. Someone had pulled her into the
elevator and then the lights had gone off and the doors
had closed. She'd felt a knife at her throat, and her attacker warned her to keep quiet or he'd kill her. Just
before they reached the basement, he whispered in her
ear that he had a message he wanted her to pass on—to
me.''

''The same message you'd been getting all along?''
Quinn sounded grim.

''I Know Who You Are,'' Jane agreed dully. ''But
this time there was an addition. The message Martine
gave me was two sentences.''

"What was the second one?"

Her stricken gaze met his. *"And I Know What You Did."*

He drew in a sharp breath. "How the hell could the police ignore you after that, dammit? What did they say when they came?"

"They weren't called. The incident wasn't reported." At his incredulous expression she leaned forward, her words coming out in a rush. "I *told* you—the people I worked with weren't about to draw attention to themselves. I'm pretty sure Martine was an illegal immigrant, and when I told her I was going to call the police, she said she would deny everything. The rest of the crew backed her up. They all liked me, but not enough to risk being deported. And not enough to continue working with me, either," she finished hopelessly. "I was fired that night."

Quinn grimaced. "Sooner or later your stalker's going to stop playing around."

"Playing? You call what he's done so far *playing?*" Shocked, she stared at him. "He's turned my life into a *nightmare!* He obviously knows everything I do, everywhere I go, and he's either right behind me or just one step ahead of me, day and night!"

"That being true, he could have killed you by now," he said brutally. "But he hasn't. That's why I say he's just playing with you."

"If driving me slowly out of my mind is *playing,* then yes, I suppose you're right, McGuire." She could feel the tears spilling over, and she knew that people nearby were looking at her, but she was past caring. "But you're forgetting one vital component in his game plan—he knows who I really am. That gives him a weapon to use against me, and I can't fight back!"

"Sure you can. You've got the same information he has, only you won't admit it." He crossed his arms, the short sleeves of the T-shirt he was wearing straining over his biceps. "I could agree to take on the job of keeping you safe, and while I was by your side, you would be. But as soon as I left, you'd be in danger again. The only person who can find out who your stalker is and why he's targeting you is yourself. And for some reason you don't want to do that."

"Haven't you heard a word I've said? I *can't* do that. My memory's a blank!" She was shaking again, Jane noted with a detached part of her mind. But this time it was from anger.

"It's a blank because you want it to be a blank." Those pale eyes met hers emotionlessly. "I told you, true amnesia's so rare as to be almost nonexistent. Besides, if you really wanted to find out who you were and why someone wants to harm you, you'd tell the police the truth and let them investigate you—and you haven't, have you?"

"No." She looked down at her hands. "No, you're right. I haven't told them the truth. I haven't asked them if I match the descriptions of any missing women, and I don't intend to." .

"Then your stalker will just bide his time until you're unprotected again." He shook his head. "The best advice I can give you is to disappear into yet another life, lady. I can help you get out of town without being followed, but that's all I can do for you, since you're so determined not to help yourself."

He was turning her down. After everything she'd told him—and except for the amnesia, he hadn't seemed to doubt her story—he was turning her down. She couldn't believe it. She said the first foolish thing that came into her head.

"Is it the money? I don't have much, but Serge gave me a couple of weeks termination pay so I'd keep quiet about what—"

"It's not the money."

"But you're not on an assignment right now." She heard a shrill edge to her voice, and attempted a more reasonable tone. "If you're between jobs, why can't you take this on?"

"I'm only between jobs because I took your phone call today, instead of making one of my own." He shrugged. "If you'd called half an hour later, I doubt that we'd ever have met. If you call again tomorrow, I won't be there to answer."

"You're going off to fight another war," she said slowly. "I guess I should have known mine would be too insignificant to interest you. My little war doesn't have the elements you're looking for."

"And just what the hell is that cryptic comment supposed to mean?" His gaze had been idly glancing around for the waitress. Now it sharpened.

"You seem to think I'm not willing to put up a fight, McGuire—that some part of me is willing to die. I think you're putting your own motives onto me." She felt for her purse, her movements jerky and awkward. "You're the one who keeps letting yourself be led to the slaughter. Every time you walk away alive there's a little twinge of disappointment in you, isn't there?"

"I go into an assignment *aiming* to walk out alive. You don't know what you're talking about." His stare was flat, his posture rigidly tense. He raked a hand through his close-cropped hair. "Dammit, I'm not the one who hated my life so much that I sealed it up in a box and buried it six feet under.''

"Even if your theory's right, at least I want to hold onto some kind of existence. That's the difference between us.'' Getting out of her seat, she stood, looking down at the man she'd hoped would be her salvation. "You won't admit it, but that's the reason behind every choice you make. I want to live, but deep down, you want to die. Did she realize that, too—that sister of yours who won't leave you alone?''

"You just crossed the line, darlin'. Back off.''

He'd half-risen, and with the difference in their heights, that brought his gaze on a level with hers. His face was inches from hers, and even at that moment Jane felt her focus slipping away. His eyes were like crystal, she thought, her breath catching in her throat. Everything else about the man was harshly masculine, but those mesmerizing eyes and those thick, sooty lashes belonged on the *parfit gentil* knight she'd wanted him to be.

It was one more reason not to believe in fairy tales. She drew back, suddenly uncomfortable at his nearness.

"Have a nice war, Mr. McGuire,'' she said coldly. "I doubt that our paths will ever cross again.''

For one long last moment their gazes remained locked, his still brilliant with anger, and hers, she knew, showing nothing at all. She'd tried, Jane told herself tiredly. She'd tried, and failed. Now her Pandora's box of troubles had lost its only saving grace. All of a sudden she knew that the tears that had been threatening all night were about to burst forth in a humiliating flood.

"Let me get you out of town, at least,'' Quinn began. His anger had faded as completely as hers had, and there was a rough sympathy in his voice.

"I'll arrange something myself.'' She shook her head

furiously, wanting only to get away before she dissolved right in front of this man and a whole roomful of strangers, most of whom were already casting interested glances her way. "You're right, it probably is the best option. Goodbye, Mr. Mc—" She saw a tiny muscle tighten at the corner of his mouth, and changed what she'd been about to say. "Goodbye, Quinn."

Even before his name had left her lips she'd turned abruptly on her heel. The next second she was blindly making her way through the crowded tables toward the back of the room where the washrooms were, both hands clenched around the strap of her shoulder bag, her face averted.

If she was lucky—and God knew she deserved *some* small scrap of luck tonight—there would be no one in the ladies' room. She would lock herself in a cubicle and cry until she couldn't cry anymore. Then she would get up, splash cold water on her face, and leave—preferably without running into Quinn McGuire.

She'd only known the man for an hour or so. For most of that time they'd been antagonists. If he was right, and she could wipe her memory at will, then it should be easy for her to forget that moment when his hand had touched her arm and his thumb had stroked her skin.

But Quinn's theory was wrong. And she had a feeling she'd be proving it wrong for a long, long time to come.

Chapter Three

She'd been about to cry. No, Quinn corrected himself, she'd already started to cry by the time she'd spun around and taken off from him in that clumsy half-walk, half-run that had nearly cannoned her into a handful of bar patrons and at least one waitress before she'd disappeared into the washrooms. He'd seen the tears shimmering at the corners of those dark blue eyes, and they'd made him feel like a dog.

He'd done the right thing, there was no doubt about that. "No doubt at all, McGuire," he murmured under his breath. "Someone had to make her face facts." He downed the last of the whiskey in his glass, and wondered if he was drinking out of the same side as she had. She hadn't been wearing lipstick—as far as a mere male could tell, she hadn't been wearing any makeup at all on that poreless, creamy-pale skin—so there was no way of knowing what part of the rim her lips had touched. But he thought he could taste her.

He drew himself up sharply. He'd been heading for drunk tonight. Obviously he'd achieved his goal, if he was sitting here trying to persuade himself that under the smoky, peaty flavor of Bushmills he could discern a hint of crushed strawberries. But that would be what she'd taste like, he thought unwillingly. Like the wild straw-berries he could just barely remember picking when he'd been a boy—the small, sweet ones that had looked like tiny jewels against the green, green grass.

The woman had stirred up far too many memories, he thought abruptly. He needed another drink.

Like magic, his waitress appeared, her smile a little harried as she set down a new glass, but then turning to a puzzled frown as Quinn stopped her from taking the empty one away.

"Humor me, Molly. Leave the glass here, and take this." He dropped a thick wad of bills on the round cork-topped tray she carried. "That should cover the tab I've been running. The rest is for you."

This time her smile was real. He'd made one woman happy tonight, he thought ruefully, as he lifted his glass and stared into the golden liquid. He'd made one happy, and he'd torn another one's world apart.

Actually, if he were honest with himself, the odds were more like two to one. He was forgetting the nun.

…you owe me, Mr. McGuire—and it is high time you paid up.

He'd welshed on his debt. He could call it whatever the hell he wanted, but what it came right down to was that Quinn McGuire had weaseled out of an old debt. He closed his eyes, and there she was in front of him, the way he always remembered her….

In the antiquated conditions of the jungle hospital, she'd worked miracles. Of course, she hadn't taken credit for them. There'd been a gleaming brass crucifix above her packing-crate desk. It had been the only thing in the place, besides the few surgical tools, that hadn't been allowed to tarnish in the tropical humidity.

She'd been changing his dressing. Whenever he

thought of her, that was how she appeared in his mind's eye, but she looked like no one's idea of an angel of mercy. If truth be told, Quinn had often thought, she'd always seemed forbiddingly unapproachable in the heavy black habit that she persisted in wearing. She had a slight limp, the legacy from a bout of polio when she'd been a child, he'd learned, and besides her bat-like attire, she'd been as blind as one. Her speech was sharp, and her English, though good, was heavily accented.

"You want to die. I want you to live. We'll see who wins, Mr. McGuire," she'd said grimly the first time he'd drifted up out of unconsciousness. One look at those angry brown eyes, ludicrously magnified behind the thick lenses she wore, had been enough to send him spiraling down into oblivion again. But she'd dragged him back, again and again, pitting her faith and her steely strength of will against the shadowy figure with the scythe. Only once had she even come close to losing hope, and that had been the day that his fever had climbed to its highest. He had been delirious, and whatever he'd been babbling, it had shaken her badly. All he could remember of that delusional day and night were two things.

He'd had wings, and he'd known if he only let himself go he would find himself soaring straight up from the sweat-soaked sheets he was lying on into a colder, lighter sky than the blazingly blue one that hung over the hospital. He'd heard them calling him, and he'd felt himself rising to meet them—

—and the second thing he remembered was Sister Bertille's angular face, her mouth working soundlessly, huge tears standing out behind her crooked glasses, pressing a heavy, chilling weight against his forehead and bringing him crashing back down to earth. Just before dawn the fever had broken. He'd opened his eyes and she'd been sitting beside his bed in a golden pool of light from the gas lantern above her, her rosary in her hands and her mouth slightly open in exhausted sleep. He could still feel the heavy weight on his forehead, and with returning lucidity, he'd reached up and removed it. It had been the cross she usually wore around her neck.

You will know when the right case presents itself…

She'd been right. He had known. And still he'd done his level best to get out of it. *Hell.*

"You're a stupid man entirely, Quinn McGuire," he said out loud. "A stupid, bad man. A debt's a debt, and you must have been crazy to think that you could get out of paying it with a clear conscience."

He'd catch her on her way out and tell her he'd changed his mind. She didn't have to know why, and although the nun was part of it, Quinn wasn't sure he knew the whole reason either. If anyone needed someone to protect her, though, Jane Doe did.

Even if only half of what she'd told him was the truth.

"*…know who you are.* It was creepy!"

"It had to be some crackpot. I kept expecting some jerk to look over the stall partition, for God's sake."

The two young women passing his table had taken a couple more steps before what he'd overheard them say registered. Before they'd taken a third, Quinn was up and out of his seat and somehow blocking their way. One of them was a blonde, and she gave a little jump.

"Hey, you scared me!" Her gaze took him in, and she relaxed visibly. "I think he should buy us a drink to make up for it, right, Kathy?"

Before her friend could answer, Quinn's hand shot out and held her lightly by the shoulder. "I heard you say something just now—*know who you are*. What were you talking about?''

''Do you mind?'' The blonde's flirtatiousness was instantly replaced by peevish annoyance. ''The hand, mister. Get it off me.''

''It's important,'' he said impatiently, letting her go and curbing his own irritation with difficulty. ''What did you mean by that?''

''We saw it in the washroom.'' The blonde's companion had been watching his face. Now she spoke quietly and quickly. ''Those words were written on the mirror over the sinks in lipstick or something. It gave me a bad feeling—''

But already he'd dodged around them, and was heading toward the back of the room. He elbowed a beefy young man in a Yale sweatshirt out of the way, and heard an aggrieved shout and the crash of breaking glass behind him. He felt a hand on his shoulder, trying to pull him back, and without looking around he grabbed it and threw it off.

He was about ten feet away from the entrance to the washrooms when the lights went out. The whole room was plunged into pitch-blackness, and he heard a woman's terror-filled, choked-off scream coming from somewhere ahead of him.

''No need to panic, people. Sure, and we'll have the lights back on in a minute. Everybody just stay calm and remain where you are.''

Someone was trying to stem the panicky hubbub that had started up. The women's washroom had to be nearby, Quinn told himself in frustration as he fought his way through the crowd and felt along the wall. There was a flimsy, freestanding partition that had shielded the washroom entrances from the view of the main room, so he hadn't been able to note the exact location previously, but this was where Jane had gone. He came to a dead end, and realized he'd gone the wrong way.

Her scream—it had been hers, he knew it in his bones—had ended abruptly. That meant that even now she could be beyond his help. What had he told her? Something about if her stalker were serious, he would have killed her by now? Something criminally callous like that?

If the nun had ended up where she'd hoped, she could damn well *bully* God into giving him some help, he thought harshly as he felt a knob, turned it and swung the door back on its hinges with a crash.

Moonlight streamed through high-set, slightly open windows. Along one wall was a shadowy line of cubicles, each one of them open. Along the other wall was a long vanity, with sinks set into it and a mirror stretching its whole length. The place was empty.

He caught a reflection of movement in the darkened mirror, and instinctively looked around. There was nothing there. He looked back at the mirror, and the same wavering reflection caught his eye again.

Then he was whirling around and looking up at the ceiling just beyond the last stall and his heart was turning over in horror.

She'd been hanged by the neck, and even as he realized what he was looking at, her feet stopped twitching.

"Mother of God and all the saints…" The sickened prayer came automatically, but Quinn wasn't relying on divine intervention. Already he had smashed open the door of the last stall, was clambering up onto the back of the toilet tank and hoisting himself to a precarious balance on the metal partition. The open ceiling was crisscrossed with pipes, and he grabbed one to steady himself, even as he wrapped his other arm around Jane's limply dangling body. He lifted her up to ease the pressure on her neck, and her head lolled over onto one shoulder.

The lights—why hadn't they gotten the damned *lights* working yet? Her dress had come undone, most of the buttons that had marched primly down the front probably somewhere below on the floor, and he could feel bare flesh against the forearm he had around her chest.

He had to get her down, lights or no lights. Whatever was around her throat was no longer cutting off her air supply, but if she still had a heartbeat, he couldn't feel it. One-handed, he couldn't fumble with a knot in the dark and keep her supported at the same time, which meant he wasn't going to be able to get her down the logical way.

The building wasn't new. The plumbing, in the washrooms at least, would be either zinc or lead, and neither of those metals was known for its strength. Judging from the trickle of cold water that was dripping onto him, there was a leaky joint only inches away from her noose. If he let go of his pipe, and grabbed hers as he jumped from the top of the washroom stall, the weight of one oversize Irishman would be more than enough to break the join and send them both, pipe and all, crashing to the floor.

All he had to do was hope the break was clean, and close enough to the knot that she slid straight off. Anything else didn't bear thinking about.

He had a whole cartload of Belgian nuns praying for him, apparently. Surely that should buy him some grace.

Quinn let go of the pipe that had kept him balanced. He grabbed intuitively for the one that was Jane's makeshift gallows and again jumped into darkness, his grip around her as tight as fear and muscle could make it.

As his hand found the second pipe, he gave it a massive downward tug, and for a moment he had the terrible conviction that the damn thing was built more solidly than he'd guessed. Then he heard a sharp cracking noise, and all of a sudden it was as if he and the woman he was holding had pitched off the top of a cliff and were riding a waterfall.

It wasn't much of a drop, and he hit the floor immediately, breaking her fall with his body. The water was cascading from the broken pipe above them, and at any other time he would have taken a moment to drag her away from the icy flow. But he didn't have moments, Quinn thought grimly. If her heart had stopped beating, he was going to have to get it started again.

He straddled her, pulling the two halves of her dress open and hearing it rip farther down than he'd intended. Impatiently he shoved aside the sodden scrap of cotton bra that was in the way, and bent down to her, listening for the sound he wanted more than any other to hear right now. There was no heartbeat. His own seemed to stop.

So this was how Sister Bertille had felt, all those years ago, he thought coldly, placing the heels of his palms flat on Jane's chest. It *was* personal—him against the blackness that already had wrapped around her like a shroud. "I want her to live," he muttered, pressing abruptly and forcefully down on the fragile bones beneath his hands. "We'll see who wins."

The cold water continued to stream down onto his back, turning his T-shirt into a second skin, but he was shielding the brunt of it from the woman beneath him. As seconds turned into minutes, and still he felt no answering echo under his palms, he began to think of her heart as an entity all to itself. As he continued in his desperate attempts to get it started again, he began to address it—not Jane, but her heart.

He was going a little crazy, he knew. He didn't care.

"She doesn't remember, but you do," he grunted. "You *must*. There would have been a first kiss—remember how you sped up, how you felt as if you were going to melt? There had to have been times when she was a girl, catching the eye of a boy, and looking away. You beat faster then, didn't you? And tonight when I held her and stroked her skin, and felt that velvety softness beneath my fingertips—don't tell me you weren't putting in a little overtime then, because I knew damned well you were. I could feel you, for God's sake. No matter what she said, *you* were responding to me, weren't you? Respond now, dammit!"

Two things happened at once.

Suddenly the lights went on. And as if the surge of power that had run through the electrical system had transferred itself to her, at that instant Jane's eyes flew open. They were glazed and unfocused, but they were open—and her heart was beating, Quinn realized, all by itself.

Around her neck was a bright yellow nylon rope, like some obscene necklace, and her hands went up to it reflexively. She still hadn't spoken, and neither had he, but for the minute there was no need to. Sliding his hands gently from her exposed breasts, Quinn pulled the two halves of her ruined wet dress together, his eyes on hers.

"I had to. You understand?" he asked softly. She'd shown panic earlier when his touch had been much less intrusive. He was suddenly worried that after all she'd been through, finding him over her like this would shock her into hysteria.

"Take it—" Her voice was a painful croak. Her eyes held a plea. "Take it off my neck, Quinn. Get it *off* me."

The note of hysteria he'd worried about was there, but understandably so. Lifting her cautiously to a sitting position, he pushed aside the swath of sodden chestnut hair that obscured the back of her neck. His mouth was tight with anger as he saw the slipknot that had been fashioned in the yellow nylon. He drew the loose end of the rope through, flinging it as far across the room as he could. To cover his outrage he hoisted her a foot or so to one side, out from under the direct flow from the pipe above.

"Why are we wet? Where did all this water come from?"

She could barely speak, but he knew she needed to. She was distracting herself with non-essentials, trying to keep the horror that she'd just lived through at bay, if only for a few more seconds.

"I broke a pipe to get you down, but that's not important right now. Do you want the police involved?" He brought his hand to her chin, tipping it up so that her gaze locked on his.

"The police?" She shook her head, violently enough so that wet strands of her hair clung to her cheekbones. "No. I told you before, I—I don't want them asking questions. I just want to get out of here."

"I know you do. But what's happened tonight would make them take you seriously now. If you caught a glimpse of your attacker they could have a sketch-artist—"

"I didn't see him. All I saw was that—" Her glance darted toward the scrawled message on the mirror and quickly away again. "Then the lights went out and he— and he—"

"Don't try to talk about it now." He shot a worried look over his shoulder. "Look, any minute now some- one's going to come through that door. We'd better get moving."

For the first time she looked down at herself. He was no longer straddling her, but his arm was still around her back, supporting her. He sensed the instant that she finally took in her revealing state and the fact that she was pressed up against a wet male body. Without con- scious volition, he glanced down too.

Although he'd tried to cover her up a few minutes ago, the ruined dress no longer could conceal the body beneath it—a body that was all graceful contours and surprisingly ripe curves. Creamy-pale breasts were tipped with a soft wash of pink, that even as he watched deepened to a rose blush. He'd thought of wild straw- berries earlier. He was thinking of them now.

And it was a damn good thing he knew how to per- form CPR, because he was pretty sure his own heart had just stopped.

"*Please*—please don't look at me!"

Her voice, high and thin, was shot with panic. He ripped his gaze away immediately, silently berating him- self. He hastened to redeem the situation before it got completely out of hand.

"Here, cover yourself up with this." She was hunched over, her arms crossed in front of her, and he sat back on his heels, quickly stripping off his T-shirt. The thing was nothing more than a wet rag—an oversized wet rag that would hang down nearly to her knees—but it would hide what she wanted to hide.

Still averting his eyes, he tossed it in her direction.

"Thank you." Her reply was barely audible. He waited until he figured she'd put it on, and then turned back to her—and once again his heart missed a beat.

He wasn't going to tell her, but there was a reason why wet T-shirt contests were popular with a certain kind of crowd. She was demonstrating that reason right now, though she seemed unaware that the soaked cotton of his shirt was clinging lovingly to her every curve, and that her nipples were tautly outlined.

"I'm sorry." Her words were still no more than a whisper. "I know you just saved my life."

"Forget it. Now that you're decent, let's try to slip out of here without attracting too much attention." He sounded brusquer than he'd intended, and he could also hear that he'd fallen into the broad brogue that he thought he'd grown out of years ago. He cleared his throat awkwardly. "There's got to be a back exit somewhere around—"

He broke off, disconcerted by the expression on her face. Her lips were slightly parted, and the flush he'd seen lower down on her body had crept up to her cheeks. Her eyes were wide, and so dark that they looked almost a true navy blue. She was looking at him. She was looking at—

He was acutely conscious of the fact that he was naked from the waist up—not shirtless, not unclad, but buck-naked. There was something about the devouring way she was gazing at his chest that made that term the only appropriate one. But for God's sake, there was nothing shocking about peeling his shirt off, even in front of a woman. This wasn't the Victorian era.

She looked as if she was about to swoon.

"You're very...very large," she said faintly. "I hadn't realized..." Slowly she brought her hand up.

Lightly her fingertips ghosted across the surface of his skin. Between her parted lips Quinn realized that her breathing had shallowed and quickened.

She wasn't the kind of woman he was used to. When he was on assignment, he found it easy to stay away from the sexual roulette of picking up a partner for the night. If the urge became absolutely unbearable, he resorted to fantasy, and despite what he'd been told as a boy, he hadn't gone blind yet. But when he was back in Boston, he usually had some kind of short-term, casual relationship going. That was the kind of woman he looked for—someone who wasn't looking for permanence, who took sex not irresponsibly, but lightly.

This emotionally fragile, sexually repressed woman wasn't his type. But the hesitant, questing touch of her fingers on his chest was setting his blood on fire like no other female ever had. Worst of all, he doubted that she had any idea of what she was doing to him—but at any moment she'd be bound to. It wasn't something a man could hide for long, especially in wet khakis that were plastered to his body.

Her glance travelled downward just as he'd feared, paused, and flew up again. Her face had been pink before. Now it blazed with color as her eyes met his.

Then her lashes came down, her head tipped back on her neck, and she moved infinitesimally toward him. Quinn found himself closing the tiny gap between them, found his hand cupping the back of that delicate, seal-wet head and found his own eyes closing like a boy moving into the mystery of his first kiss.

Her lips were cool, and beaded with water. He felt water running from the short ends of his hair, down his face like tears, to join up with the drops he could taste on her. He felt water dripping from her scalp to his hand behind her neck, felt water splashing from the pipe above them, felt it soaking through the fabric of his khakis as he kneeled there.

It wasn't like kissing a woman. It was like kissing a mermaid.

And then her lips opened beneath his, and there was suddenly no doubt that he was kissing a woman—the essence of woman, distilled and condensed, so unadulterated that he knew that he'd never had anything this real before. He'd never come close to this. He tasted her, felt her taste him, and his grip tightened on the back of her neck, bringing her closer. His other hand came up to her face, and he was certain he felt her sigh softly against his mouth.

Then everything changed. He felt her stiffen, and opened his eyes just in time to see hers fly wide with shock. She pulled away from him, her hand going to her mouth as if to shield it from his.

"No!" She stared at him as if she'd never seen him before. "No—I don't *do* this. This—this isn't me!"

She wasn't playing coy. There was real denial in her eyes, and her face was chalky-white. Quinn suddenly saw himself as he realized she was seeing him—too big, too male, too much tanned, battered hide showing. He felt as if he was looming over her. He knew he only had a split second before the situation spiraled out of control.

"It's not you," he agreed, careful not to make any move that she might construe as threatening. His hands hung loosely at his sides. "It was the shock of what you'd just been through. That's why it happened—it was just a reaction."

"But you kissed me back!" She was hugging herself, as if she was afraid she would fly apart if she didn't hold on tight, and his heart turned over.

He'd thought compassion had been burned out of him long ago. It seemed he was wrong. He had no idea what had turned this beautiful, warm woman against her own nature, what had made her shrink from a mere touch, let alone the passion she'd displayed only moments ago. But someone, sometime, had damaged her. It would have been a man. Quinn felt his hands tighten into fists, and it took an effort to relax them.

"I kissed you back," he admitted. "It won't happen again. Can you accept that?"

Her gaze searched his face. Slowly the arms she'd wrapped around herself became less rigid, and she nodded, her eyes never leaving his. "I can accept that. I think you're a man of your word, McGuire."

There were a few different answers he could have given to that, but Quinn didn't get the chance. Even as he began to get to his feet, holding out his hand for her to take or not, as she chose, he heard a perfunctory knock and the door behind him burst open.

"Mother of God—what's been happening in here?" The outburst came from a short man with thinning red hair and astonished blue eyes. The green vest he wore strained over a paunch that probably owed much of its existence to the beer on tap in the bar. Quinn had seen him once or twice during the evening, and had guessed he was the owner of the place.

"I come in here to check that the lights have come on all right, and what do I find but a complete disaster area!" the man sputtered. He looked with appalled confusion around the flooded room, frowning in bewilderment at the lipsticked message on the mirror. "I Know Who You Are? Okay, I'll bite—who the hell *are* you?"

The man's tirade stopped as Quinn rose to his full height. Jane, to his surprise, had taken his hand and had risen with him. She stood beside him, almost, but not quite, touching him, the enormous T-shirt she was wearing making her seem more insubstantial than she was. She was tougher than she looked, he thought abruptly—just like another woman he'd once known.

I surrender, Sister, he thought in wry defeat. *It was a losing battle I was fighting from the first, wasn't it?* Very carefully, he put a protective arm around Jane's sodden shoulders.

"What the hell does it look like?" he growled. "I'm the lady's bodyguard, of course."

Chapter Four

"What did you think having a bodyguard meant, for God's sake? Of course I'm staying overnight—from now on I don't let you out of my sight, lady."

"That's out of the question." Without looking at the furious man beside her on the porch, Jane opened her purse and took out her keys. "And could you please keep your voice down? Most of the tenants here don't keep late hours, and I'd prefer them not to hear me arguing on the front steps with a man at this time of night."

He took the keys from her hand. "Why are you so determined to fight me every step of the way? Didn't I go along with you back at the bar when you said you didn't want the police involved, even though it took all the damn charm I had to convince the owner that he didn't want the publicity?"

"Charm? You blackmailed the man."

"Yeah, well, that's my version of charm. No one ever dangled me by my heels over the parapet of Blarney Castle, just so I could kiss a bloody stone. Which key fits this door?"

The house was a converted Victorian, and like the big Irishman towering over her, it had no charm at all. They were standing right beneath the one light that illuminated the front entrance, and with a sinking heart Jane saw a curtain twitch at a ground-floor window.

Quinn was still bare-chested. Even the taxi driver who'd brought them here had stared so the vinegary old lady who'd rented her room to her would certainly have something to talk about if she saw them here.

"It's the brass one," she whispered angrily. "You can come in and wait while I change out of your T-shirt, but that's all."

"We'll see about that." The porch light picked up the glints of pewter in his hair and carved grim shadows around his mouth. He started to insert the key in the lock and then scowled, turning the knob. The door opened. "Top-notch security you've got here," he said briefly, shooting her a glance.

"Sometimes people get careless and leave it open," she retorted. "There's nothing I can do about that, but my own door's got dead bolts and a chain on it. I'm safe enough there."

"But you've still got three sets of stairs to climb. Didn't you say you were on the top floor?"

He went ahead of her into the old-fashioned vestibule, and she fell in behind him as he started climbing the first flight of broad wooden stairs. He was right about the way she was acting, she thought unwillingly. Back at the bar, there'd been a few moments of solidarity between them when he'd confronted the outraged owner, but during the silent and increasingly uncomfortable taxi ride she'd felt the numbness that had enveloped her since the attack start to dissipate. She'd been acutely aware of his presence beside her, even though he'd barely spoken.

She had no idea why he'd changed his mind about

taking on the job of protecting her. She knew exactly why she was having second thoughts about it.

Twice now—twice in one short evening—she'd behaved completely out of character with the man. The first time had been when he'd touched her. The second time had been when she'd touched him.

She couldn't understand what had happened to her. All she knew was that the way she'd reacted to him had been almost as frightening and inexplicable as the mind games her stalker had been playing the last few weeks— maybe even more so, in a way. Having some unknown person destroy the security of her world was bad enough, but tonight she'd started fearing herself.

"The landing light's burned out. This would be a perfect place for someone to lay in wait for you." Quinn glanced over his shoulder at her as they reached the second floor. "Dead bolts on your door won't be of much use if you never reach your apartment."

She didn't reply. His features tightened in annoyance, but he didn't push the subject. He began to climb the last set of stairs, his gaze taking in the peeling wallpaper and the broken slats in the banister with silent disapproval.

She'd felt safe here before tonight. Despite what he seemed to think, she couldn't believe that a stranger hanging around the hallways or lurking by her door trying to break in would have much chance of success. For one thing, Olga's niece Carla and her boyfriend, Gary, in the apartment next door would be sure to confront him.

She'd imagined Quinn's role to be that of an intimidating escort when she was out in public, a visible sign to whoever was watching her that she was no longer unprotected. In the back of her mind, Jane admitted, she'd hoped that after a day or two of that, her unknown adversary would lose interest in her.

There was still no reason why it wouldn't work out that way. In fact, maybe his attack on her tonight had been the culmination of his twisted game. He'd been close enough to her to experience her terror, he'd fed his obscene impulses when he'd strung her up and left her to slowly lose consciousness. Even though Quinn had appeared in the nick of time to cut her down, her pain and fear might have been enough to satisfy her attacker for good.

She wanted to believe that. She *had* to believe that, because after what had happened between them, she didn't want to spend any more time alone with Quinn McGuire than was absolutely necessary.

Except that right now he was standing in front of the door to her apartment, unlocking it. In a second the two of them would be inside, the door would close behind them, and he'd be telling her that he didn't intend to leave. She felt the familiar bubble of panic begin to rise in her chest.

"I'll go in first. Where's the light switch?" He handed her keys back to her and paused before pushing the door open.

"Just inside, on the—the left." She heard the tremor in her voice and swallowed dryly. "But no one's tampered with the locks, so I don't see what—"

"I admit, the knob's not surrounded with splintered wood and the door's not hanging off its hinges," he ground out. "For God's sake, what's your problem? I'm doing the job you wanted me to do. Give it up. You're not going to win."

There was an edge to his voice, and his eyes were devoid of the brief warmth he'd shown earlier that evening. She felt her panic subside. This Quinn—the cold, professionally curt man confronting her at this moment—she could handle. She stood aside and let him enter the apartment.

It was small—only a single room, really, since the bathroom was so miniscule it hardly qualified. But as soon as he stepped over the threshold the place suddenly seemed even more cramped and claustrophobic than it actually was. It didn't help that the ceiling only rose to its full height by the entrance, and then sloped down from there. At the point where it met the far wall where the sofa bed was, it was impossible even for her to stand without hitting her head.

But normally it was livable. With Quinn's broad-shouldered six foot three or four rising from the scarred and painted floorboards, it was immediately obvious that he'd *have* to concede he couldn't share this space with her.

"Very compact." He looked around him with what seemed like approval. "I'll feel at home here. It reminds me of military quarters."

She blinked in dismay, but already he was moving toward the door that led to the bathroom, bending a little as the ceiling slanted perilously close to his head. He opened the door and glanced in, flicking the light on as he did so. Behind him, Jane saw those massive shoulders stiffen.

The next moment he'd turned back to her, crossing the few feet between them with two swift strides.

"He's been here," he said evenly. "No, don't go in—"

But his urgent warning came too late. Already she was flying toward the bathroom, her eyes wide with shock. She stood at the open doorway and froze.

Over the small sink was a mirror, just as there had been in the women's washroom at the bar. The similarities didn't stop there. The smaller mirror also bore a message in scrawled red letters, but this time her tormenter had written the second half of his cryptic threat— *I Know What You Did*. And this time the words were still tackily wet, running in thick dark rivulets down the surface of the mirror. She swayed forward, her arm extended and her splayed fingers outstretched.

"Don't touch it." His rough grasp pulled her back before he released her. His expression was unreadable. "Yeah, it's blood. I've smelled it often enough to recognize it."

"Oh my God." She hardly recognized her own voice. "Dear God, Quinn—he's *killed* someone! He's finally killed someone—and if I'd let you call the police earlier—"

"He didn't kill anyone—not for this, anyway." His hands gripped her shoulders again, and this time he kept them there. He gave her a shake. "Jane—it's animal blood. I'd bet on it."

"How can you tell?" Her wide eyes darted once more to the mirror. She shuddered and wrenched her gaze back to his face.

"I can't. But he's not interested in killing anyone— not even you. Not yet, anyway." He propelled her away from the door. "And as for the police, they should be on their way here already. You might want to get out of those wet clothes before they arrive."

It was lucky that she was only steps away from the sofa, she thought numbly as she let herself collapse onto it. Her legs seemed strangely detached from her body, and her brain wasn't working the way it usually did, either. She stared up at him blankly.

"The police are on their way here? How could they be?'' She shook her head in confusion. "You haven't even called them—'' The dull fog that was obscuring her thoughts lifted, and she drew a quick breath. "You called them from the bar.''

"I pulled the owner aside, gave him your address and told him to send them here to question you.'' He looked away, and she could see a muscle clench at the side of his jaw. He looked back at her. "You're thinking I betrayed you, but that's not the way of it at all—''

"Oh, that's the way of it. That's the *only* way I read it, McGuire.'' Her hands were shaking so badly that she could hardly grasp the edges of the T-shirt. "Turn around. I want to get out of your damned shirt and into something of my own. Then I'm going to do what you suggested and catch the first bus out of Boston.''

Beside the sofa an open closet was built into the wall. It was no more than a metal rod between two joists, but since there were only a couple of garments hanging there, the lack of room didn't matter. Jane stood up and pulled a sweatshirt off a hanger. Quinn's back was to her. He'd respected that request, at least, she thought with dull anger.

"What the hell did you expect me to do?''

She started as he spoke, the T-shirt half over her head. Pulling it off hastily and watching him all the while, she stripped the ruined bodice of her dress to her waist and quickly put on the sweatshirt. On the single shelf above the clothes-rod was a pair of baggy sweatpants. She grabbed them.

"That's a good question.'' She kicked off her shoes, peeled the dress and her panty hose down to her ankles, and stepped out of them. Immediately she pulled on the sweatpants, keeping her eyes on his broad back.

Just by his left shoulder blade, the flesh was marred by a faded, jagged scar that she hadn't noticed before. She blinked. Whatever had caused it must have come close to taking his life. That wound, if it had penetrated to any depth at all, would have missed his heart by an inch or two at the most.

Her mouth tightened and she knotted the waistband cord of her pants with a jerk. Quinn McGuire's safety and survival was none of her business—just as her safety no longer had anything to do with him.

"First of all I hoped that you'd take on the job of guarding me for a day or two," she said tersely, pulling a pair of sneakers from the closet and jamming her feet into them. She bent over to lace them. "Then you turned me down in no uncertain terms, so I didn't expect ever to see you again. After you saved my life and told the bar owner you were my bodyguard, I expected that you were going to be on my side. What I didn't *expect* was that you would do the one thing I'd told you I didn't want."

"Can I look now?" His tone was sarcastic. Without waiting for her reply he turned, picking up his T-shirt from the arm of the sofa and putting it on. He grimaced as the wet material touched his skin. "You were attacked, dammit. You weren't supposed to die in that washroom tonight, but that's not the point. He's getting closer—"

"That's the second time you've said that," Jane snapped. "I nearly *did* die, McGuire. If you hadn't come in when you did I would have."

Suddenly the fight went out of her. Sinking onto the sofa, she brought her clenched fist to her mouth.

"He was so *strong*," she whispered. "You have no idea how strong he was. I might have gotten a scream out—I don't remember. All I know is that before I even had the chance to react he had that rope around my neck, and then something hit me on the back of the head. When I came to, my feet weren't touching anything and I could feel his arms around my waist, holding me up. Then he let go.'' She squeezed her eyes shut. "Don't tell me he didn't want me to die. He had no way of knowing you would come looking for me.''

"He nearly did kill you, but that wasn't his plan. That was his mistake.'' Quinn sat down beside her, dwarfing the small sofa. "Before we left I had a look at the rope. It had been sawn nearly through where it looped around that rough pipe. If your struggles had gone on for another minute or so, it would have parted completely and you would have fallen to the floor before you lost consciousness.'' He frowned. "Added to that, he must have seen me at your table. If he really meant to kill you, why pick the one time when you had someone with you? He had to know that when he blew the fuses and the whole place went dark, I'd be concerned for your safety.''

"He was the one who blew—'' She stopped. "I guess it makes sense,'' she said dully. "I hadn't even thought about it.''

"The fuse box was on the opposite wall between the two washrooms. He blew the fuses after he saw you enter and the bathroom had cleared out, knowing that in the confusion he'd have a few minutes before I got to you. He must have climbed out through one of the windows. As far as he's concerned, he's still playing games,'' he said, his voice harsh. "But the games stop now. You've got to tell the police everything—including the fact that you don't remember who you are, and your stalker does.''

"Don't forget the second part. He knows what I did.''

Jane pushed herself off the sofa. Her shoulder bag was on the card table by the handkerchief-size kitchen counter, where she'd dropped it as she'd come into the room. She walked over and picked it up. Then she turned, thinking that he was still seated on the sofa. He was standing in front of her.

"I can't let you run. Not like this, without any plans or precautions." He looked down at her, his gaze intent. "You do remember, don't you? You remember something. That's why you're so afraid of being part of any serious investigation."

"That's not true." Her denial was too swift, and his eyes narrowed.

"Tell me what you're hiding from me, and if I can, I'll back up whatever story you choose to tell the police. But you'd better hurry, because that sounds like them now."

She could hear it, too—a peremptory banging at the building's front door and then the querulous, high-pitched voice of her landlady. She bent her head in defeat.

"I told you the truth back at the bar. I really don't remember anything—nothing concrete, at least." She raised her head and met his disbelieving expression with a hopeless one of her own. "You don't believe me."

"Of course I don't believe you. You refuse to help the police get a lead on who your stalker might be by trying to identify you, but you still haven't given me any good reason why." He paused, tensing. "That's them coming up the stairs, darlin'. You can keep on lying— it's your choice. But if I think you've finally told me the truth I'll go to the wall for you."

He'd lowered his voice so as not to be overheard, but there was no mistaking the unwavering conviction in his words. She stared at him, her eyes suddenly sheened with unshed tears.

"Why?" she whispered. "Why would you do that for me?"

"Because I said I'd protect you, and I will—from everything and everyone." He reached over, his fingers brushing lightly against a strand of her still-damp hair, but then he caught himself. "Because that's what having a bodyguard means, up to and including dying for you, if that's what it takes. But you have to be straight with me. What is it you're hiding?"

The sound of heavy footsteps reached the third floor landing and started down the hall toward them. Jane's gaze darted to the door and then back to the impassively silent man in front of her.

He'd just said he'd die for her. Even though she couldn't remember her past life, she knew no one had ever made such a vow to her before. And all he asked in return was her trust. She took a deep breath.

"It's the second part of the message, Quinn." She shook her head, her expression tortured. "I think—I think I might have killed someone. I think I might be a murderer."

"WE'LL BE IN TOUCH." Sitting on the small sofa, Detective Jennifer Tarranova had warm olive skin, sharp brown eyes and was obviously pregnant. Her partner was built on Quinn's lines, and, like Quinn, he'd kept to the middle of the room during the interview.

"I still don't like it that you didn't stick around at the Trinity Tavern, McGuire," he said now. "If we hadn't found you here, we'd have gone looking for you. What's your address these days?"

"This'll be my address for the next little while, Fitz.

And I know you stay in touch with Terry Sullivan, so don't give me any grief about not being able to find me if you want me." Quinn's grin was tight. "Terry's still my contact whenever I'm in town."

"You two go back a ways, or what?" Tarranova arched a curious brow. She looked at her partner. "Donny, you didn't tell me you knew him."

"We were a regular band of brothers once." The big detective shrugged shoulders that were almost as wide as Quinn's. His blue eyes darkened. "But that was long ago and far away, as they say."

"The nun died, Fitzgerald." Quinn's comment was abrupt, as if he had been of two minds whether to make it or not. Then his voice softened. "I thought you might want to know. She was a part of your life too, wasn't she—long ago and far away?"

"Sister Bertille?" For the first time, the edge of antagonism that the other man had displayed since he'd arrived vanished. His broad face clouded. "I'm sorry to hear that. I'll light a candle for her."

"You do that. Me, I went out and lifted a glass to her memory." Quinn's voice was brusque again. "Anyway, see what you can do with the butcher shop lead, though I'm guessing it won't go far."

"You're sure it—" On the sofa Jane swallowed. She tried again, directing her question to Tarranova. "You're sure it was animal blood? It didn't come from—from—" Again her voice failed her. She fixed her eyes on the female detective beseechingly.

"It's not human blood, Ms. Smith. We'll have it analyzed, but it's watery. It's been frozen for a while and then defrosted, so although you can stop worrying about that particular aspect, I don't think we'll be able to trace your stalker by trying to find out where he bought a couple of sirloins in the last few months. Although with the price of top-grade beef, that list of suspects wouldn't have my name on it."

The woman smiled, obviously trying to lighten Jane's mood. As if she realized it was an impossible task, she shrugged, suddenly looking tired. "No prints, no witnesses, no known enemies—I hate to say this, but I wouldn't hold your breath. You did the right thing by asking your friend to hang around for a couple of days, though. Maybe just the sight of him will scare our nutbar off."

Jane mustered a weak smile. "That's what I'm hoping. But what if he tries again?"

"Next time you call us right away. And I mean pronto." Fitzgerald looked at Quinn. "Got it?"

"I was never under your command, Fitz, so drop the sergeant-major act," Quinn said softly. "She needed to get away from there. I wasn't going to have you grilling her in front of a bunch of half-snapped gawkers, right where she'd been attacked."

"Point taken," the other man said grudgingly. "But though I'm not under your command anymore either, I still remember that you used to take crazy chances—"

"Never with my men's lives, boyo," Quinn said sharply.

"Never with our lives, no," Fitzgerald conceded. "But you put yours on the line more times than you should have. All I'm saying is let us handle things. Your old pal Sullivan has a bad habit of getting in the way of police business, and I don't want you doing the same."

"You knew me when we were both young and foolish, Fitz. I promise to follow procedure, if that's the way you want it."

"Why don't I believe you, Quinn?" The detective

sighed. ''Maybe because you've broken promises to me before—like the time with the Swede in that bombed-out village, when we decided that if any one of us managed to get out alive, there would be no going back for the others. But after you'd taken out that sniper and made your escape, what did you do?''

''Ancient history never was my subject.'' Quinn looked away.

''You turned back. You were safely away, but you came back for me and the Swede.'' Fitzgerald shook his head. ''You know, I can't even remember his name.''

''His name was Swenson. Karl Swenson.'' Quinn's voice was low. ''We took turns carrying him on the way back to camp, but he didn't make it.''

''I knew you'd remember. You always remembered the names.'' Fitzgerald's gaze was intent. ''You remember all the faces too, don't you, Quinn? You should take Sullivan up on his standing offer of a job before it's too late.''

''Too late came some time ago for me.'' Quinn pushed himself from the counter where he'd been leaning. ''Maybe it was always too late.''

He grinned suddenly, and turned to Tarranova, who'd been watching them curiously. ''See, Detective—you get two maudlin Irishmen in a room together, and within ten minutes we're talking about fate and death. If we'd had a few beers under our belt we would have gotten around to the subject even sooner, and ended up singing 'Danny Boy' and sobbing.''

''Either that or throwing punches in the parking lot,'' Fitzgerald said dryly.

''Been there, done that—and once or twice with you, if I recall correctly, Fitz.'' Quinn sobered. ''Keep me in the loop on the investigation, okay? If only for old time's sake.''

"If we turn anything up, I'll let you know." Fitzgerald slanted a glance at his partner. "I shouldn't but I will. The Swede was a good kid. I liked him."

"They were all good kids," Quinn said briefly. "I appreciate it, boyo. And if anything more happens I'll call you in right away."

"We'll hold you to that, McGuire. You too, Ms. Smith." Tarranova got up with some difficulty from the sofa, her hand at the small of her back. "You're doing the paperwork on this one back at the precinct, Donny. I've got to get home and get some sleep so I'll be bright-eyed and bushy-tailed for my daily bout of morning sickness tomorrow."

"You're going to milk this pregnancy gig for all you can get, aren't you?" her partner growled, but Jane noticed his hand on Tarranova's elbow as she steadied her balance.

"You bet, sweetie." Her brown eyes were warm with humor, but as she reached the door she turned back to Jane with a puzzled look. "You know, I keep thinking we've met before. I just can't remember where or when. Unless—"

She broke off, frowning. Then she spoke again, her words thoughtfully slow. "Don't tell me—I've seen your face on a most-wanted poster recently, haven't I?"

Chapter Five

The long, sleepless night was nearly over. Through the narrow, slit-like window beside her bed Jane saw that the sky was now dark gray instead of totally black. Without moving, she cautiously looked over at the sleeping figure of Quinn in the armchair across the room.

His quick thinking had saved her twice last night. The second time had been when Tarranova had dropped her bombshell.

I've seen your face on a most-wanted poster recently, haven't I?

The light tone in which the words had been delivered had completely passed her by, and she hadn't seen the smile on the female detective's face. Quinn had taken one look at her stunned expression and had immediately stepped in, easily displaying the charm that he swore he didn't have.

"What about me?" There was a teasing note of complaint in his voice and his whole attention had been focused on Tarranova. In any other circumstances, he would have looked like he was flirting with the woman—in fact, he *was* flirting with her, Jane had thought numbly. "If she gets to be Bonnie, I get to be Clyde. I want to be a dashing criminal, too."

Jennifer Tarranova had looked startled for a moment, and Jane couldn't blame her. She hadn't heard Quinn's velvety purr before, but now that she had, she realized that it was a weapon even more devastating than his rarely seen smile. There was an answering purr in Tarranova's voice when she answered.

"Oh, I'll bet you're on quite a few most-wanted lists yourself, McGuire," she drawled. Her eyes held his, and she gave him a wicked little smile. "If I wasn't a happily married pregnant lady, you might even make it onto mine."

She'd turned her attention back to Jane. "Sorry, it's an occupational hazard. I told my mother the other day that she was the spitting image of a female who'd hit several banks in the area. I told her I wouldn't turn her in, but that I was expecting a Porsche for my Christmas present this year."

By then Jane had regained her composure enough to smile at the joke, and within a few minutes the two detectives had left. After Quinn had locked and bolted the door behind them, he'd turned to her.

"That was a bad moment, wasn't it?" There'd been rough kindness in his voice, and before she'd been able to answer him he'd gone on. "We've got a lot to talk about, you and I, but what you need right now is rest. Everything else can wait a few hours."

That had been hours ago. Throughout the night he'd remained restlessly awake while she'd pretended to sleep, but his breathing had been regular for some time now. If she didn't act soon it would be too late.

She swung her sneaker-clad feet to the floor soundlessly, still wearing the sweat suit she'd slept in, with this moment in mind. She rose, darting an apprehensive glance over at his sleeping form.

In the half-light she could just make out his features. His eyes were closed, and in repose his mouth had lost the grim set it usually wore. He looked at peace, as if only in unconsciousness did he lay down his weapons. She had the unsettling notion that Quinn McGuire's soul was no longer in this room with her, but had flown silently away sometime during the night, never to return.

She didn't have time for this foolishness. Shaking off the ridiculous premonition and berating herself for her jumpiness, she tiptoed past him, holding her breath as she did so. His own breathing was so light she could hardly see the rise and fall of his chest, but he didn't stir. Gaining confidence, she reached for her purse on the card table, and then hesitated.

He'd emptied his pockets before he'd settled down in the chair last night. There on the table was a plain key ring with a couple of keys on it, a collection of change and a thick wad of bills in a stainless steel clip. In her purse was less than forty dollars.

Whatever else she'd done, she hadn't been a thief, she thought shakily. The thought of taking any part of his money was repugnant to her, but with an extra fifty dollars or so, she would be able to go far enough away so that no one would ever find her. She reached for the money clip, her fingers unsteady, and darted a glance over at him.

He was still sleeping. Quickly she peeled off the first few bills from the clip, not even glancing at their denominations, and then she stuffed the money into her purse. He would understand, she thought sickly. He would *have* to understand, and as soon as she got to wherever she ended up, she would find a job and send her first paycheck to Sullivan Investigations, with a note attached informing them to forward the money on to

Quinn. She didn't want him to remember her as a thief. She made her way hastily to the door and reached for the first bolt.

"See, a murderer I could take. But when I sleep with a woman and wake up to find her taking my money, I've got to wonder if I read her all wrong the night before."

Jane whirled around, her purse falling from her shoulder to the floor with a thud. In the armchair behind her Quinn's eyes glinted. He didn't move.

"Not a moonlight flit." He glanced over at the window, where the first light of dawn was just showing. "But damn close to it."

His tone was sardonic. The guilty explanation that she'd been about to make was instantly replaced by defensive anger.

"I would have repaid you." She turned to the door and fumbled clumsily with the top bolt. "But if I have to walk out of here with nothing but the clothes on my back, I'm still leaving, Quinn. It's the only way."

The bolt shot across, and she turned her attention to the second lock. "Don't you understand? When Tarranova made that joke about the most-wanted poster, I felt *trapped.* I was sure she was going to bring out the handcuffs and read me my rights, and I knew anything would be preferable to that."

"I told you I'd protect you." From across the room, his voice was uninflected. "That includes keeping you from being clapped behind bars."

The second bolt snapped back. Jane slid the chain lock free and put her hand on the doorknob. She turned to look at him, her posture rigid. "That's beyond even you, if there's a good reason for me to be behind bars. And I think there might be. If there is, I hope I never know for sure."

She turned back to the door and started to open it, but even as she did his hand was covering hers, pushing it closed again. She started. He was at her shoulder.

"Would you please stop *doing* that?" Her voice was high-pitched and wavery, and in frustration she tugged at the doorknob again. "Every time I think you're somewhere else, I turn around and you're right there. Why can't you just leave me alone!"

"Because I don't think you've done anything so terrible that not remembering it is any kind of a solution." Quinn's grip on her hand tightened. "So get used to turning around and finding me there, angel."

"I'm not your angel, I'm not your darlin' and I'm not your *sweetheart!*" Goaded beyond endurance, she brought her face to within inches of his, her cheeks tracked with tears but her eyes blazing with anger. "Why can't you call me by my *name,* for God's sake!"

"You haven't told me what it is." He glared back at her, his own temper obviously fraying.

"You *know* I won't remember it. How many times do I have to tell—"

"That's right. You won't remember." Even as Quinn picked up on her mistake, she realized what she'd said. Hurriedly she tried to recover.

"It was a slip of the tongue, McGuire—" she began, but he didn't let her finish.

"If it was any kind of slip, it was a Freudian one," he said implacably. "You could remember, but you won't. You told me last night that I was at war with myself—that some part of me went looking for death." He shrugged, his expression grim. "The truth is that you were the one at war—but your war's obviously over. You went looking for death, and you found it."

There was a chilling finality to his words, and she felt

the blood draining from her face. "What do you mean, I found it? I'm not dead, I'm trying my best to stay alive!"

"You're trying your best to stay dead. You had a life once, but something happened in it—something that made you decide to destroy the woman you'd been."

"You said it yourself—you don't even know me." Her whisper was desperate. "How can you be so sure that I didn't do what I think I did? How do you explain the *guilt* I feel every time I see that second message, Quinn?"

Without realizing it, she was clutching at his shirt, her fists wrapping themselves in the olive-drab cotton. He looked down at them, and then seemed to come to a decision. Releasing her grip gently, he enfolded both of her hands in one of his. His other arm went around her shoulders, and slowly he pulled her against him. Jane tensed. It took all her will not to pull away.

"I do know you," he said.

His breath was warm against her hair, but she felt brittle inside, as if a wrong move from him could break her. She waited for him to make it, hardly daring to inhale.

"I knew the kind of woman you were within minutes of meeting you, although I wouldn't let myself admit it. You gave yourself away when you apologized for bringing up old memories, right after I'd been a total son of a bitch to you."

His hand was no longer on her shoulders. She thought she could feel it, very lightly, on her hair.

"Too damned softhearted to bear hurting a man who deserved it. Not exactly the profile of a stone killer." He hesitated. "Why don't you tell me what you think you remember?"

She recoiled instinctively. "I don't want to talk about it," she said automatically. "I don't want to think about it."

"But you do think about it. It's there, just below the surface, all the time." His eyes sought hers, and as their gazes met she was shocked to see the raw pain that flashed, like heat lightning, behind the clouded pewter irises. "You dream about it and you relive it, over and over again, in your mind. It's the backdrop to everything you do, isn't it?"

His voice was intense. She nodded slowly. "You're right. It's like being stuck in a nightmare. But how did you know?"

He blinked, and the heat left his gaze. Once again his eyes were opaque. "That doesn't matter. What does matter is bringing it out into the open. It's like crawling through a jungle at night—sometimes the noises that scare you so much turn out to be nothing at all."

"And sometimes the noise is a lion," she retorted with shaky defiance. "What then?"

"Then at least you're on your feet and facing it." He smiled wryly. "It's not much, but it's better than having it jump you from behind, darlin'."

This time his use of the endearment didn't bother her. Having him so close to her wasn't as frightening as she'd thought it would be either, Jane realized. In fact, if she was about to face a lion, she wanted to do it with Quinn's arm around her. She closed her eyes, let herself breathe in the scent of him, and peered through the single chink she had in the barricaded fortress that was her memory.

"I don't see what he looks like, but he's tall." Her voice was almost inaudible against his chest. "He's so tall—and he's angry, Quinn. I don't know what he's angry about, and I don't think he's even angry at me. But I know that at any minute he could turn his rage my way. I'm—I'm terrified."

Her heart was thumping erratically. She swallowed, and this time there was no doubt that he was stroking her hair.

"And then what happens?" he asked calmly. She made herself go on.

"We're in a bedroom—it's hard to see, but there's a little light shining from somewhere near the floor. I know that there's someone else in the bedroom, too. It's this other person he's looking for. He's yelling at me, asking me where this other person is. I'm crying and telling him that I don't know. But I'm lying."

"You know where the person he wants is? You're covering up?" Quinn's hand stilled, and then resumed its slow, reassuring stroking.

"The other person is someone I care for, I think. No—I'm sure of it. I *love* him. He means everything to me. And he loves me, too, so I can't betray him. He's hiding under the bed, and the tall shouting man is standing over me, getting angrier by the minute."

Her eyes were still closed, but Quinn had been right. It was as if the scene was unreeling against the backdrop of her mind, like a horror movie being played in excruciatingly slow motion. "I can see the shouting man's belt buckle," she went on, more tentatively. "It's in the shape of a truck, an eighteen-wheeler. His hands go to the buckle and he starts to undo it, and I know he's going to whip me with his belt. He smells funny and his eyes are all shiny and his face is dark red from anger, and the belt looks like a snake sliding out of the loops of his jeans, and I *know*—I just *know*—he's going to use it on me."

Her voice was thin. Even to her own ears it didn't sound the way it usually did, although it was recognizably hers. She drew her brows together tightly, and dug her nails into the palms of her hands. The grip that Quinn had on her clenched fists was a welcome anchor to the real world, but the horrors unfolding in her mind were still growing. She looked up at him, her eyes open but unseeing.

"Oh, Quinn," she said in a high, thready whisper. "I think it's a lion."

"I think it's a lion, too, sweetheart." His own voice caught, and then steadied. "But we'll face it together."

She gave a shuddering sigh, and her lashes drifted back down onto her cheeks.

"He's going to use it on me unless I tell. So I tell." She shook her head against his chest. "I tell him where my friend is hiding, and then he stops yelling at me and he smiles. He folds the belt up in half in his hands and he snaps it, and it goes *crack!*—just like a gunshot. And from under the bed I hear my friend trying to get away, but the big man is too fast. He bends down and grabs him by the ankle and starts dragging him out. And I know that I can't stop him—I've never been able to stop him before—but this time it's going to be bad and this time it'll be my fault. I look around the room, but I can hardly see because I'm crying so hard. I'm afraid, and I haven't got much time, and I see the baseball bat in the corner of the room, but my legs are too shaky to go over and get it."

Her voice was coming faster now, her words running together. Quinn was no longer stroking her hair. His hand was cupped protectively around the back of her head, as if he were trying to shield her.

"I see him being pulled out. His pajama legs are

shoved up to his knees, but he's not wearing a top, and I can see his back. The marks from the last beating still haven't scarred over, and I know he won't be able to take another one so soon. The bat is in my hands—I don't even know how it gets there—and I lift it up as high as I can. It's heavy, Quinn. I can hardly hold onto it. And then I bring it down on the back of the man's bent head, and I hear it make a terrible noise, like the noise the melons make when Mama thumps them in the supermarket, and I'm scared. But then he lifts his head and looks at me, and I'm even *more* scared, so I bring the bat up again, and down again. This time it comes down right on his face and blood comes out of his nose, and he falls onto the floor. I know that I've killed him and someone starts screaming—''

Her flood of words came to an abrupt halt.

''And that's all you remember?'' Quinn asked quietly, after a moment.

''That's all. Everything ends there.'' The high, thready tone of a moment ago was gone. Jane's voice was dead and flat. ''But that's enough, isn't it? I brought a bat down on a man's head with all the force I could muster, and not just once, but twice. I must have killed him, Quinn. Whoever he was, I murdered him.''

''What did the little light by the floor look like?'' His question was sharp, and she answered without thinking.

''It was in the shape of a bear—oh!'' She looked up at him, a spark of life returning to her eyes. ''I hadn't recalled that before. But what does it matter? I still—''

''And your friend's pajamas—what color were they?'' Again he shot the question at her, and again she answered promptly.

''Blue. Blue with red—'' She stiffened. ''Blue with

red trains," she said slowly. "But that can't be right. That sounds like the kind of pajamas a—"

"And how was it that you could see the belt buckle so clearly? That's the clearest picture in your mind, isn't it? *Why?*"

"Because it's right in front of me when he's standing there. It's just a few inches above the level of my..." Her voice trailed off. "It's just a few inches above the level of my eyes," she whispered. "He's an *adult,* and I'm a—"

"You're a little girl." Quinn drew back a little, and both his hands went to her arms. He gripped them tightly. "It's a child's memory—not something that happened recently. It's the most frightening memory from your childhood, but a little girl swinging a child's bat that she could barely hang onto couldn't have killed a grown man. He was drunk, and you probably knocked him out, but you wouldn't have killed him. You just stopped him from abusing another child." His gaze held hers. "You were the lion. You had the heart of one."

"I'm not a killer." A weak little laugh bubbled up in her throat. "Quinn—I'm not a killer. I didn't murder anyone!" The last of the tenseness left her limbs, and she blinked back the moisture from her eyes, her smile brilliant. "You don't know what it's been like, thinking I was responsible for causing the death of another person."

He gave her a brief smile back, but his eyes were shadowed and he didn't answer her. She went on unheedingly.

"If that's what was blocking my memory, then it should return completely, shouldn't it? And then I'll know why—" She frowned, her smile dimming. "The little boy with the scars on his back—he must have been my brother. And the shouting man would have been my father. No wonder I didn't want to remember my childhood."

"It made you the person you are today," he said. "Good or bad, it's part of you. Somewhere out there you've got a brother who loves you."

"But somewhere out there is someone who thinks he has a reason to hate me."

Suddenly she realized that she'd been standing in the circle of his arms for minutes, and she took a clumsy step back. Avoiding his eyes, she bent over, picked up her purse from the floor and walked over to the small table. She shot him a shamefaced smile as she took out the handful of bills and replaced them in the clip.

"I really did intend to pay you back. I just thought that running was the only solution," she said in a low voice. "But now I don't know what the solution is. Who could he be, Quinn? Who's stalking me, and what did I ever do to make him hate me so? And how did he follow me from my old life to this one, when even I can't bring the two together yet?"

"We're going to have to ask Terry Sullivan for some help, I guess."

She frowned. "Help? What kind of help?"

"I'm just a one-man army. Terry has the weight of Sullivan Investigations behind him, and a whole payroll of contacts—some of them on the police force. I want the list that you didn't want Tarranova and Fitz calling up on the computer, angel."

"What list?"

"The list of women who've gone missing recently." He looked at her. "We're going to find out who you were, and then we're going to find out what was happening to you during the last few weeks of your previous life. Unless your memory comes back in the meantime,'' he added.

He'd just called himself a one-man army, she thought nervously. The description was apt. But now he was getting ready to take the war into the enemy's camp—with her tagging along behind him.

"Do you know how to use a gun?'' His question broke into her worried thoughts, and she turned a startled face to him.

"A *gun?*'' She gave a shaky laugh. "Of course not. I'm terrified of them.''

"How about any form of self-defense?'' He shook his head before she could answer. "I guess not. Besides, in the time I've got to teach you, a weapon's a surer bet. I'll take you to Sullivan's practice range this afternoon and show you the basics.''

She found her voice. "But that's what *you're* for, Quinn. Why do I need to know how to use a gun?'' She pressed her lips together in firm denial. "I'm sorry, I can't. It's completely alien to me.''

"That's why they call it a practice range,'' he said shortly. "After you practice for a while, it won't be so alien.'' He was about to say more, but suddenly he cocked his head to one side.

"There's someone at your door,'' he said, so quietly that she had to strain to hear him.

"Jane? You home?'' The hushed query from the hall outside her apartment was accompanied by a muted tapping on her door. "You okay in there?''

"That's Carla.'' Letting out a relieved breath, Jane attempted to take a step forward, but Quinn's grip held her back.

"He used Martine to get to you.'' He strode past her to the door, his shoulders set as he opened it.

"Oh—I didn't know you had company." Past Quinn's solidly immovable bulk Jane could see her neighbor furiously blushing. "Gary and I were worried. We came home late last night and Mrs. Quantrill told us that the police had been here."

Carla was tall, and although she gave the impression of being heavy, most of her weight came from muscle. But for all her size, she could be shy with strangers, Jane knew.

"I took your advice and went to a security firm yesterday," she said, as the bigger woman edged past the silent Irishman with difficulty. "They gave me Quinn's name."

Carla beamed at him, her reserve melting. "Whew, that's a relief. Carla Kozlikov. Good to meet you, Mr. Quinn." She stuck out her hand.

"It's just Quinn. You told Jane she needed a bodyguard?" His hostility ebbed slightly.

"That's why I say it's a relief." She nodded. "Gary and I have been worried sick about her. When Gary met me at the gym last night, we even thought twice about coming back here to see if you were home yet, instead of going out to dinner and a movie. But it was our anniversary—not a wedding anniversary or anything," she said swiftly. She blushed again. "Just of the day we met, but it was still a special occasion."

"Celebrating the luckiest day of my life? Special is an understatement."

Gary stood in the doorway, shooting an affectionate smile at Carla. He grinned at Quinn. "Gary Crowe. I'm glad Jane found someone to keep an eye on the situation. That old battle-ax Quantrill was waiting up, and she told us about the police being here." His brows drew together in concern. "Not another one of those stupid messages, I hope."

His voice was edged with anger, and Jane gave him a grateful glance. "Another message," she admitted softly. "But that wasn't the worst of it." She gave them a condensed version of the attack at the Trinity Tavern.

"I don't like it," Gary said worriedly. "I'm going to look into an alarm system. Obviously this guy can pick locks."

"Does Quinn know about the amnesia?" As Gary asked Quinn's advice about security systems and the two men moved over to the window, Carla directed her question to Jane in an undertone.

"He knows. He thinks I could regain my memory if I really wanted to," Jane said doubtfully.

"He's probably right." The big woman's response was unexpected. "From the start I always thought there was a reason you couldn't remember who you were. I thought maybe you'd been trying to escape from an abusive marriage."

There was a slight query in her voice, and for some reason her curiosity made Jane uncomfortable. She owed Carla a lot, she knew. While her aunt had seen nothing wrong with helping Jane make her unofficial departure from the hospital, as a nurse, Carla's position had been different.

Her neighbors were warm and caring people, Jane told herself. But they knew as much about her as she did herself. It was unsettling.

"I don't feel married." Wanting to change the subject, she smiled. "And besides, you already snagged the perfect guy. So what should I have gotten you for your anniversary yesterday—something paper or something in silver?"

Her little joke had the effect she'd intended. Carla's freckled skin colored again, and she gave a flustered laugh. "Not silver, anyway. It hasn't been nearly long enough for—"

"Weren't you going to make cinnamon rolls for breakfast this morning?" Gary strolled over, a pitifully hopeful expression on his good-natured face.

As he linked his arm in hers Carla giggled, and a few minutes later Jane saw them out into the hall. Even while she locked the door behind them, she could still hear their laughing voices as they let themselves into their own apartment next door.

She turned to Quinn. "Did it relieve your mind a little, meeting them?"

"I don't know about him, but she's damned dangerous," he said flatly. "She doesn't like you at all. You're staying at my place tonight."

Her mouth dropped open in shock. "Who—*Carla?*" she sputtered, when she'd found her voice. "Are you crazy? She's a sweetheart! If it hadn't been for her I wouldn't have gotten this apartment, and she and Gary have gone out of their way to—"

"She's jealous as hell. Anytime her boyfriend addressed even the most casual remark to you, she was watching both of you like a hawk. I'd like to know where she was at the exact moment you were attacked in the Trinity last night." Quinn frowned. "Pack what you need. I'm getting you out of here now."

"You took an instant dislike to the woman, before she'd even stepped over the threshold," Jane protested heatedly.

"Sure, and she was eavesdropping, that's why!" His voice was low and intense. "She's certainly got the heft and the muscle to have strung you up at the Trinity. I'm not saying she did. But if you're looking for enemies, you don't have go any farther than next door, darlin'.''

"I admit, she's probably a lot stronger than most men. Stronger than a normal man, like Gary, anyway—'' she began, but Quinn was in an arguing mood.

"Well, there you're wrong again." He shook his head decisively. "He's no ox, but he's all hard muscle. Except he wasn't givin' you the evil eye every time you weren't looking, so I think we can forget him."

"I've got a better idea. Let's forget this whole stupid conversation," Jane retorted. "But there's just one thing that maybe you *should* remember—Martine said that the person who held a knife to her throat was a man."

"I hadn't overlooked that, but she also said that he spoke in a whisper. I doubt that she could have known for sure from a few words whispered in the dark." He glanced at the chronometer on his wrist. "If you want a quick shower, you've got five minutes. After that I'm coming in and hauling your sweet butt out of there, phobia or no phobia. We've got a full schedule today. Got anything else to wear besides that?"

"What's the matter with what I'm wearing?"

"Those sweats are too baggy. Jeans and a T-shirt are more appropriate for the firing range," Quinn said shortly. "If you haven't got any, we'll pick some up for you downtown. I want to be able to watch your stance and the way you position your arms, and right now everything's obscured."

"But I still don't see why it's necessary for me to do this," Jane protested. Her eyes darkened with apprehension. "If anything happens, you're going to be defending me. You *are,* aren't you?"

For a moment he didn't answer her. His gaze met hers

grimly. "Until my last breath," he said. "But if anything happened to me, I'd want to know you had a fighting chance. You're still going to learn how to handle a gun."

Chapter Six

"How's she doing?"

Quinn looked around, taking the empty clip from the Glock and setting the weapon down on the stainless steel shelf that ran the length of the barrier behind the firing range in the cavernous basement of Sullivan Investigations. Beside him, Terry Sullivan grinned, his hands in the pockets of an exquisitely cut dark suit.

Quinn smiled wryly as he looked at him. Sullivan, despite the trappings of success, hadn't changed. He still slouched as casually as if he were wearing fatigues instead of Armani, he drove his Jaguar like it was a Jeep, and he went through women like a soldier on leave. One of these days the boy was going to take a long, hard fall, Quinn thought sardonically. But that day hadn't come yet.

"She's in the latrine," he said. "She took one look at the Glock, went green, and headed off at a run. By the way, thanks for sending me the business."

"My pleasure." Sullivan rubbed his jaw, trying to hide his smile and not succeeding. "She's afraid of guns?"

"Yeah, but somehow I just don't buy it." Quinn frowned. "I told you she had amnesia? It's as if she not only lost her memory, but her own personality. Every once in a while she reams me out like a drill-sergeant. That's the real Jane coming through. Or she looks at me with complete understanding, like she can see right into my—'' He broke off, appalled at himself.

''You're doing a little revealing yourself, there, McGuire.'' Sullivan looked as shaken as he felt. ''You're the last of the tough guys. Don't tell me you've gone and fallen for Miss Jane Doe.''

''Her name's Smith for now,'' Quinn snapped. He jabbed the button that replaced the target, and watched in silence while the fresh one, a silhouette of a male figure, slid into place. He felt Sullivan's appraising eyes on him and let out an impatient breath.

''I'm a freakin' soldier, Sully.'' He turned and gave his old friend a flat stare. ''You got it right—I'm the last of the tough guys. Love and marriage aren't in the cards for someone like me, and I know it.''

''Oh, right. I'd forgotten.''

Now Sullivan's expression was hard, his blue eyes just as icy as the pale gray ones they met. The two men were almost equal in height, and at the same moment, they both shifted their weight slightly onto the balls of their feet.

''I'd forgotten the damn *cards*,'' Sullivan said, his voice low. ''I'd forgotten them and your crazy Irish fatalism, McGuire. Or maybe I was just hoping that you'd come to your senses. Your death won't bring them back—not Jack, not Paddy, not even the kid, whatever his name was.''

''Haskins,'' Quinn said without emotion. ''I know I can't bring them back.''

''But you think that you should have gone in their place. You always thought it should have been you, instead of any one of the men you were responsible for. And you won't be at peace until you join them.''

"You don't know what you're talking—" An indrawn breath whistled through Quinn's bared teeth like a hiss. He stood motionless, only his eyes slowly moving down to where Sullivan had grabbed a fistful of his T-shirt. Then his gaze slowly traveled up again to the other man's face. "You're my best friend, Sully," he said. His arms hung loosely at his sides, but his stillness had an ominous quality about it. "Get your hands off me. I don't want to hurt you."

"Remember Aquaba—that little cantina on the outskirts of town? We were pretty evenly matched back then, McGuire, and I've stayed in shape. I'll take my chances." Sullivan didn't release his hold. "Goddammit, Quinn, I don't want to be raising a glass to *your* memory in the next month or so, and I've got a terrible feeling that's exactly what I'm going to be doing."

The blue eyes blazed with sudden pain. "I don't want to hear them flying overhead one night, and know that you're up there with them, boyo."

"Myths and legends." Quinn's voice was even. "I didn't know you believed in that kind of thing."

"Most of the time I don't. But when I see the road you're heading down, I wonder if there isn't some truth to those legends. Because you believe in them wholeheartedly, Quinn—you *need* them to be true. That's the only way you can be free of the guilt."

Sullivan looked down at his hand as if he'd forgotten that he was still gripping Quinn's shirt. Slowly he opened his fingers and let go. "Little Miss Jane Doe," he said, with a strange smile. "Are you sleeping with her?"

"Dammit, Sully—watch what you're saying, or so help me—"

"I didn't think so." Sullivan looked past him. "Here she comes now. You know, Quinn, the lady may never have handled a gun before, but I've got a feeling she's already hit a nerve. See you around, tough guy."

Even as Sully strolled away, Jane was beside him again. Her face was the color of cheese.

"Ready?" he asked shortly, pretending he didn't notice her pallor. Sullivan's little theory couldn't be more wrong, he told himself. *Both* his theories.

"I—I can't go through with this." Wearing the new T-shirt and the jeans he'd insisted she buy, Jane wrapped her arms around her body, not meeting his eyes. "I know I'd never be able to use a gun in a real situation. I'd panic, or I'd forget to take the safety off, or—"

"The only way you'll ever be able to use it when you need it is if you practice until it's second nature. The Glock's unloaded." He nodded at the weapon. "Go on, pick it up. Get the feel of it."

"I don't—"

"Pick it up."

He felt like a total bastard, and for a moment he considered dropping the whole idea. She was probably right, he thought wearily. She'd freeze if she ever had to use it to defend herself. A picture flashed into his mind of the way she'd looked last night hanging from that damned pipe—helpless, more dead than alive, and an easy victim for the twisted monster who'd put her there.

She hadn't had a chance. If he gave in to her now, she wouldn't have a chance the next time she was alone and unprotected. If playing the bad guy was what he had to do to avert that, then so be it.

"If we never learn who your stalker is and you relocate to another city under another name, you'll probably be safe.'' His voice was toneless. ''But what if he never gives up? What if the town where you live gets a new ice rink, say, and your face is in the background of the news photo of its opening? Or you get married and your husband wants to take you with him on a business trip to Boston?''

Her eyes were open now, and she was staring at him fearfully. She still had her arms wrapped around herself, and her body was slightly hunched over, as if she felt sick, but he forced himself to ignore that part of him that wanted to walk out of here with her, to hold her as he'd done this morning, to tell her that she didn't have to worry, he'd always be around to keep the danger away from her.

Because that would be a lie. And suddenly he realized that Sullivan had been right on one thing—she *had* touched a nerve with him. Enough so that he didn't ever want to be less than honest with her, anyway.

''One day it could come down to you, him, and whatever weapon you can use against him,'' he went on implacably. ''And I want you to walk away alive from that encounter. Pick up the—''

''No!'' The exclamation burst from her with a vehemence she hadn't displayed before. No longer hugging herself, her arms were now at her sides, her hands balled into fists. Her face was still white, but her eyes blazed with a mixture of anger and fear. ''I was just in that washroom getting physically *sick* at the thought of having to go through with this, Quinn! I'm afraid of guns! They kill people, and I don't even like *looking* at—''

''Pick up the damned gun.'' Out of the corner of his eye, Quinn saw Sullivan pause a few feet away, watching them, but Jane didn't seem to realize that they had an audience. She was shaking, her gaze locked on his, the skin tight over her delicate cheekbones.

"I'm not getting out of here until I do, am I?" she asked, her voice ragged with hopelessness.

"No." His one-word answer seemed to hit her like a blow. She'd actually flinched, Quinn thought, and all of a sudden he knew he couldn't continue. He was just about to speak when he saw her reach slowly for the Glock.

"You're sure it's not loaded?" Her voice was an almost inaudible thread.

"I'm sure. But that's not good enough. You have to be sure." He was standing a little behind her, and he reached around the shaking shoulders and released the empty clip. "Rule number one—assume a weapon's loaded until you see for yourself that it's not."

She nodded. The gesture was so controlled it was almost imperceptible. "Then what?" she asked, her lips barely moving.

"We'll do a dry run first, just to get you used to the feel of it. You're right-handed, so that's your shooting hand." He wrapped her fingers around the handgrip. "The Glock's safety is built into the trigger—pull it back. Can you feel it?"

Step by step he took her through the basics. Sullivan had come closer, but he didn't interrupt them. She couldn't seem to get her body position quite right, so at one point Quinn hunkered down and moved her feet for her.

"The first time you feel the recoil you're going to think someone just pushed you backward, so you want the best balance you can get. Right foot slightly forward, left foot slightly back. You got it. Elbows still bent?"

He looked up and saw her incline her head a fraction.

She was wearing the shooting glasses, and although the hearing protectors were still just hung around her neck, already she was unrecognizable as the woman of this morning. Her jeans fit her in all the right places, and they were cinched around her waist by a plain leather belt. The only T-shirt she'd been able to find in her size had been black, and the severity of the color suited her. It contrasted with the creaminess of her skin, and without the distraction of bows and ruffles and lace, her fine-boned elegance suddenly was apparent.

Quinn realized he was still holding her leg. He let go hastily, and cleared his throat. "The target's thirty feet away. It's just a torso, because that's what you want to hit in a real situation. This isn't the movies, and no one's going to be aiming for the bad guy's trigger finger. See the circles? That's his heart, but I don't even want you trying for that." He looked at her, his face serious. "If this was for real, you'd just aim for the middle of his body, and keep pumping out those nine millimeter rounds until the clip was empty."

"There's a circle on the head outline, too," Jane began, but he cut her off.

"Forget that. That's for the professionals, and even they aren't going to get inside those circles every time." Casually he reached for the loaded clip on the shelf beside them. He held it out to her. "Put the clip in like I showed you."

He saw her shoulders slump forward again in that curious, hunched attitude. She'd been holding the Glock in her right hand and gripping her right wrist with her left for steadiness, as he'd shown her, but now both hands were trembling again. She set the gun down on the metal shelf with a clatter. She turned to him, her eyes panicky behind the shooting glasses.

"I know how it works. You've taken me through everything, and if I ever have to use one I should be able to. I don't see why I have to fire off real bullets." Her voice was low and intense. "What it all comes down to is that I'm practicing to kill another human being."

"You're practicing saving your own life, lady. And Quinn here's the best damn teacher you could have." Sullivan had come up behind them. He stood a few feet away, his fists shoved negligently into his pockets, a hard light in his eyes. "Maybe better than you deserve."

"Sully, stay out of this." Quinn glared at his friend.

"What do you mean, better than I deserve?" Jane turned to face the detective, her stance off-balance and somehow precarious. The hearing protectors slung around her neck suddenly reminded Quinn of the rope from the night before, and he started forward.

"Sullivan, it's none of your business—" he began, but neither of them was listening to him.

"What do you mean?" Jane demanded again. She stared at Sullivan, and the corner of his mouth lifted in a tight grin.

"I mean that you seem to think McGuire's your enemy, instead of the bastard he's trying to protect you against. Yeah, he's teaching you to take down a man— *if* you have to, and if that's the only option you have. But you're too goddamned sensitive to even contemplate that possibility, aren't you?" He shook his head, his gaze never leaving her shocked face. "So along with trying to keep you safe from a psycho, he's going to have to worry about keeping you safe from yourself, because you refuse to face reality. That could get both him and you killed—and if it did, I'd only be holding one wake, believe me, lady."

"Get the hell out of here, Sullivan!" Quinn's voice

was like a whip-crack in the silence. "You're way out of line, talking to—"

"No. He's right." Her words were barely above a whisper, but they overrode his louder tones. "From the start I've wanted you to make this all go away for me, without any effort on my part. I just wanted to close my eyes and pretend it had nothing to do with who I am."

She turned and picked up the Glock. Beside it was the loaded clip, and she picked that up, too. "But I don't really have a choice anymore, do I?"

One-handed, she pulled the hearing protectors up and over her ears, and even as Quinn started to speak he stopped, realizing that she wouldn't hear him. He flicked a furious glance at Sullivan, who stared impassively back.

"She's terrified of actually shooting the thing, for God's sake," he snapped. "I shouldn't have forced her into this in the first place, dammit!"

He turned back to Jane, intending to put an end to it, but even as he did he heard the clip snapping smartly into position. Her whole attention was focused on the gun in her hand, and something about her posture and attitude made him pause. He frowned.

"She's terrified? It doesn't look like it to me," Sullivan said in an undertone. "I knew you were a good small-arms instructor, but I didn't know you were as good as all that."

He hadn't known either, Quinn thought. Holding the gun in both hands, pointing at the floor, she gazed straight ahead at the silhouetted torso thirty feet in front of her, and an almost unnatural relaxation seemed to come over her.

A vision flashed through his mind. He saw again the awkward way she'd run toward the washrooms last night, her knees together and that clumsy purse impeding her. That woman was gone. The woman standing in front of him was somebody else entirely.

He wanted to stop this *now*.

But he was already too late. He checked the half-step he'd taken toward her as he saw the Glock come smoothly up into firing position, her elbows slightly bent to take the recoil as he'd taught her. And then she fired off the first shot, and the spent cartridge flew from the chamber to her right—and Quinn knew that nothing he was seeing was the result of his teaching.

The recoil jerked her aim up, but as if she'd been anticipating it, already her left hand was steadying her shooting wrist back into position, and the second shot rang out with a deafening explosion even as he was hastily pulling on his own hearing protectors. The third shot was a split second later, and then the fourth, barely a heartbeat between them. Spent cartridges were ejecting from the side of the Glock, one following the other almost mechanically, and dancing to the floor around them.

Five. Six. Quinn knew that a detached part of his mind was automatically counting off the shots, but his attention was fixed on Jane as if there was nothing else in the universe but the woman and the gun and the steady crashing explosions that kept coming. *Seven.* Her grip went up and came down fluidly, and then her trigger finger squeezed off another shot. *Eight.*

The knuckles of her left hand were white where they tightened around her slender right wrist, keeping her aim true. There were two cartridges left, he knew. *Nine.* Her face was unreadable, and from his vantage point on her left he saw that she showed no reaction to the noise, the acrid smell of cordite that surrounded them or to the powerful recoils that were jolting her arms with every pull of the trigger.

Her hands came down into position again, her grip steadied, and she pulled the trigger of the Glock. The tenth and last shot rang out.

She lowered the weapon without pause. Quinn realized that she'd been counting too, and somehow this seemed almost more disconcerting than all the rest. What happened next was just as unsettling. Without even looking at the gun in her hand, she snapped the magazine release at the side, popped out the empty clip and placed them efficiently back on the shelf beside her. With her thumb she jabbed the button that activated the cable to bring the target to the shooting booth—he hadn't even shown her what it was for, he realized disjointedly—and while the silhouetted torso moved toward them, she took off her glasses and slid the ear-protectors down around her neck.

She still hadn't looked at him. She hadn't spoken. In fact, he thought edgily, it was as if she was unaware that there was anyone else around. He opened his mouth to say something—*anything*—to break her eerie silence, but he was beaten to it.

"Sweet St. Barbara." Sullivan came closer, his invocation more awestruck than profane. "Or I think it's St. Barbara who's responsible for this. She's the one the artillerymen call on, isn't she?"

But Quinn didn't answer. The target was close enough now to see, and at first he didn't realize what he was looking at. She'd missed every single shot, he thought, confused. The concentric circles over the heart hadn't been pierced at all. The target trundled to within a foot of the shooting barrier and jerked to a stop. Jane reached out and pulled it closer, her gaze not on the torso, but higher, and then he saw.

She'd been right, he thought helplessly. There *was* a circle on the silhouette's head, of course. But now it was riddled with crisp, neat holes, and he knew if he took the target from her and counted them himself he'd find that all ten of her shots had found their mark. The proof was right there in front of his eyes, but he still didn't believe it. It was impossible.

"Watch her!" Sullivan said urgently, and he tore his attention from the target as it fluttered from Jane's nerveless fingers. She was swaying, and his arm went around her just in time to keep her from falling.

"What's the matter—are you going to be sick?" he asked sharply. The navy blue eyes were glazed and staring, but even as he watched he saw the clouded confusion leave them, and she focused on his face.

"I did that, didn't I?" She gave an almost imperceptible nod at the target, still clipped to the cable.

"You did that," he agreed tightly. "I've never seen anything like it. Do you know where you learned how to shoot like that—has any part of your memory returned?"

"No. But I think I just caught a glimpse of the kind of person I was," she said hoarsely.

A shudder ran through her. She closed her eyes and then opened them again, meeting his gaze.

"Oh, Quinn—I think it's a *lion,*" she whispered unsteadily.

Chapter Seven

The small black-and-white picture was so blurry that it was hard to make out the features of the woman it was supposed to portray. Jane squinted and drew back a little. A wide, happy smile, shoulder-length dark hair, and eyes that seemed somehow not to match the smile.

"Forget her."

Startled, she looked up. Terry Sullivan had entered the room. His manner toward her held a touch of stiffness, but the cardboard cup of coffee he set down in front of her seemed to indicate that he was willing to call a truce.

"Quinn's still using the phone in my office. Do you need anything?"

Prying the lid from the coffee container, she mustered a smile. "Nothing, thanks." She sank back in the leather chair and made a vague gesture that encompassed her surroundings. "It's comfortable in here."

"It's one of our interview rooms." He glanced around. "When you've got a wealthy blueblood who suspects her husband's cheating on her and wants to cut him off at the knees or maybe a little higher, you keep the decor soothing. I thought it might be appropriate for what you're going through, too."

"I knew it wasn't going to be pleasant." She looked

at the pictures and typewritten descriptions that covered most of the tabletop and picked up the photo she'd been studying. "But I hadn't realized that it would affect me as much as it has. Why did you say forget her?"

Sullivan plucked the sheet from her. "I didn't mean to put this in with the rest. She was found. Her husband was charged with her murder." He looked down at the picture, his jaw set, and then he sighed. "Any likely possibilities? It's too bad they don't all have photos."

"Even the photos aren't much help." Jane tried to shut her mind to the tragic fate of the woman whose face had just been smiling up at her. "Most of them could be anyone. Sullivan, how long have you known Quinn?"

Her abrupt change of subject obviously took him by surprise. "Long enough," he said guardedly. "Why?"

She hesitated, and looked down. "He saved my life last night," she said finally. "It's natural that I'd want to know a little more about him than his name, rank and serial number, but somehow I think that's all I'd get out of him if I asked."

"So what makes you think I'm about to spill his secrets, if he won't?" He leaned against the edge of the table and surveyed her quizzically, but his casual attitude dissipated with her next words.

"I know his secret already. You know it, too." She looked up at him calmly. "About the only person who doesn't is Quinn himself. He's consumed with guilt over something that happened in the past—so consumed that he thinks his own death is the only way he can atone for what he's done. I'm right, aren't I?"

Sullivan's stare was shuttered. "This conversation is over," he said coldly. "I don't know why I let it begin in—"

"He kissed me last night. I kissed him back." Jane flushed, but she kept her eyes on his. "I don't even like being touched, but I wanted his hands all over me. I still do."

He'd pushed himself away from the table. Now he leaned back against it and gave her a slow stare. "Little Miss Jane Doe," he murmured after a long moment. A corner of his mouth lifted. "Who'd have thunk it? So what are you trying to tell me, lady—that you've gone and fallen for a crazy Irishman?"

"No. I don't know." She stopped, and the anguish in her eyes sobered the dark-haired man watching her. "All I know is that for those few minutes in his arms I felt like I'd come home—like I finally knew who I was, and where I belonged. Except I don't know who *he* is, and the little I do know scares me, Sully." Unconsciously she used Quinn's nickname for him. The blue eyes watching her closed for a moment, and then opened again.

"He never knew his father, and his mother left Ireland with Quinn when he was just a kid. She had family in Boston, and she thought she could make a new life for him here. She died only a few months after they arrived, and for the next ten years he was shunted from relative to relative, until he lied about his age and enlisted. I think the army was the first home he'd ever had." He shrugged. "I know he thought of the men he fought alongside as his only real family."

"Why didn't he stay in the army? What made him become a mercenary?"

"He got promoted." Sullivan grinned reluctantly. "He got promoted a few times, and after a while he began to feel like he was losing touch with the ordinary soldier. So he asked to be busted back down a rank or two, was told that the army didn't work that way and quit in disgust as soon as they let him. But being a soldier was all he knew, so he became a freelancer. I'd served under him in the army, and when I got restless I joined him. For a while there were a few of us who always seemed to end up together.''

His voice had grown reminiscent, and he fell silent. Then he shook his head, as if to clear his thoughts.

''But it's not like working in an office. You don't put in your time for thirty years and then collect a gold watch and a pension and retire to Florida. Mercenaries either quit, like I did in the end, or else they get killed on the job.''

Picking up the lid that she'd removed from the coffee container, he idly snapped a piece of the plastic from it. ''Jack Tanner went first, and I know that was a blow to Quinn. They'd been together right from the start. The next one of our merry little band to go was Paddy Doyle, and shortly after that I got out. Next to Quinn, Paddy was my best friend. Hell, Paddy was everyone's best friend. His ashes were sent back here, and once when I visited his grave I saw Quinn just leaving. We pretended we hadn't seen each other.''

Sullivan broke another piece of plastic from the lid and let it drop to the floor. ''Like I said, after Paddy's death, my heart just wasn't in it anymore. A few others quit, and that just left Quinn and young Haskins.''

His mouth tightened and he looked at her. ''He feels responsible for all of them. But Haskins's death is the one he'll let himself get killed over. Ask him to tell you about the wild geese sometime.'' He opened his hands and shreds of plastic fluttered to the floor like confetti. Dusting his palms against his pants, he straightened. ''If he tells you, then maybe you're the one who can help him. But I don't think he'll tell you.''

"Tell her what?'' Quinn was in the doorway. He crossed over to the table and slid some rolled-up sheets of paper over to Sullivan, frowning. "These came in by fax while I was on the phone. Tell her what?''

"About the time we got into that all-night poker game with those crazy Russian officers,'' Sullivan said smoothly, casting a wicked glance at Quinn. "He's terrible at cards—and this was strip poker. He was down to his skivvies and his boots, and he bet everything on four of a kind. Except the Russian had a full house.''

"For God's sake, Sully, you left out the most important part,'' Quinn growled. "They were *female* officers,'' he said hastily to Jane.

Sullivan grinned and picked up the faxed sheets that Quinn had given him.

"Any luck?'' Quinn met her eyes.

"More than some of these poor women seem to have had,'' she said, sighing. "But no, I haven't come across anything that's rung a bell in my memory. Like I was telling Sully, any one of them might be me.''

"I'll leave you to go through the rest of those,'' Sullivan interjected. "Quinn, there was something I wanted to talk to you about. Got a minute?''

"Can it wait?'' Quinn had pulled one of the photocopied sheets toward him and was studying it. "This might be worth following up on,'' he said to Jane. "She disappeared just a few days before you were admitted to the hospital.''

"It can't wait.''

There was an edge to Sullivan's voice, and both Jane and Quinn looked up from their task. Quinn's gaze held a touch of impatience, but as Jane realized that Sullivan wasn't meeting her eyes, she felt a sudden foreboding.

"What is it?" Quinn frowned. "For God's sake, this is going to take us hours as it is."

"I don't think it's going to take hours, Quinn." She had been holding a photo, but now she put it down carefully. "I think Sullivan just shortened the list of possibles down to one. You did, didn't you?" she asked him. He didn't answer her.

"What's the big mystery, Sully?" Quinn's impatience held a touch of anger. "If you think you've got a lead, let's have it." He pushed back his chair, but even as he started to rise Sullivan spoke.

"I guess Jim down at the station realized he hadn't sent me this description the first time—probably because she's not a missing woman, strictly speaking." With difficulty he peeled one of the faxes free from the others.

"Read it out." Quinn was standing now, but he made no move to take the paper from him. "If you think it concerns Jane, then she should hear it, too. Go on, read it."

His ex-comrade met his gaze and held it. Watching them, Jane saw a muscle in Quinn's jaw suddenly tighten. "Read it out, Sully," he said softly, his anger gone.

"Name—Jan Childs. Age—26. Weight—116. Height—5'6". Missing from Raleigh, N.C. since August 30."

Sullivan's voice was a monotone.

"This woman is likely armed and should be considered extremely, repeat extremely, dangerous. Childs is a marksman-class shooter, especially adept with small arms and handguns, and is a rogue police officer.''

Dimly Jane realized that in her two bunched fists she was clutching wadded-up photos and papers. Beside her she heard Quinn draw a harsh breath.

"Detective First-Class Childs is wanted for the murder of Richard Stanwell Asquith.''

"It's not you.'' Quinn snatched the fax from Sullivan and scanned it, as if he needed to see it for himself. "There's not even a photo, for God's sake,'' he said angrily, turning to Sullivan. "A rogue cop? Armed and dangerous? A damned *murderer?* How the hell could that be Jane?''

She looked up, her features unnaturally still. "I Know What You Did,'' she said woodenly. "Do you want to phone Tarranova and Fitzgerald, or should I call them myself?''

QUINN'S APARTMENT, though it wasn't huge, gave the impression of space and airiness—aided, Jane realized, by the fact that it was uncluttered to the point of sparseness. She glanced over at him. He was on the phone, as he had been since they'd arrived here a few hours ago. He'd called Sullivan several times, but from the curtness of his conversations and the frustrated way he'd hung up, it was obvious that if his friend had any news for him, it wasn't what he wanted to hear.

He'd insisted she stay here overnight. He'd wanted her to reconsider her decision to contact the police, and to her surprise, Sullivan had agreed with him. The two of them had persuaded her to put it off for twenty-four hours.

"I'll run some background checks on this Childs woman, see what I can dig up about her and this Richard Asquith she's supposed to have killed. I've got a man in Raleigh. He can get right on it," Sullivan had said. "A photo's our first priority."

"I don't believe you're a murderer. I didn't before, and I still can't," Quinn had reiterated stubbornly.

"How can you say that with any certainty?" she'd asked him. "What happened on that practice range was as much a shock to you as it was to me, Quinn, so what else might there be about me that you don't suspect?"

"I don't know." His face had been set and determined. "But just because you've got abilities I hadn't known about doesn't mean I read your character wrong. Dammit, Jan—my life depends on knowing what another human being is—"

He'd stopped dead, and she'd seen the swift apology in his eyes.

"The name fits me, doesn't it?" she'd said softly. "I'll give you your twenty-four hours, Quinn. But at the end of it, I think we both know I'll be calling Jennifer Tarranova."

She wished now she hadn't agreed to the delay. It was only putting off the inevitable.

"Hungry?" He was off the phone, and standing over her.

Barely raising her head, she shrugged. "Not really."

"Tough. Scrambled eggs and toast sound okay?" He reached down. Before she knew what he intended to do, he'd taken her hand and was pulling her to her feet. "Come on, let's talk in the kitchen while I'm cooking. I don't want you moping around in here all by yourself."

If that was his idea of a pep talk, it fell far short of the mark, she thought with a spurt of irritation. She followed him unwillingly, and slumped down on a straight-backed chair. "I'm not hungry," she said again, her voice dull. "And I wasn't moping. But after what we learned today, you can't expect me to be Little Mary Sunshine, Quinn."

"You can't go without eating, and I'm damn well not going to sit down to a meal by myself," he said shortly, slapping a frying pan down on the stove with more force than necessary, and pulling a carton of eggs from the refrigerator. "And all we learned today was that you're a pretty slick shot. Hell, you're almost as good as me."

"Almost?" She looked up swiftly. The kitchen was longer than it was wide, with a Dutch door at the end of it that opened onto a fire escape leading down from the second story to a little grassy courtyard, Quinn had told her earlier. Now he opened the top half of the door, and glanced out into the gathering dusk.

"Okay, if it came to a contest, it might be a tie," he conceded off-handedly, taking a deep breath of the chilly air. "Look at the sparrows. They're settling down for the night."

"I'd beat the pants off you, and you know it," Jane said with more energy than she'd shown since her world had been shattered a few hours before. She frowned, suddenly remembering. "And since we're on the subject of birds, Sullivan told me to ask you about the wild geese. What did he mean by that?"

Quinn's back was toward her, his forearms resting on the ledge that topped the bottom half of the door. He didn't answer her immediately, and as the silence lengthened into seconds she regretted her impulsive question. "Forget I asked," she said awkwardly.

"Hell, it's no big deal," he said, still looking out into the November evening. "It's a legend, that's all. It's just that it's not worth talking about."

On the other side of the small square was the sister building to the one they were in, another old-fashioned six-plex. From where she was sitting, Jane could see warm yellow rectangles of light glowing from the other apartments across the way, and she could hear the restless cheeping of the tiny birds that Quinn was watching so intently.

Just outside the door hung a feeder and a net-covered lump that had to be a suet ball. At the sight of them she blinked.

He'd intimidated her when she'd first met him last night. Looking at him now, she saw again the controlled stillness that, combined with his size and solidity, had given the impression of precariously leashed force. He lived in a violent world, and he'd had to become violent himself to survive in it, so her initial image of him hadn't been wrong. It had just been incomplete, she thought slowly. He got pleasure from watching a handful of city sparrows. He'd put out seeds to make sure they didn't go hungry.

And he'd stubbornly hung on to his belief in her—a belief that even she could no longer sustain.

She blinked again, this time because of the ridiculous prickle of tears she could feel behind her eyelids, and felt the tension that had gripped her all day slip away. Maybe this tentative peace wouldn't be enough to see her through the ordeal that lay ahead of her, she thought. But it was enough to see her through tonight. She couldn't ask for more than that. She rose, and quietly crossed the few feet of brightly lit kitchen that separated them.

He didn't look around as she joined him, resting her arms on the ledge as he was doing and staring, like him, out into the rapidly gathering darkness.

"It looks like smoke," she said softly. "Like maybe somewhere far away a world is on fire, but all we get here is a few wisps of drifting smoke. I like this time of the year."

"I do, too." Quinn's voice was as quiet as hers. "My mother always said that autumn was her favorite season. She used to take me for walks just before dark, and we'd watch the lights come on in the houses we passed. Then we'd go home, and she'd put our lights on and say that maybe someone passing by on the street was watching over us." He glanced at her and then back again. "I don't remember much about her, but that always stuck in my mind."

"Sullivan told me she died when you were young," she said tentatively.

"Sully's as bad as my old Aunt Bridget for running off at the mouth," he said evenly. "I can see I'm going to have to have a chat with him about that."

There was a sunflower seed on the ledge. She picked it up. "It was my fault. I told him I wanted to know more about you."

"Why?" His query was mild, but she was close enough to him to see the slight tensing of that square-cut jaw. "I'm a beaten-up Irishman who's been fighting other people's wars for them for too long. Why would you be interested in me?"

She stifled a frustrated sigh. It seemed that she not only had her own barricades to tear down if she wanted to initiate any kind of conversation with him, but that she also had to somehow surmount his. The irony of it struck her. Really, she thought wryly, if they'd met under different circumstances, they might well have found that they made a perfect match. Maybe it was time to end the skirmishing with a direct approach.

"Are you fishing, McGuire?" She slanted a look at him through her lashes. The cold air had brought color to her cheeks, and a strand of her hair had drifted against the corner of her mouth. She hooked it away carelessly, not taking her eyes from him, and after a moment he turned and gave her that rare smile that seemed to transform him into a completely different man.

"Maybe I am, at that." They were face-to-face, and she could feel his breath, warm against her cold lips. "But tell me anyway. Why were you asking that gossip Terry Sullivan about his old friend? What was it about me that sparked your—" He hesitated. It was a calculated hesitation, she was sure. "Your *interest?*" he ended softly.

She'd thought she'd seen him flirting with Jennifer Tarranova, Jane thought disconcertedly. But if his voice had been velvet then, now it was cream—cream with a rough splash of Irish whiskey. What would it feel like to have that voice beside her in bed, pouring all over her in the dark?

Like nothing you've ever known. Like everything you've ever been too scared to know until now, she told herself breathlessly. She took her courage in both hands and answered him.

"I wanted to know who had kissed me. I wanted to know who it was that *I'd* kissed." She felt as if there was barely enough air in her lungs to get the words out, and when he didn't immediately reply, the squeezing sensation in her chest intensified.

Someone in a nearby apartment must have turned on a radio, because suddenly the faint sounds of big band music drifted upward into the night. A corner of Quinn's mouth lifted.

''Now, isn't that something? Mrs. Lavery's got her Tommy Dorsey records out again, and if I'm not mistaken, that's her old heartthrob Mr. Sinatra singing 'In the Blue of the Evening.''' He tipped his head to one side. ''No, I'm wrong, entirely. It's 'Fools Rush In.' Even more appropriate, considering what I'm dying to do.''

The invisible band around her chest snapped suddenly free, and she looked up at him. His eyes, usually so pale, were dark gray, with only a silvery sheen to them. He'd cleaned the Glock after she'd used it at Sullivan's firing range, and she could smell the sharp-sweet scent of solvent on him.

''I may know next to nothing about you, McGuire, but I do know that the last thing you are is a fool,'' she said calmly. ''A risk-taker, maybe, but not a fool.''

Quinn shook his head slowly. His smile faded to seriousness. ''Oh hell, I'm probably both, angel. Watch me.''

When she'd kissed him last night she'd been able to persuade herself that it wasn't really happening. For those few moments, everything that she'd just gone through had made it easy to lie to herself. When reality had set in he'd continued the comforting lie by letting her blame her reaction on shock, on relief—on anything but what she'd known in her heart it really was.

But last night she'd been someone else. Today it was no longer possible to hide behind the fearful facade she'd been wearing for these past few months. It had been irrevocably shattered a few hours ago, and if she was truthful with herself, she knew that even last night it had been badly cracked.

He wasn't giving her the chance to pretend anything this time anyway.

His mouth came down hard on hers—so hard that if his arms hadn't gone around her at the same time she would have taken an involuntary step backward. He was making it very clear what was happening between them, she thought dazedly—this was pure want, pure desire, and there would be no way in the future that it could ever be excused as anything else. And that was exactly the way she wanted it.

Her head tipped back to receive him. One powerful arm was around her waist, his hand spread down low enough so that it was cupping the tight denim of her jeans. His other hand slid into her hair, straining it away from her face and clutching a handful of it at the back of her head. Her own hands were trapped between their bodies, her fingers splayed against the solid wall of his chest.

And then she felt his tongue in her, immediately and unhesitatingly deep, and she met it with her own.

It didn't matter that she was being crushed against him, Jane thought hazily. She felt as if she was expanding, opening, *ripening* against every hard inch of him. An airy, weightless sensation possessed her, and it was a moment before she dimly realized that it wasn't her imagination. Without any effort at all he'd lifted her off her feet, holding her closer to him, the hand that had been cupping her derriere now supporting her in the most intimate hold she could conceive.

Yesterday a casual touch on the arm from him had made her retreat in nervousness. Today she wanted what he was giving her right now, and more.

The chill air surrounded them like cold silk, but where they touched it instantly heated, melted—became *liquid,* as if they were creating a bubble around them. Her hands slid up Quinn's chest, her fingertips reaching blindly for his face and finding it by touch alone. His jawline was roughened by stubble. It scraped the smoothness of her skin, but she barely noticed.

He was drinking her in, she thought with the one part of her mind that was still capable of thinking. His head bent, his mouth more than covering hers, there was an insatiable, forceful immediacy to his kiss, as if he was determined to get as much of her as he could before he was torn away. She felt as though he was filling her with the night, as if a soft darkness was splashing through her, running like mercury from her lips, to her breasts, to her thighs, and pooling like some dangerously volatile liquid at the point where his palm supported her.

At that same point she could feel him pressing up against her. He wanted more. His body, hard and straining, was making that urgently obvious. She heard a small sound, like the mewling growl of a tiger cub, and it took a second before she realized that it was coming from her own throat.

Quinn's mouth lifted reluctantly from hers, and as she opened her eyes she saw that his were still closed, the thick lashes dark against the deeply tanned cheekbones.

He opened them. They were unfocused and opaque, and his lips were parted, his breathing shallow. Then slow awareness returned to his expression, and he gently set her back down on her feet.

"Like some randy, hot-handed boy," he murmured hoarsely. "No finesse at all, McGuire." He looked down at her in chagrin, his fingers still trapped and woven through her hair. "It was supposed to come off a lot more subtle than that, angel. But you tasted so sweet, and I got stupid."

"You promised last night that you wouldn't kiss me ever again. You lied," Jane breathed. She was still close enough to him that her lips brushed against his as she spoke, and that glazed look returned to his eyes.

"That makes me a terrible man, then, doesn't it?" Quinn said softly. "You can't trust me, can you?"

"Should I, McGuire?" She brought a finger to the corner of his mouth and traced the shape of his bottom lip. He caught her finger lightly between his teeth, and flicked against it with his tongue. With it still in his mouth he shook his head, his gaze on hers.

"No." He spoke around her finger, not letting it go.

"Was I right to be nervous around you?" With her other hand, she ran her fingertips slowly past his rib cage, the flat hardness of his stomach under the thin cotton of his T-shirt, and stopped at the worn leather of his belt. Then she slipped her fingers past it, pulled his shirt from his jeans, and felt the heat of his bare skin.

His gaze wavered. She took her finger from his mouth, but kept it pressed against his bottom lip.

"No," he said huskily. "I'm no threat at all, right now. You've disarmed me entirely, you have."

"You're lying again, McGuire." She glanced down, and then up again to his face. "We make quite a pair."

"I think we might, at that." There was a sudden seriousness in his voice. "But you haven't lied to me. And I trust you more than you trust yourself, darlin'."

She shivered slightly, suddenly aware of the crispness of the night air, and he immediately propelled her to one side, away from the slight breeze that was coming in. "See, I know how to handle a woman," he said, turning from her and closing the top half of the Dutch door. "Manhandle her and then give her pneumonia." His glance fell on the carton of eggs and the pan on the stove and he grimaced. "Another surefire ploy—offer her dinner and then let her go hungry. Come on, we'll find you a sweater and then you can sit down and watch me make good on one of my promises, at least."

His brogue was back in full force, and he wasn't meeting her eyes. Suddenly she knew why. As he started past her she reached out and touched him on the arm.

"You still don't want me to go to Tarranova tomorrow." It was a statement, not a question, but he answered her anyway.

"I signed on to protect you. Watching you hand yourself over to the authorities wasn't what I had in mind when I agreed to this job, and it's even less to my liking now."

He stood motionless in front of her, as overwhelmingly large and muscular as always, but his solidity no longer intimidated her. Some part of Quinn McGuire had thawed, Jane thought. Deep inside he was still coldly controlled, because that control had been part of him for so long that it was integral to his persona, but what he felt for her wasn't based solely and completely on physical need. She knew that for a fact, because she felt the same way.

Like she'd said, they might have made quite a pair, she told herself. But neither of them would ever know for sure. It just wasn't fated to work out that way, and no matter what he might hope right at this moment, in his heart he knew that was true as well as she did.

"I think I'm Jan Childs, Quinn. And Jan Childs killed someone. I have to turn myself in." She lifted her shoulders. "It's the only way this whole thing makes sense— the fact that I was so terrified of finding out what kind of person I really was, the way my stalker seems to be trying to punish me for the crime he keeps referring to in those damned messages. Even the drugs could well have been my way of trying to eradicate the guilt I obviously couldn't handle. I've got one last night of being Jane Smith, and that's all. I want to spend that night with you.''

"And what if I said one night wasn't enough? What if I told you I wanted more?" His gaze was clear and direct.

She looked away. "Then I guess it all began and ended with a couple of kisses. No harm, no foul, McGuire, and we both go our separate ways tomorrow."

"I don't buy that—" His heated retort was interrupted by the sound of the phone ringing. "We're not finished here," he said shortly. "Don't get any bright ideas and try to take off on me, darlin'."

She wasn't even going to have the one night with him, she told herself as he strode from the kitchen and snatched up the phone in the living room. She had no illusions about what lay ahead—arrest, a trial and a conviction, a sentencing that depended on the details and extenuating circumstances, if any, of the murder she'd apparently committed. She'd wanted something to hold onto during the nightmare she was stepping into—something that she could take out and hold and examine in secret when everything else was gone.

Except at the eleventh hour, just when she'd needed him to take what she was offering, Quinn had turned into the white knight she'd originally hoped he would be.

He was hunched over the phone, his voice curt, and so low that she couldn't hear what he was saying. She saw him pass a hand across his forehead tiredly, and suddenly she realized she was wrong. She had what she needed. There would be some memories and images to sustain her through the dark days ahead.

She would always be able to close her eyes and see a big man leaning out into the dusk, intently watching a handful of tiny birds settling down for the night. She would be able to recall the look on his face as he'd spoken about his mother. She never would forget that heartstopping smile he'd given her when they'd both been standing by the door. And he'd kissed her twice.

"They found her."

She hadn't noticed him hanging up the phone, but suddenly he was right there in front of her, his hands gripping her shoulders. His features were taut, his eyes in shadow as he looked down at her.

"They found her, Jane. She was caught at the Canadian border, trying to cross over using a false passport."

She looked at him, not understanding. "Canada? Who was trying to get into Canada?" Her hand flew to her mouth. "Dear God, Quinn—do you mean—" She stared at him, too afraid to finish her question. He completed it for her.

"Jan Childs." He held her disbelieving gaze unwaveringly. "They picked her up and arrested her a few hours ago. Which means that you obviously aren't her, darlin'."

Chapter Eight

Mama's face was all wet and shiny, and the stuff she put on her eyelashes had made black rings around her eyes, Li'l Bit thought. Mama's glass was filled right up again, and it was the fourth time Mama had filled it up that night.

Mama had that Goddamned Cheating Bastard's picture on her lap, the way she always did when she got like this.

Really the picture was of Daddy. Except sometimes he was Daddy, and sometimes he was that Goddamned Cheating Bastard. If he ever came back again, Li'l Bit wanted to ask him what name he liked better.

But he wasn't ever coming back again. And it was all her fault.

Mama always said that men liked their women to be pretty and sweet and dainty—and that went for little girls, too. Little girls were supposed to be Daddy's li'l bit of honey-pie when he came home from the factory, with their best dresses on and their hair curled up with a bow on top. Little girls were supposed to help Mama set the table just right while Daddy had a second beer and watched the news.

But little girls *weren't* supposed to play baseball, or

ride a bicycle with Joey and Davie down the street or get into a fight at recess with the big girl from fifth grade who'd stolen their milk-money. It wasn't ladylike. *She* wasn't ladylike, no matter how hard she tried, and that's why Daddy had left. She knew that was true, because Mama had told her.

That's what Mama was telling her right now, her wet mouth open so wide and her angry eyes all squinched up and hard, while Li'l Bit sat on the sofa and felt like she was shrinking inside.

He never would have gone if it hadn't been for you! After you were born he didn't even want to be around. Li'l Bit? Li'l bit of stupid, maybe. Li'l bit of selfish! He left because of you—it wasn't because of me! He didn't leave me, he left you!

JANE SHOT bolt upright, her heart crashing against her ribs and her eyes wide open. At first she couldn't make anything out in the darkness, and then Quinn was beside her, swiftly snapping on the bedside lamp and bending over her in alarm.

"What is it?" His voice was edged with concern. Disoriented, she looked down at herself, and back at him, her eyes still adjusting to the softly shaded light. She shook her head to clear it.

"Just a dream. It's gone now."

She took a deep breath and started to slide back down under the covers. The next minute she was ramrod-straight again. "Is this your bed?" She plucked in surprise at the unfamiliar garment she was wearing. "This isn't even mine. You *undressed* me. What's going on here?"

"You fell asleep at the kitchen table, right after my scrambled eggs with toast and just before I'd finished brewing the tea,'' he said dryly. ''I cleaned the butter out of your hair, carried you in here, and got your clothes off. I had sex with you and then I put one of my old shirts on you. What was the dream about?''

''It was—'' She jerked her head up. Then her gaze narrowed. ''Oh. Was I any good?''

''Undemanding and compliant. But I was amazing,'' he said.

''Undemanding and compliant?'' There was mild indignation in her tone, but it was forced. Indignant wasn't actually what she was feeling right now, Jane thought. She let her lashes dip a little, as if she was tired, and studied him from under them. Tired wasn't what she was feeling either.

She'd been tired earlier, obviously—or perhaps it was more accurate to say that the roller coaster of emotions she'd been riding had so exhausted her that she'd simply crashed. Her system had been on overload for weeks now, and thinking that she might be Jan Childs had been like having her worst nightmare come to life. The shock and relief of finding out that it wasn't true seemed to have been the signal for her body and mind to collapse for a time, and even in sleep the tension she'd been under had produced that unpleasant little dream.

But dreams or no dreams, she'd gotten enough sleep so that tired wasn't what she was feeling. She was in a strange bed—Quinn's bed. She was wearing a man's shirt—Quinn's shirt. And despite her banter with him a moment ago, learning that Quinn himself had put her in his shirt and his bed was extremely…*unsettling*.

Oh, who was she trying to kid? She hoped that the lamplight was subdued enough to hide the color she could feel mounting her cheeks. Being in Quinn's bed and Quinn's clothes wasn't unsettling, it was downright *erotic.* The shirt was swamping her, and the man who usually wore the shirt she had on—the man sitting only about twelve inches away from her—was very, very male. His voice was pure sex, those thick dark lashes were pure sex, and that mouth was the hottest thing she'd ever seen on a man.

"Lick it if you want." He was watching her, a bemused expression on that tanned face.

She was clutching the collar-point of the chambray shirt in one fist, Jane saw. She'd been inhaling the scent she thought she could smell on it—his scent. And Quinn was right. She'd wanted to touch it with her tongue. Guiltily she snatched her hand away.

"I don't know what you're talking about, McGuire." She glanced swiftly downward to hide her confusion.

The bed she was lying in was covered with what looked to be some kind of handwoven spread, and it provided one of the few touches of color in the room. In the low light it glowed with muted shades of green and blue, bordering blocks of scarlet. It had the silky softness of mohair.

"See, and there I thought you never lied to me. You know what I'm talking about, and I know what you're thinkin'. And both of us stare wide-eyed at each other and lie our heads off, denying it. What are we going to do about it?" He made it a serious question, but as she looked up at him, she saw resigned humor on his face. He sighed. "I'm a coward, I am. And so are you, angel. Damn good thing we both shoot straight on the firing range, because in the bedroom we seem to be doing a hell of a lot of dodging and weaving."

"Maybe we should put it to a test, McGuire." Feeling slightly bolder, she picked up on his serious tone. Her brows drew together in a faint frown. "A couple of cowards and liars? I can't let that one go by without trying to clear myself. Truth or dare.''

He looked at her, the corner of his mouth lifting slightly. ''And what's that?''

''Cut the bull, McGuire.'' Now she was smiling too, but there was a challenge in her gaze. ''Even a simple Irish lad like yourself knows how to play truth or dare. If you choose truth, then I get to ask you a question and you have to answer truthfully. But as a liar, you might not want to make that choice. Maybe you'll pick dare. In that case you have to do whatever I dare you to do.''

''I can't see how I could lose.'' He leaned back lazily onto his elbows, his glance lingering on her, and again she hoped that the heat she could feel wasn't visible. ''You did say that all this applies to you as well, right?''

''If we were playing the game for real, yes.'' Jane saw the trap he was laying. She went on hastily. ''But in this case—''

''I like to get the rules of an engagement clear in advance,'' Quinn cut in smoothly. ''Since this is war— well, war games,'' he amended, ''—then both sides should be bound by the same restrictions. Which reminds me—we get to take prisoners, don't we?''

Maybe she was reading more into that last sentence than he'd intended, she thought, unable to tear her gaze free from his. But she didn't think so. Despite his off-handed tone, there was a relaxed alertness about him that suddenly made her feel like a mouse who'd blithely suggested a game of tag with a cat. A *big* cat, she thought, swallowing. A big *tomcat*.

She could play the game all by herself. The truth was she didn't dare take this any farther.

''You know, I think I could go for that tea right about now,'' she said feebly, thanking God she still had her bra and panties on under the chambray shirt. Flipping back the plaid spread, she swung her legs over the side of the bed, only realizing a second later just how bad a tactical error she'd made.

"I dare you to stay."

Quinn hadn't risen from his slouched position on the bed, and a tautly muscled thigh was now against her bare one. His face was in shadow, but it was impossible to miss the swift white gleam of his teeth, and she hesitated, her feet just touching the floor.

She'd started this. And earlier, when they'd kissed, she'd wanted it to go farther. So why was she preparing to scuttle away now? What had changed?

She had, Jane thought with an unwelcome flash of insight. She'd changed—or at least, her situation had. A few hours ago she'd not only had no past, but she'd been convinced she had no future. A woman with no future could afford to be reckless. A woman with no future was entitled to grab whatever she could of the present, without worrying about the consequences.

But she wasn't Jan Childs. And if she spent one night with Quinn McGuire, Jane thought slowly, for her it would mean more than just two bodies coming together in a physical act. She wasn't asking for any promises from him. She just wanted to know that it was a little more than that for him, too.

"I accept your dare, McGuire." She met his shadowed gaze. "Now you have to tell me the truth. Why?"

"Why what?" He still hadn't moved, but his motionlessness had an edge of tenseness about it.

"Why do you want me to stay?"

The quality of stillness about him seemed to intensify. Then he unhurriedly shifted his position and half-turned toward her, his weight now supported by only one elbow. His other hand bridged the gap between them, and rested lightly on the skin of her leg. Slowly he traced an invisible line down it with one finger, stopping at her knee, and although his touch had never gone higher than midthigh, Jane felt as instantly faint as if he'd thrust it upward toward the prim line of lace at her panties, had slipped under that lace and was even now exploring farther. She realized that her lips had parted, and that the room around her had lost focus. With an effort she forced the flood of sensations back and waited for his reply.

"Because I showed up drunk the first time we met and that wasn't good enough for you," he said finally. A smile ghosted across his features. "You were out of options, and I was your final hope, but you still made it damn clear I'd screwed up royally. You accused me of being a rye-drinker, if I recall rightly, and then you said you'd never be on a first-name basis with me."

He paused. Her brows drew together. "That's why?" she said, confused. "I reamed you out and you *liked* it?"

"Hell, no. I hated it," he corrected her. "I thought you were way out of line."

"But—"

"I hated it because I knew you were right. I'd let you down and I knew it and I felt like a cur. Naturally I blamed you for the way I was feeling." His grin flashed out again, this time ruefully. "Even I knew how unfair that was, so I made up my mind to hear your story out, tell you thanks but no thanks, and go back to my interrupted bout of solitary drinking. Except then I touched you. Everything changed after that."

"You still turned me down," she protested. "You let me walk away from you."

"Yeah. But even at that point I knew I was lost." He

shrugged. ''Courage under fire. A refusal to admit defeat. And just when I'm beginning to tell myself that a woman like you is tough enough to handle it all without my help, I catch a glimpse of the vulnerability underneath all that strength.''

He didn't know it—he probably wouldn't even admit it—but everything he'd just said was equally applicable to himself, she thought. He'd told her once that what she saw was what she got with him, but he couldn't have been more wrong. If all there was to Quinn McGuire was a tough, rangy, good-looking Irishman, then she wouldn't be here in his bed.

''That's why I want you to stay,'' he said quietly. His finger was lightly stroking her thigh again. ''Now it's your turn to choose, darlin'. Truth or dare?''

''Dare.'' She'd answered without thinking, because it was getting hard to think straight, but immediately she knew she'd made a mistake. ''No—truth,'' she said quickly.

''Too late.'' His fingers trailed idly up her thigh, and then down, as if he was unaware of what he was doing. The silvery gaze grew thoughtful. His hand brushed against the lace of her panties. ''I dare you to do the one thing you want to do more than anything else right this very second,'' he said finally, looking at her. ''Whatever it is.''

She felt a silky feather of anticipation trail down her spine.

''Stand up.'' Her voice broke on the soft command, and he shot her an appraising glance. Again the white teeth gleamed briefly, and then he rose slowly to a sitting position. Taking his time, he got to his feet, his arms hanging loosely at his sides, one corner of his mouth still lifted wryly. He turned to face her.

The shaded pool of light from the lamp beside the bed softened the starkness of the room and glinted on the polished wood of the blinds at the window. It grayed into shadows just a few feet away from Quinn, but he was standing right in it. For a moment he seemed burnished, even the short strands of sun-bleached hair at his temples glowing more gold than pewter in the warm light.

She was still sitting on the edge of the bed, but as the lamplight caught the wicked gleam in his glance, she made up her mind. She stood up, as slowly as he had, and took a step toward him. She had to tip her head back to meet his gaze.

"This is what I've been wanting to do more than anything, McGuire," she said, her hands going to the top button on his shirt. Carefully she slid it from its buttonhole, exposing a small vee at the top of his chest. Her fingers moved down to the next button. "I've wanted to undress you, just like you undressed me earlier."

"Solely in the interests of fair play?" Quinn murmured. She knew he was looking down at the top of her bent head, but she kept her concentration focused on her task.

"Not entirely." She undid the second button and let her hand linger on the smooth tan of his chest. "Besides, if it was fair play, I wouldn't be taking all this trouble. I seem to remember you ruined a dress on me last night."

"I didn't like it anyway, angel."

Casually Jane ran the tip of her nail from the hollow at the base of his throat to the top of his breastbone, and she looked up in time to see him catch his breath.

"But then, I've never cared for this shirt that much, either," he said huskily.

"So you don't mind if it loses a button here or there?" she asked, her tone detached. "Like this?"

As she spoke, she gave a little tug at the next button, and with a tiny tearing noise, it ripped free. She looked up at him.

"Or like this?"

She pulled again, and the shirt tore a little farther. The pulse at the side of his throat was visible, Jane saw with fascination. It was definitely beating faster than it had been a moment or two ago. She placed her palms against his chest, looking up at him through her lashes.

"You feel a little warm, McGuire. Can't you take heat?"

"I thought I could." His own lashes dipped as she ran her palms down to the next obstructive button. "But I've got a feeling you're going to make me sweat before we're over."

"You're right," she said promptly. "I owe you for that 'undemanding and compliant' remark."

"Yeah. It's the part about me being amazing that haunts me, though." A small tremor ran through him as the tips of her nails pressed lightly against the flat of his stomach. "How in the world am I going to live up to that, especially when you've got me on the edge right now?"

His hands had been rigidly at his sides, but as he spoke he brought them up abruptly. "Oh, hell, you win this one," he said hoarsely, impatiently tugging at what remained of his shirt until it parted. "Is this what you wanted?"

She held her breath and looked at him in silence. In front of her was what seemed like yards of wide, McGuire chest, looking as if it had been carved out of ironwood. Under the bulge of pectoral muscle, she could see the shallow rise and fall of his breathing. It wasn't wood she was gazing at, it was solid male. The shaded light gleamed on his skin, refracting off the almost-invisible sheen of moisture that slicked every square inch of him, and turning the sprinkling of dark hair there to a shadowed tangle of silk.

His arms were held to his sides by the shrugged-off shirt. There was nothing he could do to prevent her from indulging in the other fantasy she'd been unable to carry through earlier. She leaned forward, and with feline delicacy, flicked the tip of her tongue once across that sheened surface.

''Yes.'' Her one-word answer was almost a whisper, punctuated by another little flick of her tongue.

His hands were on her shoulders, his grip tight. When he spoke, it was as if the words were being dragged out of him.

''I'll take the same dare. This is what I want more than anything, right at this moment.''

Before she knew what was happening, his grip had slid down to her waist and under the chambray shirt she was wearing. She could feel the hardness of his hands spanning the softness of her skin, his fingers meeting behind her at her spine, and then without the slightest change in his breathing he was lifting her.

Raw desire spilled through her like sparks from a live wire, electrifying every nerve ending, momentarily shorting out every synapse in her body. His very lack of effort was erotic. He was so *strong,* she thought disjointedly. It wasn't something he worked at or thought about, it was simply a part of him, like those pale eyes, that tanned mouth, those heavily muscled shoulders. There was a sensuous thrill in letting herself be carried away by his bigness, his hardness, his basic and unconscious masculinity.

Automatically her bare legs wrapped around him. He shifted his hold, one hand easily supporting her under her derriere. His other hand came up and touched her lips, his fingers spread as if to shush her, and he brought his mouth close to her ear.

"I'm changing the rules, darlin'. You don't get to choose, you just have to answer me truthfully. Do you want this?"

His whisper was warm against the sensitive line of her neck, and even as he finished speaking she felt his tongue lick slowly around the curve of her ear. She drew in a sharp breath, her eyes closing and her head tipping back.

"Uh-huh," she managed, amazed that she'd even been able to say that much.

"It's a two-part question. I told you I was going to cheat." There was a thread of urgency in the low voice. "Do you want everything?"

Despite what he'd just said, Jane realized, giving her a choice was exactly what he was doing. She knew with sudden certainty that if he caught even the faintest echo of the woman who'd flinched from his touch only twenty-four hours ago, he would step back. But that woman was gone. It was important that Quinn know that.

Slowly she opened her eyes. Her arms had been twined languidly around his neck, but now she brought her hands to the well-washed shirt that was covering her like a robe.

"I want everything," she said softly. One by one she undid the buttons that marched down the front of her garment, feeling as she did the heat emanating from him meeting her uncovered skin. "I want you everywhere on me."

She spread the two halves of the shirt open, and saw his gaze waver. All that was keeping her from total exposure to his eyes was the scrap of white cotton that covered her breasts and farther down, at the flare of her hips, the lace-trimmed cotton of her panties. Then Quinn's hand moved slowly from her throat to her shoulder, his eyes never leaving hers. Without looking, he slid first one of the pristine white straps, and then the other, from her shoulders.

"I'll start here then," he said, his brogue thicker than she'd ever heard it, his words slightly slurred. "And I'll just keep going."

He bent his head, and his mouth was immediately on her, seeking and finding the tautness at the center of one breast, opening wide to take in as much of the surrounding softness as possible. Just as immediately, she arched her back toward him reflexively and her fingers slid through the short blunt blades of his hair. She felt *suffused* with liquid heat, she thought dazedly. Every part of her was hot, as if she was only inches from a fire and her skin was already starting to redden from the flames. He was still holding her to him one-handedly, and his free hand was cupping her other breast, tracing her nipple with his thumb, teasing it to a tightness that she hadn't known was possible. He lifted his head, but just enough so that she could hear his murmur.

"I was right. They're like strawberries, angel. Sweet and lush and ripe." He circled her with his tongue.

"Do you want me, McGuire?" She knew what his answer would be, but she wanted to hear the words come from his lips in that slurred purr. His gaze met hers, and the light at the back of those silvery eyes told her that he knew exactly why she'd asked.

"You like hearing it?" There was a trace of teasing humor in his voice, and as she nodded the corner of his mouth lifted briefly. "I'll have to remember that. Yeah, honey, I want you. I lust for you. I want to see you under me, your hair spread out all over my sheets. And I want to see you on top of me, your head thrown back and your thighs on either side of me. I want you to talk dirty in my ear, I want to have you tell me what you want and I want to work it for you, darlin'. Anything else?"

"Just one more thing," she breathed. "Do all Irishmen talk as much as you?"

"Yes." His reply was prompt. "Our women only put up with us because we can talk and act at the same time."

Even as he spoke he was lowering her to the bed behind her, but before she could lie back he was stripping the too-large shirt from her with one hand and unfastening her bra with the other. Straightening again, he peeled his own shirt completely off, letting it fall to the floor. His hands moved to the front of his jeans.

"No." Jane looked up at him. "Let me." Swiftly she rose to a kneeling position, the mohair cover soft against her bare legs. She could feel his gaze on her, and as her fingers brushed against the zipper of his jeans she heard him draw a quick breath.

"Honey, I was still hoping to try for amazing, not totally humiliating," he ground out.

Even at this moment he could startle her into laughter, and she bit her lip, holding it back, but unable to keep her expression completely straight. He looked down at her, and a corner of his own mouth lifted. His hand went to her hair, gently brushing a stray strand away from her forehead.

"Don't we make a pair," he said in that whiskey-and-cream voice. "Don't we make one hell of a fine pair, angel? You make me feel as nervous as if I'm fifteen again, and it's the first time."

Her heart did a slow acrobatic roll in her chest. Quinn McGuire was the kind of man women fell in love with, even though they knew they shouldn't, and she was halfway there, Jane thought tremulously, meeting his eyes. His lashes made thick spiky shadows on his cheekbones, and the hard angles of his face were softened by the diffuse light. There was a golden sheen over the muscular torso and those incredible shoulders. Not halfway there, she told herself with reluctant honesty. Only about a yard from the finish line, and putting on a burst of reckless speed. How smart was that?

It wasn't smart at all. And she didn't care. They did make quite a pair—she made him feel like he was starting all over again, and he made her feel like a femme fatale, experienced enough to drive him out of his mind with a touch.

Her eyes widened suddenly.

"Quinn, I just realized—" She stopped, not knowing how to go on. "I could—that is, I don't know if I've ever been with—" She took a deep breath. "For all I know, I'm a virgin, Quinn," she said in a rush. "You saw what I was like yesterday. Maybe I've never—never done it before. Maybe I'll be terrible at this."

"A virgin. Yeah, that would turn most men off," he said dryly. He reached down for her hands and put them back on his jeans. "Unzip me. Take these off me. Pull me down on the bed with you. I'll let you know what comes next when we get there, okay?"

Just like that, she crossed the finish line.

"Okay," she said, her voice still a little shaky. "Unzip. Am I doing this right?"

"Exactly right." His hands hung at his sides. He made no move to help her.

Under his jeans he wore plain white briefs. Her fingers slipped under their waistband at the same time as she grasped the denim of his jeans. "Both off together, Quinn?" she asked breathily, looking earnestly up at him through her lashes.

"Time's probably of the essence, especially if you keep batting your eyes at me like that," he rasped. He wasn't letting a flicker of emotion cross those carved features, she noted. She wondered just how much of an effort it was costing him, and decided to find out.

Leaning forward, she pulled the waistband of his briefs down an infinitesimal degree, closed her eyes, and quickly flicked her tongue at him. Immediately his hands were on her shoulders, gripping them tightly, and she felt a convulsive shudder run through him.

"We still don't know if you're a virgin, sweetheart," he rasped. "If you are, and if you don't stop improvising like that, the odds are pretty good that you'll still be one after tonight."

"*Not* something I expected to hear from the amazing Quinn McGuire," she said in mock disappointment. She tugged at the waistband, lifting it over him, and then the breath left her lungs in a rush.

He was…he was *fabulous,* she thought dazedly. The arrowed trail of dark hair that led from his chest to his groin, here became a dense thicket, and the part of him that rose from that tangle of hair and strained against the still-confining jeans was—

—it was as big as the rest of him, Jane thought. And

it was beautiful. Unthinking, she ran the tip of her finger down his length, and felt the tightness nestled close against his body at the base.

"Play nice, angel," Quinn gasped. "In fact, I'd better finish this myself." In the shadowy light she saw him push his jeans down with an impatient gesture, saw him step out of them, saw him come toward her on the bed.

"Lie back. Now I'm going to tease you," he said softly.

All she had to do was feel. All she had to do was let wave after wave of sensation lap over her. His mouth was on her ankle, and then it was trailing up her calf, the back of her knee. She heard herself making an incoherent little sound of pleasure.

And then his mouth moved higher, his hands parted her legs a little, and his tongue was wet against the soft skin of her inner thigh. Her fingertips were tingling, clutching convulsively at the mohair spread, bunching it tightly into her fists, and her hair had fallen across her face.

"See, this is what I wanted. You with your hair spread out over my pillow, angel. You telling me what you need." With a smooth, unhurried movement, he lifted her hips. Hooking a finger into the lace of her panties, he pulled them down her thighs.

"I need you to make love to me, McGuire," she said softly, looking at him through her lashes and feeling the slow, heavy pressure building up inside her. "No— that's not it. I need—" She raised herself on one elbow, pulling him down to her mouth with her other hand. Putting her lips to his ear she whispered into it, one short, pithy sentence.

She sank back on the pillows, watching him all the while. "Your wish-list included that, didn't it?" she said innocently. "In fact, there was only one more thing on it, as I recall."

"I was getting around to it. You talking like a bad girl threw me off my stride there, that's all," he said, the pulse at the side of his throat quickening. "Sweetheart, this is ground zero. Let me know now if you've got any doubts about this—any doubts at all."

He was close to losing control, Jane saw. As close as she was, or closer, but still he wanted to make sure that nothing he was doing would cause her regrets in the future. He was big and gorgeous, but he was so much more than that.

"I picked the right man, didn't I?" she said softly, looking up at him. "Even last night I knew I had. No, Quinn—no doubts. No turning back." She touched his mouth with a light finger, and her lips parted slightly. "But like I said, I don't know if I've done this before. Maybe you've got doubts."

"Because this might be your first time?" Grasping her wrist, he pressed his lips to her palm. "You're a virgin, angel. No matter who you slept with before, this is the first time you've had me in you."

He lowered his head to her even before he'd finished speaking, and his last words came out in a whisper. Her hair was still across her face, but without pushing it away he covered her mouth with his, one arm going around her back, lifting her to him. He was straddling her. She could feel his tongue, hard and urgent, on hers, and that dense thicket brushing against her belly.

He tasted raw. He tasted like salt and skin, with no civilized refinements. Suddenly she knew she didn't want to wait another second. She dragged her mouth from his and met his gaze.

"Give me my first time now," she breathed. "Let me know what it's like to have you in me, Quinn."

"My first, too." His voice was almost inaudible. "Nothing before this ever counted." Not breaking their gaze, he leaned over and pulled open the bedside table drawer. Still holding her with his eyes he ripped open the small foil square with his teeth, flashed her a quick ironic smile, and pulled the condom from the foil, putting it on with brief efficiency.

Then his mouth came down on hers again, but this time he was lifting her hips at the same time, gently lowering himself, gradually entering her. She felt herself opening to him, her parted thighs parting wider, her nails digging into his shoulders, her mouth wet and covered by his, and she knew a moment's panic.

He filled her. He more than filled her. She felt as if a slow fuse was being lit deep within her, and then he moved farther into her and the fuse caught and started to burn.

He was supporting himself above her, those broad shoulders rigid, his arms corded with heavy muscle. He was watching her, a shadow of worry on his face. She saw it, and knew what he was concerned about. She shook her head, feeling the room spin around her with the slight movement.

"No, don't stop," she breathed. "Let's take this as far as we can, McGuire."

He went even deeper, and then he was withdrawing, but before he withdrew completely he was filling her again, and this time she felt like a glove around him, a soft suede glove that had been made for him and for no other man. He was right, she thought dimly. Nothing before this counted. He was making her his with every slow, powerful thrust. Every time she received him, every time she gripped him and delayed his withdrawal she was making him hers. This was the first time, the only time for both of them.

Her hips rose to meet him, her arms stretched up to grasp those solid shoulders. One strong hand was around the back of her head, and his mouth was at the corner of her lips, his breath coming in shallow gasps. Again he filled her, again he withdrew, and without lifting his head or opening his closed eyes he spoke, his voice slurring.

"Let's bring it on home, now, angel. Let me give...let me give you everything now."

She couldn't speak. The most she could do was nod, and even that was almost too much of an effort. She saw his eyes open above her, knew that the blank glazed look in them was a reflection of her own, and felt her nails press into the smooth skin of his shoulders. Quinn gasped, and then that incredibly sexy smile flashed down at her one final time.

"But you like hearing it, don't you?" he breathed.

His mouth was at her ear, his breath hot in the curve of her neck, his whisper ragged and erotic; and all the time he was moving into her, then out, their bodies coming together in a steadily increasing tempo. Jane felt bombarded with sensations—Quinn inside her, Quinn's taste on her lips and Quinn's voice, as soft as velvet, wrapping around her and igniting every smouldering fantasy she'd ever had.

She felt herself soaring upward.

Behind her closed eyelids she saw again the ink-black darkness of the sky she'd watched earlier with him, but this time there were no comforting squares of light to pierce it, only icy splinters of stars, so many millions of light-years away that their heat had burned out long ago.

She thought she could hear the stars singing: a thin, wild, high cry that inexplicably disoriented her. Blindly she reached for him.

His voice was once more in her ear, closer than before, and at the sound of it the universe suddenly wasn't vast and lonely anymore.

"—cold and dark there, angel." His words were so broken they hardly made sense. "Bring me home. Let me come home to you."

The darkness lit up with a searing trail of light. Jane felt his grip on her tighten until she could hardly breathe, but there was no need for breath, no need for anything. Her own arms wrapped around him, holding him to her as if she would never let him go, and then another burning trail of light burst behind her eyes, and another, and another. The heat was all around her, and the blackness was shot through with glittering ribbons of sparks, garlands of light. She was drenched in light, she was *drowning* in light, she was drinking it in and feeling the sparks pour through her. She was dissolving into a glittering, starry constellation herself, with Quinn a part of her.

The Lovers, Jane thought disjointedly. *We're stars, we light up the night so brightly that sailors will steer their ships by us for a thousand years to come. We'll shine for eternity, together forever in the sky.*

And then the stars were rushing apart again, and she was falling through the night with Quinn's arms around her....

Eventually she opened her eyes. The darkness was merely shadows, the light only the soft glow over his shoulder from the bedside lamp.

Those thick dark lashes, only inches away from hers, were still fanned across the high cheekbones, but even as she watched they lifted. His gaze was silvery and unfocused until it fixed on her. Quinn drew a shuddering sigh, slowly bringing his hand up to her face and gently stroking a damp tendril of hair from her temples.

"This has to be heaven, angel," he said softly. "I just never thought they'd let me in."

Chapter Nine

He slept on his stomach, and he was a sprawler, always with one arm flung across her and holding her to him. She'd learned that over the last three days and nights—three days and three nights in which the two of them had seldom left the bedroom, let alone Quinn's apartment. Jane came out of the bathroom, still towelling beads of water from her skin, and looked at him.

He was probably asleep. He should be—they'd hardly gotten any last night. A small, secret smile curved her lips as she remembered. The man was insatiable, or maybe she was insatiable when she was with him, but for whatever reason, they just didn't seem to be able to leave each other alone. After the first time they'd made love, she'd drifted off in his arms. Before dawn she'd awoken, and without speaking a word, the two of them had begun again, their bodies entwining, their mouths seeking and finding each other's in the dark, their hands clasped together tightly, like two wanderers lost in an enchanted forest. The first time had been—well, *amazing*. Her eyes lit with amusement as she recalled his teasing arrogance. But the second time had been even better, and every time after that had built on what had gone before.

She'd gone looking for a bodyguard. She'd lost her heart.

It was too soon to tell him that, especially since she didn't know for sure if he'd lost his. He wanted her, there was no doubt about that. And when they weren't actually in the bedroom, he found any excuse to touch her, even if it was only putting his arm around her shoulder and holding her to him. He loved just sitting with her and talking with her, telling her what he remembered about his early childhood in Ireland and his mother, glossing over what must have been years of upheaval after her death and emphasizing the scrapes and escapades that he'd gotten himself into as a boy.

He'd talked of Sister Bertille, too, and his eyes had been bleak as he'd told her of the letter he'd received, informing him of her death. He'd held something back about that letter, Jane knew, but that was hardly to be wondered at. The nun had been important to him, and her passing was obviously still a fresh wound. It was enough that Quinn was sharing so much of himself with her.

The one thing he wouldn't talk about at all was the subject that Sullivan had told her to ask him about, but Jane had come to the conclusion that Sully had been off base about that. Whatever the story was behind the wild geese, that was all it was—a story. Or as Quinn had said so dismissively, a legend, not worth discussing.

She'd wished she could share more of her life with him, but her memory still hadn't returned.

She bit her lip, blotting the water from her hair with the thick towel. That wasn't quite true. She'd had that sad little dream twice since the first time, and she'd come to realize that the child called Li'l Bit was probably herself.

Mama had been the type of woman who needed a man. In Jane's dream she'd been overly made-up, fussily dressed, completely shattered by the loss of the husband she obviously had built her life around...so shattered that she'd freighted her little daughter with guilt and failure, blaming her—*me,* Jane thought angrily—for her Daddy's departure. She would have felt incomplete until she'd found another male to take her absent husband's place, even if that male had a penchant for drinking and violence.

But he wasn't the only one Mama lived with after Daddy left. There were more—in the end, too many to remember. You only remember him because of Garnet.

Jane froze, the towel forgotten in her hand.

"What is it?" Quinn's voice came from the bed, and at it her head jerked up. She looked at him. He hadn't been asleep, she could tell. His gaze was alert.

"I just remembered another part of my childhood," she said slowly. "I remembered my stepbrother's name."

On shaky legs she crossed over to the bed and sat abruptly down, needing suddenly to feel his touch. He leaned back against the pillows and put his arm around her, hoisting her closer to him. She laid her head against his chest, breathing in the scent of his skin and feeling obscurely safer.

"The boy you saved from being beaten?" he asked gently. "He was your stepbrother?"

"His name was Garnet Vogel, and his father lived with my mother for a while." Her voice was hollow. "His father was the man I hit with the baseball bat, and he beat his son all the time. I can still see Garnet's poor back."

She shuddered. The muscles in his arms tensed, and she looked up at him.

"Sorry, angel." With an obvious effort he relaxed his hold on her slightly. "But men who hit children or women—" He took a deep breath, his jaw tight. "The boy had been scarred?"

"Badly scarred. He must have carried those scars with him into adulthood," Jane said, her eyes dark with pity. "I remember that he and his father lived with us for about a year before even my mother had had enough. She'd started drinking pretty heavily by then, and it was no place for a couple of children," she faltered. "Garnet and I tried to protect each other. We were all we had."

"Where was your own father?" Quinn was frowning, and she realized he knew nothing of the dreams she'd been having. She filled him in swiftly. There really wasn't that much to tell, she thought regretfully—out of a whole lifetime, just these few unhappy memories.

"The frilly dresses, the insistence on being 'lady-like.'" He was looking at her, his expression unreadable. "Not even being encouraged to stand up for yourself. Any of this ring a bell, darlin'?"

She stared at him uncomprehendingly for a moment. Then it all made sense. "I reverted," she said flatly. "I reverted to being the good little girl that I thought I was supposed to be. That's why I didn't even try to fight back when my stalker attacked me at the Trinity Tavern."

She was shaking, she noted dispassionately. "I almost got *killed* that night, all because I was trying too hard to be my Mama's good, obedient Li'l Bit!" Her eyes flashed at him. "I can't even remember her calling me anything else but that stupid, demeaning name. How could she have done that to a child?"

"If she's still alive, she's got a lot to answer for, I agree," he said quietly. "But if she was an alcoholic and attracted to abusive men, maybe she's been called to account already. The main thing is that sometime in the past twenty years or so you changed from being that scared little girl. You got strong, sweetheart. You went out and got yourself a gun and some shooting lessons, and became a regular Annie Oakley."

She smiled unwillingly. "I did, didn't I? I must have been trying to put my past behind me with a vengeance." Her eyes clouded again. "Which means that it must have taken something pretty traumatic to make me revert back to my childhood persona. I didn't like being that ladylike little girl the first time—I only did it because I felt so responsible for my father leaving, and I thought that was the only way to make everything all right again. My mother had made me feel so damn *guilty!*"

"There could be a thousand reasons why you chose that persona to take on after your amnesia," Quinn began, but Jane had tensed in his arms.

"That's it—the guilt. I've always been certain that I can't remember who I am because I don't *want* to know that woman. Even when I tried to deny it to myself I knew deep inside that I'd done something terrible that I was blocking out." Pulling from his clasp she sat on the edge of the bed, yanking the belt of the terry robe she was wearing tighter around her waist. "If I had been Jan Childs that would have explained everything."

"You're barking up the wrong tree entirely," Quinn said shortly. "There's no way you killed anyone or committed any other crime heinous enough to swing for, darlin'. If anything, your memory's being blotted out because someone did something terrible to you."

"*I Know What You Did.* Your theory doesn't explain that, does it?" She shook her head. "I've wanted to stay here with you and pretend that if I never regain my memory it doesn't really matter. But it *does* matter."

"For God's sake, why?" There was a harsh edge to his tone. "It hasn't mattered the last three days. I don't need to know your true name to know that I—" He stopped abruptly. His eyes met hers. "Hell, I've got nothing to offer you, angel. I never expected to have even this much with you."

"I never expected this either." Impulsively she reached for his hand. "But at least you've got yourself to give me. You've got a past. You've got a future. I don't have any of that, Quinn. What if we decide we want to make a life—" She flushed, but then went on doggedly. "For heaven's sake, who knows what will happen between us? All I'm saying is that I have no future to give—to you or to myself. Two weeks from now, two *years* from now the police could show up at my door with a warrant for my arrest. I can't do that to you. I can't build any kind of new life until I find out what I was running from in my old one."

"The future." His strong fingers enfolded her hand almost painfully. "No one can guarantee that for any of us. The best we can do is make the most of the here and now, angel. But you want more, don't you?"

"Is it so hard to understand?" She looked at him, alerted by something in his tone. "I'm not a child, and I know nothing comes with a guarantee, Quinn. But doesn't everyone have dreams and plans for their life? Doesn't everyone *deserve* that?"

"I guess most people do. You do, anyway, sweetheart." He held her gaze for a heartbeat, and then sighed. Before she could say anything he went on. "So do you want Sully to pull those missing women files again?'' There was defeated acceptance in his voice.

''There were too many, and the pictures and descriptions were next to useless.'' She shrugged. Aimlessly she pleated a fold of the mohair spread between her fingers. ''I meant to ask you about this,'' she said lightly. ''It's beautiful. You'd think the colors would clash but they don't. Is it some kind of tartan?'' Not meeting his eyes, she studied the scarlet blocks and woven blue-and-green border of the blanket. Beside her she heard him give an exasperated snort.

''It's the McGuire tartan—Irish, of course, not Scots. Blood, sky and the green, green grass of home. I'm not diverted, angel. What is it you don't want to tell me?''

''Oh, all right.'' She was acting like a Li'l Bit again, Jane thought, annoyed at herself. She stopped playing with the tartan spread and gave him a direct look. ''You're not going to like this, but it's my only chance. We've got to find my stalker—even if we have to use me as bait to lure him out.''

''Forget that. What's Plan B?'' he said promptly.

''That's just it—there *is* no Plan B,'' she snapped. ''Face it, he's the only one who seems to know anything about me.''

''What he knows about you may well be just the insane imaginings of an obsessed stranger, for crying out loud,'' Quinn cut in. ''He might have nothing to do with your past at all.''

''I don't accept that.'' Her face was white and set. ''Those two messages wouldn't mean anything to anyone else but me.''

''Those two messages would make just about anyone nervous.'' Quinn shook his head. ''Everyone has something they want to hide. Everyone feels guilty about what they've done or who they've been in the past, believe me.''

"Believe you?'' Her glance sharpened. "Why? Because you're talking from personal experience?''

"I'm talking generally.''

Swinging his legs over the side of the bed, he reached for his jeans, hanging over the back of a nearby chair. Standing up, he jammed first one leanly muscled leg and then the other into them and pulled them up without bothering to fasten them.

Unfair, McGuire, Jane thought, watching him and feeling the now-familiar heat rise to her cheeks. Maybe by now she should be used to seeing him naked, semi-naked, sexily half-undressed or in the act of taking clothes off or putting them on, but she wasn't. And parading around in front of her with his jeans unzipped like that was dirty fighting. She narrowed her eyes at him.

"You're such a tramp, McGuire—using your body to win an argument.''

She got off the bed herself, loosening the tie of her robe so that as she stood it fell open. Her skin was still damp from the shower. She walked past him to the plain beech dresser and picked up the wide-toothed comb that lay on its surface. Standing in front of the mirror and knowing that he could see her reflection, she drew the comb through her wet hair.

He was watching her. She brought both hands to the top of her head, her breasts lifting with the movement, and carefully worked out a tangle.

"I didn't know we were having an argument.'' Standing behind her, his own reflection beside hers in the mirror, Quinn hooked a thumb casually in a front pocket. His jeans slipped down an inch or so past the washboard-hard belly. Jane pulled too hard on a tangle and bit her lip in frustration. "And I'm not that trampy, angel. If it's bothering you I'll zip up."

"Please do, McGuire. You look like you expect me to shove a five-dollar bill down the front of those things any minute."

"I was thinking this was worth a ten, at least," he murmured aggrievedly, his hands going to his zipper. He gave it a half-hearted tug, and then raised wide eyes to hers in the mirror. "Too—too hard to pull it up," he said in a forced tone, his hands still at the zip. "I don't think I can get it past—"

"The Mighty Quinn?" she said dryly, trying to keep a straight face. "Yes, that must be a problem you face daily."

"It's my burden in life," he agreed stoically.

"Just a martyr to the cause of keeping the women of the world happy. Make that keeping *me* happy."

Reaching around from behind her, he cupped her breasts in his hands, the tan of his skin contrasting darkly with the creaminess of hers. Their eyes met in the mirror, and she couldn't hold back the giggle she'd been suppressing. He grinned, and rested his chin on the top of her head.

"I cracked first. I just had to touch them." He grimaced. "A tramp *and* weak-willed. It's a wonder you put up with me."

"I like weak-willed men in the bedroom, McGuire." She lifted her arms and laced her fingers behind his neck, still watching their reflection in the mirror. "I even like it when you fight dirty."

"Yeah, well, it was a fight I wanted to win at any cost." Suddenly serious, he frowned. "You know I can't agree to you using yourself as bait for that maniac. If you're determined to draw him out, we'll just have to come up with some other way.''

"I can't think of any other way, Quinn.'' Dropping her arms and turning to face him, she looked up at him, her eyes clouded. "He must be frantic. He's probably been looking everywhere for me, and if I suddenly reveal myself again by going back to my apartment, he might get careless enough to make a mistake.''

"Or he might be goaded into forgetting about the games he's been playing up until now and just kill you.'' His jaw tightened. "I'll help you track him down any other way, but I won't be a party to this.''

She hadn't really expected him to agree, she thought hopelessly. His eyes were as hard and as opaque as they'd been the night they first met, and there was no trace of the man who'd teased her, made love to her, laughed with her over the past few days. He wasn't going to give in on this one—in fact, aside from enlisting Sullivan's help in pulling the missing person files, Quinn hadn't shown much enthusiasm at all for the task of finding out who she might have been. His primary focus had always been on keeping her safe—which was understandable, she admitted reluctantly. She gave a small resigned shrug and turned away from him in disappointment.

"I guess you could contact Detective Fitzgerald and see if they got anything on that butcher-shop lead.''

"I already did that. It didn't pan out.''

"So we're at a dead end. Going through those photos and descriptions again probably *is* our only option, since you're so opposed to—'' In the next room the phone began to ring and she pressed her lips together in annoyance.

"The machine'll pick it up,'' he said tightly as it rang

again. "Look, you've got to understand that I'm not trying to be the heavy here. You seem to forget that I saw
you hanging from that goddamn pipe that night." The
phone shrilled out once more. He took an impatient
breath and continued. "I still haven't been able to get
that image out of my mind, and if you think—" He
broke off abruptly.

"It's not picking up. You might as well answer it."
Jane sighed as he hesitated, watching her. "Go ahead
and answer it, Quinn. I know it's impossible for you to
agree to this plan, but after all these weeks I guess I just
wanted to go on the offensive against him, instead of
waiting and wondering when he would strike next. It was
a dumb idea, I admit."

"Not dumb. Just too risky." He shot her a worried
glance. "We'll come up with something else—oh, for
crying out loud, hold on a minute while I get rid of
whoever the hell this is." Striding from the room bare-
footed, he snatched the phone up with a thunderous expression on his face.

From the bedroom doorway she watched him ruefully.
She could stay mad at him just about as long as he could
stay mad at her. Two and a half minutes seemed to be
their limit, she thought. But despite not being able to
blame him for his stubbornness, she still knew she was
right. Quinn was so attuned to her in every other way.
Why couldn't he seem to understand that?

"When did she call?" The curtness in his voice
roused her from her thoughts and she looked up sharply.
"Did she get a good look at him? Yeah, that's what I'm
thinkin' too, Sully. No, I can handle it on my own.
Right. I'll call you if I find out anything."

"Get a good look at who?" she demanded ungrammatically even before he'd hung up the phone. "And who's 'she'? Does Sully have a lead?"

"Not really." Grasping her by the arms, he lifted her lightly off her feet and moved her from the doorway. Putting her down again with a quick grin, he went past her into the bedroom and grabbed up his T-shirt from the chair. "I'm going out for an hour or so, and I want you to stay here. Lock the door behind me when I leave."

"Run that one by me again?" Her hands on her hips, Jane stepped in front of him, blocking his way. "I stay here? And while I'm here doing something girly like painting my toenails, just where the hell will you be?"

"Gotta see a man about a dog, angel." He wouldn't meet her eyes. "That's just an expression," he added weakly. "My uncle Liam used to say that when he—"

"When he didn't want you to know where he was going. I got it, McGuire," she said shortly. "Well, if you're into colorful canine expressions, then I'm sure you know what a female dog is, right?"

"A bitch?" he said dubiously. "Listen, darlin'—"

"Give the man a Milk-Bone." Sitting down on the bed, she pulled on her own jeans and reached for her bra, shrugging her robe off unconcernedly. "Which is what I'll be if you even *mention* leaving me here again. I'm coming with you. Sully got a lead, didn't he?"

"It might be something, or it might be nothing at all." Quinn looked at her. "Carla phoned Sullivan Investigations and asked them to get a message to us. She saw your stalker this morning, trying to break into your apartment."

"SHE'S PRETTY UPSET." Gary hesitated, as if weighing his words, and then went on rapidly. "It's not your fault,

I know that, Jane. But that scumbag came here looking for you, and instead he could have seriously hurt Carla. You can't blame me for wishing you'd never gotten her involved.''

They were standing on the dilapidated verandah of the old Victorian house, out of sight of Mrs. Quantrill's lace-covered window. Gary had been waiting there for them when they'd arrived, obviously hoping to talk to them privately before they went up and questioned Carla. Now Quinn looked at him. Without shifting position or even altering the expression on his face, there was suddenly a mildly menacing attitude about him.

''What is it you're saying—that Jane's somehow to blame for the actions of the madman who's been making her life a living hell? I'm sorry for what happened to your girlfriend, Crowe, but if it had been Jane who'd walked up to him when he was pasting that goddamn message on her door, I don't think she would have gotten away with a few bruises.'' His mouth tightened to an impatient line. ''But we're wasting time. Can she give us a description of the man she saw?''

Gary laughed shortly. ''They were face-to-face, until he knocked her down and ran past her.'' He opened the door to the building and paused. ''I was out of line there. I apologize. It's just that when I heard her scream and came out to find her lying there like that, I—'' He swallowed. He was paler than she'd ever seen him, Jane noted sympathetically. ''For a minute I thought the worst,'' he finished softly.

''I was out of line, too.'' As they followed Gary up the stairs, Quinn continued. ''This bastard's hit-and-run technique is enough to make anyone jittery.''

''That's what Carla said, too. She's no shrinking violet, but he took her by surprise. It wasn't until I'd got-

ten her back on her feet that she even saw the message
on your door. After, she got the key to your place from
Mrs. Quantrill,'' he went on as they reached the top
floor. ''She wanted to go in and make sure he hadn't
left any other—''

''Wait a minute.'' Quinn reached out and grabbed
Gary's arm. ''I thought she surprised him as he was
trying to break in. Was he on his way *out* when she ran
into him?''

''He was at the door. He could have been trying to
get in or he could have been making sure it was locked
again as he left. Carla didn't know for sure.'' Gary
looked down at the hand on his arm. ''What's the difference, McGuire?''

''Dear God—do you think he might have left some
kind of a booby trap in there?'' Ignoring her former
neighbor, Jane turned an alarmed gaze on Quinn, but
already he was heading down the hall at a run. Gary
looked confused, and then he was running too, elbowing
past him and pushing open the door to the apartment he
shared with Carla. He darted in, calling out her name,
and just as immediately came out into the hall again, his
face white and strained.

''She's not there. She must have—''

Even as he spoke Jane heard Carla's answering call
coming from the apartment next door—*her* apartment,
she thought with a chill feeling of dread. Without any
concrete basis for her certainty, she was suddenly sure
that something terrible was about to happen.

Quinn had covered the distance between the two
apartments already, but just as he reached for the doorknob he stopped himself. Squatting down on his heels,
he seemed to Jane to be looking at the lock mechanism.
His head jerked up.

"For Christ's sake, it's packed with explosive! Carla—stay away from the—"

Whether the woman inside heard his warning or not was immaterial, because even as he shouted it out Gary's hand was on the knob, turning it frantically.

Later, trying to remember the sequence of events, Jane found that all her mind had retained was a series of frozen images. She remembered seeing Quinn's hand desperately reaching for Gary's, even as the door started to open. She remembered him turning, as swiftly as a striking snake, rising to his full height as he did so and leaping toward her. She remembered—she thought she remembered—seeing Carla's puzzled face as the door swung open, and Gary's belatedly appalled expression as he turned to look over his shoulder at them.

Then Quinn was on her, his arms tightly wrapped around her, his momentum carrying them to the floor, and he was rolling with her like a paratrooper making a combat landing.

A moment later the world around them blew apart.

Chapter Ten

"The boyfriend's fine. That gash by his eye required stitches, but he can thank his lucky stars he wasn't blinded." Jennifer Tarranova looked at Jane, her expression somber. "There's no easy way to say it. Your friend Carla's not expected to make it."

Jane closed her eyes, trying to hold back the pain. She and Quinn had arrived at Mass General only seconds behind the ambulance that had transported Carla, and they'd been waiting for word on her condition for four hours now, although without much hope. Even the seasoned emergency attendants had blanched at the sight of the wounded woman. The wonder was that the blast hadn't killed her outright, Jane thought, sickened.

"Is Quinn still with your partner?" she asked, her voice dull.

"He's just reading over his statement before signing it. I'm sorry we had to keep you waiting all this time, but we wanted to get whatever information we could from the boyfriend first." The female detective put a tentative hand on Jane's bowed shoulder. "You're thinking it could have been you, aren't you?"

Jane opened her eyes. "No," she said tonelessly. "I was sitting here thinking it could have been Quinn. He was the first one at the door. If he'd opened it without checking he would—he would have—"

Oh, hell, she thought with a detached part of her mind. *Someone's turned off the autopilot, and I'm about to crash right here and now.*

Her shoulders were already shaking, and the hands that came up to cover her face were trembling as if she had the ague. She felt as cold as a fever victim too, but the next moment she felt faint, and she knew that beads of sweat had formed on her suddenly burning forehead. She was going to lose it. She *wouldn't* lose it, she thought distantly, willing herself to stay upright. She wouldn't *let* herself lose it, dammit—not in front of a fellow officer.

Not in front of a fellow officer... Jane froze as she realized what had just run through her mind.

"Her unlocking the door tripped a switch, priming the bomb to explode the next time the door opened. It was set to blow inward, from what the bomb squad can tell so far. The boyfriend getting hit by that flying metal was just sheer bad luck." Tarranova leaned forward. "Even if McGuire had been the one to open it, the odds are that he would have walked away with nothing more than a few cuts and bruises. Don't keep tearing yourself apart over something that didn't happen."

"You're right. I—I'm okay now." Her lips felt strangely numb. It was hard to get the words out, and when she did it seemed as if there was a time-lapse between her speaking, and her hearing herself speak.

"Did Gary give you any information that might help you find who did this?" Again it was a second before her words echoed back to her, but thankfully Tarranova didn't seem to notice anything was wrong.

"We would have stood a better chance if Carla herself

had been able to pass on the description firsthand.'' She sighed. ''But that ain't gonna happen, so we'll have to work with what little she told him. Medium-size white male, steel-gray hair, early forties maybe. Whoopee,'' she said dryly. ''Oh, and she mentioned something about a heavy gold ring, Crowe says, which sounds like a signet ring. If that's all we've got to go on, I'll probably still be working this case when this little one's graduating from college.'' She patted her rounded stomach, her expression softening. Beside her Jane sat very still.

''A signet ring. That's something to go on, anyway.'' She thought she'd kept all emotion out of her voice, and she'd thought that Jennifer Tarranova wasn't paying that much attention to her anyway. It was a shock when the detective looked up sharply at her.

''That means something to you?''

Tarranova didn't know about the amnesia, of course, Jane recalled with an effort. She would have to start working on keeping her lies straight, if she was going to pull this off. She shook her head.

''No. It just sounds like something distinctive that might narrow the search.'' She met the other woman's glance, hoping she wasn't showing any of the nervousness she was feeling. Tarranova held her gaze suspiciously for a second, and then sighed and looked down at her watch. Wearily she rose to her feet.

''Signet rings aren't that uncommon. I'm afraid that without the Kozlikov woman working alongside a police sketch artist, we're still left with the proverbial needle-and-haystack scenario.'' Unconsciously she rubbed the small of her back, giving Jane a wan smile. ''I've still got a ton of paperwork back at the precinct. I'd better round up Donny before I fall asleep on my feet like a brood mare. Do you want to come with me, or should I tell that good-looking Irishman you're waiting for him here?''

"I'll wait for him here." Looking up at the other woman, Jane's gaze wavered. "Do you know yet if it's a girl or a boy?" she asked softly.

"A girl." The brown eyes glowed. "My Vito says he figures I planned it that way, just so he'd be outnumbered. He's already bought her the biggest darn teddy bear I've ever seen in my life."

"She'll be loved. That's the greatest gift you can give her." Jane smiled, and this time it wasn't such an effort. "She's already very lucky. *You're* very lucky."

"I know it," Jennifer Tarranova said simply.

As the detective left the waiting area and walked away, Jane watched her go. They *had* met once, just as Tarranova had thought the night she and Fitzgerald had come to the apartment. It had been at a national seminar on profiling serial-killers, about four years ago.

I was a very minor guest speaker, Jane thought, forcing the details to come. *She asked me some questions after the presentation. I remember even then thinking she was someone I'd like to have for a friend.*

But of course, Jennifer Tarranova would never be a friend now. At some point, Tarranova would start hunting her down. Heavier footsteps sounded along the tiled hall that led to the waiting area, and without looking up Jane knew they were Quinn's. She could tell him from his walk. If she entered a dark room, she'd know if he was there, just by sensing his presence. She knew the way he smiled, the way he frowned, the way he kissed, the way he made love to her.

She knew him by heart. And she didn't know him at all.

"Fitz says we can go. How're you holding up, angel?'' He hunkered down in front of her, and although her head was bent she knew that those clear, silvery eyes she'd thought could hold no secrets from her, were gazing worriedly at her now. He reached for her hands, and she let him enfold them in his. Then she lifted her head and met his gaze.

"You lied to me, McGuire.'' Her voice was dead and toneless. "I *am* Jan Childs, aren't I?''

"HOW THE HELL could I have been so *stupid?*''

They were in one of the conference rooms at Sullivan Investigations. Quinn stared bleakly across the table at his friend.

Sullivan shrugged. "What choice did you have? She was ready to turn herself in when I called you that night. It bought us some time, at least.''

"Yeah, but we didn't find out anything helpful during that time,'' Quinn growled. "She didn't kill Asquith. I *know* she didn't. Someone set her up.''

"My guys say he had plenty of enemies, but they were the kind who'd try to bankrupt a man, not kill him. And besides, from what little I know, Richard was a shark himself.''

"He had a brother, right?'' Quinn tapped a thumbnail against his teeth and paced restlessly around the table. "What more did you learn about him? Could he have done it?''

"Leon Asquith's dipped his hands in blood so many times that I doubt they'll ever be clean,'' Sullivan said dryly. "But the one person he seemed to care for was his little brother Richard. Pin any other crime on him and you'll probably be right, but not this.''

"You can start by pinning that bombing a few hours ago on him.'' The voice from the doorway was light and curiously harsh. ''And if Carla dies, we'll have him for murder. But we're not going to get anywhere sitting around here and talking about it.''

Quinn turned swiftly. There, striding briskly into the room, was Jane...no, *Jan,* he thought in brief confusion. And he didn't need a second look at that closed, set face to know with dull certainty that she *was* Jan now—the Jan Childs whose photo lay in the slim file on the table behind him, the Jan Childs who'd been a cop, and one of the best, according to her evaluation reports. She'd made profiling her expertise, and from all accounts she'd been better than some of the people the FBI had on staff. But she'd turned the Bureau down when they'd offered her a job, preferring to stay in Raleigh, where she'd made her home after a childhood of being bounced from state to state with her mother and a succession of so-called stepfathers.

Jan Childs, her own profile stated, was tough. She was a loner. She was brilliant, an overachiever, and even her few acquaintances admitted she kept them at a distance; some even going so far as to call her cold. She was nothing like the woman he'd known as Jane Smith, Quinn thought. She was Jan Childs. Jane Smith was gone—perhaps for good, thanks to him.

Or maybe not... He had to know for sure. He took a step toward her.

''I screwed up,'' he said bluntly, seeking her eyes. They met his expressionlessly. ''I shouldn't have kept your identity from you. I did it because I thought we could find something to clear you before you gave yourself up to the authorities, but that should have been your decision, not mine.''

He thought he saw something flicker at the back of that dark blue gaze, and for a moment he felt as if the

Jane he knew was still there, looking out at him. Her face was pale, and he reached over and touched her lightly on the arm. "Are you okay, angel?" he asked impulsively.

The flicker he thought he had seen disappeared. The slim, straight-backed woman pulled out a chair and sat down, looking up at him dispassionately. "A couple of things, McGuire," she said, opening the file that was sitting in front of her. She switched her attention to it, but continued talking. "First off, the name's Childs— Jan, if you prefer. Secondly, personal is out. You and I had something these last few days, but now it's over. We work together, that's all." She glanced at her own photo, frowning, then set it aside and closed the file. Her eyes met his. "I thought I knew you. You thought you knew me. We were both wrong."

"No. It was probably the rightest thing either one of us ever did," he said evenly. "And I did know you—I still know you. If I didn't then I wouldn't be here, trying to figure out who killed Richard Asquith."

"That's simple, McGuire." The generous mouth that he'd kissed only hours ago thinned into a humorless smile. "I killed him."

"He's got his own reasons for not buying that story, but you don't want to hear personal, do you?"

Sullivan had been silent throughout their exchange, but now he spoke. He was sitting across from Jan, one arm draped carelessly over the back of his chair, his tie loose, and the leather shoulder holster very visible. His gaze was as coldly blue as the one that met it.

"So how about trying my reason on for size, lady— if you did kill Richie Asquith, then why didn't you turn yourself in to Tarranova and Fitz at the hospital? Hell, that's why Quinn didn't tell you that you were Jan

Childs in the first place—because he was trying to save you from yourself. Uh-uh.'' He shook his head, a tight grin on his good-looking face. "You don't remember killing Asquith.''

"That's right, Sullivan, I don't.''

She looked tired, Quinn thought with swift concern—tired and at the end of her rope. But she'd made it clear she wouldn't thank him for worrying about her.

"But I remember just about everything else. I remember my life as Jan Childs, up until about the last month. That's still pretty hazy,'' she admitted. "I remember Richard, and I remember that he was my fiancé. I remember wondering how I could have been so blind as to get engaged to him, once I found out what a bastard he was. I remember him hitting me. I remember realizing that I'd chosen exactly the same type of man as my mother always had.''

"He hit you?'' Quinn couldn't help himself. His hand was on her shoulder, and for half a heartbeat he felt her move into his touch. Then she drew away.

"Just the once, McGuire. I was going to leave him right then and there, but he swore he'd never do it again, and I—''

For the first time she faltered. That hard, self-confident facade wasn't seamless, he thought slowly.

"I knew what he was. I knew he'd started going out with me because he saw me as a challenge—a tough lady cop, who had the reputation of being impossible to get into bed.'' She gave a short laugh. "I should have given in and slept with him. He would have dumped me so fast I wouldn't have known what was happening. But I didn't. I kept telling myself that I'd finally found someone to—to love me. Someone who wouldn't leave me.'' She looked up at him, her eyes hard and bright. "Li'l

Bit had been looking for that for a long time. I even persuaded myself that he'd hit me *because* he loved me so much, and because he was afraid I was breaking off our engagement. So I stayed. But I hated myself for staying. I grew to hate *him*."

"You still can't remember pulling your gun and blowing him away, though, right?" Sullivan asked laconically.

"No, I can't. Maybe I'll never remember that moment when I violated every oath I'd ever sworn to uphold as an officer, when I crossed the line and became the very thing I abhorred." Her hands had been flat on the table. Now she was hiding them in her lap, Quinn saw. They were clenched into fists. "But it was my gun they found at the scene." She nodded at the file in front of her. "There are witnesses—Richard's housekeeper, his driver, even his brother—who can put me with him less than an hour before the time of death. And if Leon Asquith wasn't absolutely sure I murdered Richard, then why has he been stalking me all this time?"

"You said we could pin the bombing on him," Quinn said slowly. "Now you say he's the stalker. How can you know for sure?"

"Because of the description Carla gave Gary. The clincher was the signet ring she mentioned—Leon never took that off. It had belonged to his grandfather, the first baron Asquith. The first robber baron Asquith," Jan added dryly. "The one who made their initial dirty million—in armaments, I believe—and the one that Leon tried to emulate."

"I've looked into our friend Leon." Sullivan lifted an eyebrow. "He's got people on his payroll to do the dirty work for him, which is why he's never even been charged with jaywalking. Why would he risk all he has to conduct a personal vendetta against you?''

"Because punishing me *is* personal with him. He tried poaching on his little brother's preserve once, and I told him if he ever tried it again I'd make sure that Richard knew that his brother had been putting the moves on his fiancée. After that he did everything he could to turn Richard against me, and eventually he probably would have succeeded. But instead, the woman he couldn't stand killed the brother he loved." She looked thoughtful. "He *did* love Richard, in his own way. Somehow he must have found out where I was, and that I'd lost my memory. Simply informing the authorities of my whereabouts and letting justice take its course wouldn't have been revenge enough for him. He wanted me to suffer, and then he wanted me to die as violently as his brother had died. In a way, I can't blame him.''

"I can," Quinn said tightly. "But we won't go into that right now. You still haven't answered Sully's question—why didn't you give yourself up when this memory came back? You intended to before, when you only suspected you were Childs.''

"That's right." She met his eyes coolly. "Three days ago I only suspected that I might be Childs. Now I *am* her again, and Jan Childs is a cop. I've got one last killer to bring in." She paused. Her laugh was forced and humorless. "Two, I guess. Myself—and Leon Asquith. And if you still can't accept the idea of me setting myself up as bait to draw him out, then I'm going to do this alone, McGuire.''

HE'D TOLD HER she was walking into an ambush. Jan's grip tightened on the steering wheel of the borrowed sedan, narrowing her eyes against the glare of oncoming headlights and acutely aware of the solid bulk of the man beside her. Maybe he was right. Maybe Leon Asquith did have a trick or two up his sleeve that she didn't know about. But at least she was walking into this with all her senses on full alert.

McGuire had been smarter than Leon. He'd gained her trust before he'd betrayed her.

"How did you know what name he'd be going under?"

It was still the same voice, she thought, pain lancing through her. Velvet and cream, with a dash of raw whiskey. That voice had called her every endearment under the sun, had cried out for her in the throes of passion, had lied to her. Since the phone call from Sully that first night at his apartment—the phone call, she now realized, in which Sullivan had told him that the photo he'd just received of Jan Childs was the spitting image of Jane Smith—he'd never called her by name. It made sense. Since that night she'd been Childs to him even in his thoughts, not Jane. And he'd kept that information from her.

"Bill Crump was his grandfather's real name. When he emigrated from England he changed it to something he thought sounded more impressive—William Asquith. Whenever Leon travels on business and wants to keep a low profile he calls himself B. Crump."

She flicked on her turn signal and moved into the right lane. "Knowing that, and knowing his tastes, the Ritz-Carlton seemed the obvious hotel to call first, although I guess he's been staying somewhere else for part of the time, because the desk clerk wasn't sure if he'd checked in yet when I called earlier."

"How did he sound when he spoke with you?" He

was looking at her, Jan knew. She could feel his gaze on her. She kept her eyes on the road ahead.

"He didn't say much. I told him I'd been in an accident a few months ago, and since then I'd been suffering from amnesia, but that today my memory had started coming back to me. My first thought had naturally been that my darling fiancé would have been going out of his mind with worry, not knowing what had happened to me, so I'd called the Raleigh residence and been told that Richard was dead. At that point I let myself get a little hysterical."

"That was risky." Quinn's voice hardened. "Do you think he really believed you?"

"I don't see why not, McGuire. I said that when through some quirk I'd remembered the Crump name, I'd been desperate enough to call the hotels on the off-chance that Leon had been looking for me and traced me here. I acted as if I didn't remember that we hadn't been close. Even if he didn't buy it, he agreed to meet with me."

"Yeah. But not in his hotel, darlin'. He wants you to trek all the way out to some dilapidated factory that he's thinking of buying. It's a trap."

"And I'm the cheese, and you're the cat, okay?" The next exit was the one she'd been told to look for, Jan noted almost at the last minute. She swung the wheel over too sharply and just made it. Pulling to the side of the off-ramp, she brought the car to a stop.

"This isn't going to work," she said tightly, her hands still clamped around the steering wheel. "You've objected to this plan from the first, and even now that we're almost there you're still trying to talk me out of it."

"Sure I am. And if I thought it would do any good

I'd dump you in the back seat and turn this car around myself, for God's sake,'' Quinn said harshly.

"You could try, McGuire." Now she did turn to face him. "But rogue or not, I'm still a cop, for this one last case at least. And thanks to you and Sullivan, I'm armed. I'd see that as interference with a police officer in the course of her duties, and I'd react accordingly."

He stared at her. It was as if he was looking at her for the first time, she thought, suddenly uneasy.

"You fell in love with me, didn't you?" he said quietly. "I know you did. And now I'm the enemy—just another man who betrayed your trust."

It couldn't be pain she was hearing in his voice, Jan told herself. Pain would mean that there'd been something real between them, and she couldn't believe that. If what they'd had had been real, she wouldn't be able to endure knowing that she'd lost it.

The only way she could function was by telling herself that it had been a sham from the start. And she knew just how to prove that to herself.

"I didn't fall in love with you, Quinn. Jane Smith fell in love with you—and she was naive enough to think that you were a little in love with her, too. But you never gave her your heart, did you? You never shared anything more than superficialities with her."

"That's not true. I gave more of myself to her—" He swore under his breath impatiently. "To *you*, dammit—than I'd ever given anyone. I gave you my heart *and* my soul."

"Your soul? I don't think so, Quinn. I don't think I got that. I think you kept that under lock and key, and you never intended to hand it over to me."

At this hour of the night there wasn't much traffic, and none at all taking an exit that only led to a rundown industrial area. Behind them on the freeway they'd just left cars whined by, but here there was nothing to distract them, nothing to interfere with this conversation. She wished there *was* something that would put an end to it, Jan thought suddenly. She didn't want that final proof anymore.

But she'd started this. She had to finish it.

"What are the wild geese, Quinn? What's the legend, and why won't you talk about it?"

The off-ramp was unlighted. The only illumination came from the sedan's headlights, garishly throwing every piece of gravel in front of them into high relief, and the paler, colder light of the moon. It was full, or nearly full, Jan saw. It looked featureless and dead.

"I told you, it's not even worth talking about."

His eyes were equally silvery, equally unreadable. *The man in the moon,* she thought. *So far away, even though he looks like you could reach out and touch him.* Unwillingly she recalled that she'd once entertained the foolish notion that the two of them could reach the stars.

"I thought you'd say that."

She liked being Jan Childs, she decided. Being Jan Childs was safe. Jane would have let messy emotion threaten the steady, low tenor of her voice. Li'l Bit would be shrinking away to nothing inside. But Jan Childs could switch her attention away from the man sitting beside her, could reach for the steering wheel again, could put the car into gear and start pulling off the gravel shoulder back onto the road again. She could do all this and feel no pain. She could do all this even though he still remained silent. She could do all this and tell herself that Quinn McGuire meant nothing to her at all.

And if she tried a little harder, one day she might even be able to make herself believe it.

Chapter Eleven

Once the Bilt-Fine factory might have been a bustling place, and from the size of the overgrown parking lot, it had probably employed about fifty people. But the market had obviously dried up years ago for whatever product had been manufactured there. Now it was a ghost factory, on a poorly maintained road lined with other deserted buildings like it.

"He's obviously not going to show."

Jan flicked her gaze automatically to the rearview mirror as she spoke, but Quinn was out of sight, as he had been since shortly before they'd arrived at the Bilt-Fine factory. He was lying on the back seat. Any other man of his height and bulk—not that there were many built like him, she conceded—would have voiced some complaint about the cramped quarters by now. But she got the feeling that if they were stuck here for another two and a half hours, or even two and a half days, he would accept it with the same stoic indifference that he'd shown so far. He'd made a mild comment about going through worse in some mountains once, and that had been about it for conversation.

"He's gotten cold feet, or maybe he never intended

to meet me at all tonight. This could be another one of his games,'' she continued, her lips barely moving.

''That'd suit me fine.'' His words were barely audible, but the unconcerned tone in which they were delivered came through loud and clear. She stopped herself just as she was about to turn around.

''Well, it wouldn't suit me, McGuire,'' she snapped at the steering wheel. ''I need him to tell me how he set it up. I need leads that Tarranova and Fitzgerald can follow. It's just not going to be good enough to point the finger at him without any corroborating evidence, not when he's probably covered his butt eight ways from here to Sunday, and the person who's accusing him is a murderer herself.''

''That's like trying to bolster your argument by telling me that the earth is flat. I just don't accept it, and no matter how many times you say it, I still can't accept it. Think of me as Christopher Columbus, if that helps.''

In the dark she pressed her lips together angrily, not trusting herself to reply immediately. ''We're talking murder,'' she said finally, keeping her tone as level as possible. ''That's about as serious as it gets, McGuire. I don't see how you can joke about it.''

''I'm not joking. I just want you to understand that I'm operating by different rules here entirely, and I have been from the start.''

There was a gap between the two front bucket seats, and suddenly she felt his grip just above her elbow. It took all her willpower not to look around at him.

''I couldn't have chosen a stupider place to try to convince you of this, but beggars can't be choosers,'' he said roughly. ''You've got to stop assuming that you're guilty of this killing, Jan. Sure, and there's a mountain of evidence stacked up against you. But a lot of innocent people have gone to the electric chair because of evidence that was later disproved. Most of them haven't gone willingly, but you seem ready to help strap yourself in, for God's sake. You don't just accept it—you *want* it.''

''I don't want it. Nobody wants that.'' Her chest felt uncomfortably constricted, as if there wasn't enough oxygen in the vehicle. ''But I know I deserve it for what I did.''

''Li'l Bit deserves it, you mean,'' Quinn said harshly. ''She deserves punishment—she always deserved the punishment she got, because she was such a failure. She made her father go away. She was the reason why her mother couldn't face life sober. And later, when she grew up and fooled people into thinking she was tough, competent Jan Childs, she still deserved what she got— a boyfriend who hit her. That's why you stayed with Asquith. That's probably what attracted a bastard like him to you—he sensed your vulnerability.''

''So did you.'' Leon wasn't coming, Jan thought, and even if he was she didn't care if she blew their cover or not anymore. She turned to face Quinn, her face white and her hand fumbling for the door handle. ''You saw the vulnerability too, and you took advantage of it, just like he did. You let me fall in love with you—start dreaming about a *future* with you—and all the while you knew damn well you would walk away from me someday. You never intended to stay. You never even considered a life with me, did you?''

There was just enough dim light in the car's interior to see the expression on his face, if there'd been one. But there wasn't. Even his eyes gave nothing away.

''Just answer me, Quinn,'' she said, her voice suddenly quiet. She felt immeasurably weary. "You never really thought you'd have a life with me, did you?"

"No," he said slowly, holding her gaze with his own. "No, I never thought that would happen."

She'd been wrong. Tough, invulnerable Detective Childs *couldn't* take this, Jan thought frozenly. She felt like she was hemorrhaging, as if her heart's blood was spilling from her in an unstoppable flood. She looked at him, and for one moment she wasn't the child she'd once been, the cop she no longer was, or the woman who'd never existed.

She was only half a soul. She would never be complete—not now. There was only one other half that could make her whole, and he'd just done what she'd always feared he would.

Quinn was still within arm's length. But he'd already walked out of her life.

"I need to be alone," she said, her voice thready. "I have to be alone for a minute." She started to open the door.

"You'll be a prime target if Leon shows up. For God's sake, Jan, I'm your damned *bodyguard.* I can't let—"

"And I'm a damned cop," she said, hoping she could hold on to the last of her composure for just a few more seconds. "I can take care of myself, McGuire."

She was out of the car before he could answer her, and walking fast along the cracked pavement that led to the office entrance of the outmoded factory. Sullivan had lent her a peacoat, but even its thick boiled wool didn't seem to be doing anything to combat the terrible coldness that was spreading through her. Three nights ago she hadn't noticed the damp chill of the November air, she thought. Three nights ago she'd leaned against

Quinn's broad chest, his arms enfolding her, and the autumn air hadn't felt cold at all.

She reached the building. The nondescript gray sedan, with Quinn in it, was only about thirty feet behind her, and in a minute she would have to turn back to it, get in and drive back to Sullivan Investigations. She could phone Tarranova from the office, she thought. From then on procedure would take over and she could stop thinking.

Actually, you've stopped thinking already, Detective.

The faint, commanding voice in her head strove to make itself heard above the wordless keening of pain and confusion that overlaid her thoughts. Jan blinked burning eyes. She'd been mindlessly nudging the toe of her sneaker against a small clump of earth between two of the paving slabs in the walk. Beside the clump a cigarette butt gleamed whitely against the dark earth.

There was plenty of other detritus littering the area. There were even other cigarette butts. Everything else had long since had the color leached out of it. Everything else had been there for some time.

Leon was a smoker.

She was the one out in the open, but suddenly she knew with terrible certainty that Quinn was the one in danger. She whirled around, her mouth already open in a shout, but even as the words were still trapped inside her it had begun.

The night lit up with an illumination so ferocious that her arm flew up reflexively to shield her eyes, but at the same time the air was rent by an immediate and continuing cacophony so violent that it felt as if two mighty palms had just boxed both her ears. In front of her the side of the sedan suddenly bloomed, like some strange and deadly night-flowering vine, with a jagged line of punched and pierced metal, each with its own stamen of fiery sparks.

The Bilt-Fine factory was up and running again. It was churning out death.

"Quiiinnn!"

He was *in* there, Jan thought in terror. He was *in* that pierced and shattered metal box, and if by some miracle he wasn't dead already, he soon would be unless she *did* something. The shooter had to be above her, on the low, flat roof. She was running already, and for one anguished moment her sneakers dug into the ground as if to propel her toward the car and Quinn. But there would be no way she could cover even five feet before being cut down by that curtain of fire, she knew. She would be killed outright, and she would die knowing that she'd failed him.

There had to be a way to clamber to the top of the low brick structure, some protruding sill or pipe that she could use as a handhold to hoist herself up. There had to be *something*. She was sprinting toward the corner of the building—she had almost reached it—and then the blast hit her from behind.

She was on the ground, slammed down so quickly and violently that she'd barely broken her fall with her palms. She felt a piercing pain in her right hand and a sickeningly warm taste in her mouth, but she ignored everything except the need to stagger upright once again. She got to her feet drunkenly, fell back down to one knee, and stood again. Her back, even covered by the thick peacoat, felt searingly hot, and the nearby brick wall was lit with a ruddy glow, as if just behind her the sun was setting in a Technicolor blaze of glory.

She knew what she would see even before she turned around.

He'd hit the gas tank. The gray sedan was a fireball, its hellish core directly at the point where Quinn was. The air around it for a distance of at least fifteen feet seemed liquid, a shimmering wall of intense, deadly heat. It wasn't the sun going down, it was all light, all warmth being forever extinguished from her world.

She was looking at the funeral pyre of the man she loved.

"No." It wasn't a scream. It was a direct observation to God. "*No.* He can't be dead, because if he's dead then nothing makes sense. You *wouldn't* let him die, because then—"

The greasy, billowing smoke was filled with thick ash. Something danced in the roiling air in front of her, and then drifted like an autumn leaf to her feet. She bent to pick it up. Even as she touched it it crumbled crisply in her fingers, but enough remained so that she knew what it once had been. It was a scrap of blackened leather. The last time she had seen it, it had been brown. The last time she had seen this had been as part of the battered leather jacket that Quinn had been wearing.

She held it in her hands disbelievingly. Then she brought it slowly to her face, the tendons in her neck standing out like cords and her eyes wide and staring, but as she pressed it to her skin it disintegrated into nothing more than black ash. She drew her hands away and looked at them. They were covered in blood and soot.

The blood was hers, she realized. Her nose was still bleeding from her fall. But how could that be? She was dead herself. She had to be dead, because there was no way she could go on living, no way she could go on believing in a—

"*You let him die!*" This time it was a scream, hoarse

and accusing, sounding as if it was being ripped from her throat. Her head was tipped back to the night sky. "You let it happen and I want an answer! Why *him?* Why not *me?*"

"It's too late to strike a bargain with God. You should be negotiating with me." The harsh, smoke-roughened voice came from directly behind her, and at the same moment she felt something hard being pressed into her spine. "But that won't do you any good either. All deals were off the second you pulled the trigger on my brother—and please don't insult me with that amnesia story again. Come on, take your gun out and lay it on the ground. I know you have one."

She didn't move. "I said I wanted an *answer!*" Her own voice was a cracked rasp. "Why did you have to kill him?"

"Because he was there." There was a thread of sarcasm in Leon's tone. "For God's sake, Jan—because he would have stopped me from doing what I want with you, of course. He was your bodyguard, wasn't he? Now, put your gun down before I get really angry."

Slowly she reached for the Glock in her shoulder holster, her gaze still fixed on the burning wreckage in front of her. She could probably take him down, she thought distantly. She could probably get a round or two off before he cut her in half with a scythe of bullets from whatever automatic weapon it was that he was holding on her. But there was a chance that he would survive, and that was unacceptable. She released the gun from her holster, drew it out and bent over, laying it on the ground. Life was futile now. She wouldn't let her death be as meaningless.

She would wait for the right moment. When it came,

she would make sure that Leon Asquith departed this world with her.

"How did you know he'd come with me?" Prodded by the weapon at her back, she stumbled, and regained her footing.

"I was told he never left your side." Leon looked impatient. "Move it, Jan. There's a door around the corner of the building."

This had been the blue-collar entrance, she realized dully as he pushed her over the threshold a moment later and fumbled for a light switch by the door. This was the factory itself—the front walk, with its once-neat borders and shrubs, had been where the secretaries and the management went in, sequestering themselves securely away from the grime and noise of those who did the real work. Behind her, Leon found the switch, and suddenly the place was flooded with bluish-white fluorescent light. Directly above her one of the tubes flickered and sizzled, and then went dead.

"They've kept the power connected to this dump for ten years, just on the off-chance that a prospective buyer might actually turn up." Leon grunted. "I was here for about two and a half minutes four years ago, and I didn't need to turn the lights on to know that I wasn't interested. But for this particular project, I think it'll do just fine. Walk over to that piece of machinery in the corner there."

He jerked his head at an odd contraption that looked like something out of Jules Verne. Rust-flecked and hulking, it was comprised of a large flat metal bed about waist-high, and above that was a heavy arm fitted with some kind of a disk-like contraption.

"I told Richie we couldn't afford to have a goddamn cop around," he said suddenly, matching his pace to hers as she skirted another, equally puzzling and useless-looking, machine. "But he said you were blind where he was concerned. Why did you kill him, anyway? Did you find out about his little hobby?"

"What little hobby?" she asked dully. "The fact that he liked hitting women?"

"If all he'd done was hit you, I guess the relationship hadn't progressed as far as I thought it had." Leon sounded slightly surprised. "I loved my little brother, but he was a strange one. Strange and...imaginative, let's say. So if it wasn't that, why did you kill him?"

His voice had hardened. They'd reached the flat-bed machine and he shoved the barrel of the automatic cruelly against her spine. "Who the *hell* did you think you were? Do you know what you *did?*"

His words reminded her of something, and then she realized that they were a twisted echo of the messages he'd taunted her with over the last few terrifying weeks.

I Know Who You Are.

I Know What You Did.

Something inside her snapped, and disregarding the weapon trained on her, she turned to face him. "No, Leon, that's just it. I didn't know what I'd done. I didn't know who I was. Your sadistic little messages meant nothing to me, so you might just as well have killed me as soon as you tracked me—"

"The freakin' cops were all *over* us, and then the damn FBI stepped in," he hissed, as if she hadn't spoken. "They had a forensic accountant go through Richie's records on the pretext of looking for someone who might have had a grudge against him over a past business deal, someone who'd hired you to kill him. They've been wanting to pin something on us for years, and you made it possible for them."

He laughed shortly and humorlessly. "Hell, they probably would have given you a goddamn citation before they fried you, Detective. I'm going down, along with Asquith Armaments."

"You were dealing in illegal arms sales," she said with dawning comprehension. "You're the one who keeps wars going, aren't you?—who *starts* them if profits look like they might be getting a little soft."

It's what I was trained for. There's always trouble somewhere in the world....

Quinn had told her that the night they'd met, and he hadn't been able to disguise the bleakness in his voice. If it wasn't for the greed of men like Leon Asquith, Jan thought, men like Quinn McGuire wouldn't be sent into battle again and again, until they were so weary and hardened that they couldn't fit into any other way of life.

For the past ten minutes she'd been encased in a numbness so all-enveloping that even the screaming inside her head, the wrenching scream that had been shrieking from her psyche ever since she'd known for sure that Quinn had perished, was muffled, as if there were several locked and bolted iron doors between this robot-like creature who was conversing with Leon Asquith, and the real Jan Childs. With this last revelation, the iron doors clanged open simultaneously, the screaming inside her rose to a crescendo, and the unbearable grief that she'd been holding back flooded through her and spilled over.

"You killed him! You *killed* him, God damn you! And if you hadn't done it tonight, you and your kind still would have caused his death! *You don't deserve to live—*"

She lunged at him, her hands extended and reaching for his throat, taking him by surprise. She saw the shock in his eyes, and then the frightened rage as her hands found and gripped him by the neck, her thumbs instinctively sinking into his larynx.

It was over in a second. Out of the corner of her eye she saw him raise the rifle. Then she saw it come swinging down, butt first, toward the side of her head, and for a while the whole world went black....

...blood and sky, and the green, green grass of home...ask him to tell you about the wild geese... I gave you my heart....

I gave you my heart....

She would be with him soon. If there was a God, and if God was watching, surely he would forgive two lost souls who had made all the wrong choices until it had come to the final one. Maybe Quinn had been right, and they wouldn't be let into heaven. But perhaps they would be allowed to linger just outside the gates, two heartbeats away from infinity, and on cold autumn nights they would shine down upon a world full of sinners and lovers, together forever.

''The Lovers,'' Jan murmured painfully, struggling toward consciousness. "I know you loved me, angel. I know you did."

Just then her hazy thoughts were shattered. From behind her came a sudden blast of noise so overwhelming that her immediate impulse was to clap her hands to her ears, but for some reason she couldn't. Her eyes flew open, just as a massive jolt ran through her.

The first thing she saw was Leon's face, drawn and sweating, staring down at her. The second thing she saw was that she was tied securely to the flat metal bed of the machine that they'd been standing by just before she'd lunged at him.

The thing still works, she thought stupidly. *I wonder what it does.*

There was a second crashing jolt that shook the entire contraption. Instinctively she twisted her neck around, just in time to see the heavy metal arm that she'd noticed earlier jerkily lift the disk-like appendage from the steel surface she was on. It rose to its full height, ratcheted into place again, and came down with shocking force, smashing against the steel like some nightmarish metallic snake striking prey.

It was inches closer this time. Now it was about three feet behind where her head was. It rose stiffly, ratcheted into place once more, and crashed down again.

"Tell Richie hi when you see him, Detective. Tell him from me he was a goddamned fool to keep El-Hamid's correspondence on that last deal, instead of destroying it like he was supposed to." Leon bent over her. He was so close that she could smell the acrid sweat on him, mingled with the less unpleasant scent of machine oil and grease. "I knew you were bad news the first time I laid eyes on you. But I always could see what attracted Richie to you. This could have turned out differently."

"No, Leon." She flinched as the stamp-press came down with a crash behind her, but inside she felt an insane calm. She tried to keep her thoughts focused. "This was always the way things were supposed to turn out between you and me. We were meant to be enemies. It was fate."

"I don't believe in fate." He flicked a glance at the stamp-press arm behind her. "You can always change the future. What I do believe in is revenge—*punishment.* You're the one who deserves to die, as far as I'm concerned, and in a second or so you will. I'm going to enjoy watching it, Jan."

"You're wrong on both counts, Leon."

She paused, squeezing her eyes shut as the press came down, so close now that she thought she could feel the rush of its descent. She wondered why she wasn't screaming, begging for his mercy, pleading with him to release her, and knew that even if she had given in to such an impulse, it would be of no use. Leon had no mercy. He truly believed she had to die, to pay for what she'd done.

An hour ago she'd been convinced of that, too. Now she knew she'd been wrong.

"I don't remember killing your brother. But I know that it wouldn't have been premeditated. It would have been the only option left to me at the time, Leon, whether you believe that or not. I don't know if I was trying to defend myself, or if he suddenly decided to try one of his strange games on me and it got out of hand, but I'm not a cold-blooded killer. And I don't deserve to die."

She felt oddly light, as if a crushing burden, after years of weighing her down, had just rolled from her shoulders. She was a human being, she thought shakily. She had made mistakes—some worse than others. But the crippling guilt that had grown from the seeds planted so long ago was finally gone. She felt filled with a quiet peace.

She knew what she had to do.

The press came down. This time she knew she wasn't imagining the compressed air rushing past her. Two more strokes, maybe three, she thought calmly. There wasn't much time.

"You said I was wrong on both counts." He bent over her, a small smile playing around his lips. "You know,

Jan, I just don't think you're going to have the time to convince me of whatever the second one was.''

His tie was a charcoal silk with a muted red stripe running diagonally across it. It was only an inch away from her strapped-down right hand.

''That you're going to enjoy watching me die. That was the second point that you got wrong.''

He shifted slightly. The tie fell across her hand. With one swift movement she grasped it and wound both ends around her fist, jerking Leon's head down to hers.

''Because when I go, *you* go, Leon,'' she whispered, her lips only inches from his.

In a grotesque parody of intimacy, their gazes locked onto each other's. She could feel his sweat dampening her hair and she saw his eyes widen in shock as he attempted to get away. Behind them the stamp came down, and he bucked convulsively.

''Let me go! Let me *go*, Jan—I swear I'll turn it off! I was trying to frighten you—I never meant to actually kill you— *Goddammit, let me go!*''

He jerked backward as far as his short tether would allow, and the stamp ratcheted into position above them. The fear in his face suddenly turned to hate.

''You're not going to *do* this to me!''

She heard him fumbling clumsily with the rifle under the machine's bed, his freedom of movement almost nil. With his head held close to her, he was unable to see what he was doing. He couldn't let go of his weapon and use his fists against her, again because she was holding him down so tightly that even if he did allow himself to drop it he wouldn't be able to get enough leverage in his hunched-over position to put any force behind a punch.

There was only one option left to him, Jan thought,

and that was the one he had chosen. He was going to try to fire through the metal bed itself. It might work. She had no idea what he was using for ammunition, but it packed formidable firepower—possibly enough to pierce the machinery and kill her. But Leon himself could just as easily be hit by a round, and he knew that. He was attempting right now to blind-aim his weapon, and what it really came down to was time.

This time she saw the stamp ratchet into position directly above her, saw the disklike punch poised to strike, realized that her life was over. At the same moment, above the din of the ancient machinery, she heard the deadly, chattering cough of Leon's automatic weapon, and knew with satisfaction that he had been too late.

After this heartbeat she would be with Quinn. Jan closed her eyes, seeing again that dark silver gaze, that incredible smile. She would hear that whiskey-and-cream voice. He would hold her in his arms, and this time she would never, never, *never* let him go away from her again.

She heard the tiny metallic screech that meant the punch was about to descend. She saw with horror that her grip on Leon's tie had loosened. She felt him jerk away from her in triumph, his face a mask of fear and hatred; saw him raise the rifle, heard him screaming out something unintelligible—

And then he staggered. The rifle clattered from his grasp.

The punch blurred downward.

Chapter Twelve

She didn't remember the moment of impact, she thought hazily. Death must have been instantaneous, and this dark void she was now in had to be some kind of limbo. How long would it last? How long would it be before she heard Quinn's voice calling out to her?

"*Jan!*"

There it was. She'd known he would be waiting for her, waiting to guide her home. She called back to him in her thoughts, knowing that that was how he was communicating with her.

"Jan! For God's sake, angel—*say* something!"

There was pure terror in his voice, and that was all wrong. She frowned. That was all wrong, too, she thought a split second later. She'd left her body. How was it possible to assume any kind of expression?

"If she's dead, then the geese are flying for me tonight, too, dammit! If she's dead—" His voice broke off suddenly. Then he went on, almost inaudibly. "If she's dead, then take me, too. That's all I ask."

It wasn't whiskey-and-cream, it was a rasping, broken whisper, and it was coming closer. She could hear footsteps as well, and then a sudden clanging noise, as if something metal had been knocked to a floor.

The Bilt-Fine factory floor? Fear flooded through her. If she wasn't dead, then death was still to come. If she wasn't dead, then the punch-press was still suspended over her forehead. Why hadn't it smashed down yet? Was this yet another sadistic ploy of Leon's?

If she wasn't dead, then how was it possible that she could hear Quinn's voice?

"Quinn?" His name left her lips on a whisper. She'd lost her mind, Jan told herself. She was calling out to a dead man, a dead man she'd brought back to life again only in her grief-stricken imagination. Except why would the ghost she'd raised be stumbling into objects? Why hadn't she conjured him up by her side, instead of halfway across the room?

"Quiinn!" The scream tore from her throat the same instant that the realization ripped through her fogged mind. He had to be *alive.* Through some miracle he was alive—alive and coming for her.

"Quinn—Leon's got a rifle!" As swiftly as joy had flooded through her, fear replaced it. "He's here, Quinn!"

"He's dead, angel." The soft rasping voice was right beside her, and then his arms were around her and his face was next to hers in the dark. "I got him just before I shut down the power at the main box by the door." She felt him disengage one arm from her, and heard him reaching above her head. He swore. His voice shook as he did so.

"That was too damned close," he said hoarsely. "Too close entirely, for God's sake."

He took a shallow breath, and then he was fumbling with the oily length of rope that bound her. As she felt it loosen and then fall free, she heard him start to say something, but he was too late.

She raised her head slightly, wanting only to get away from the horror that had nearly been the end of her. She hit something hard and fell back immediately.

For a moment she didn't say anything. Blindly she brought an explorative hand to her head. The disk-like stamp of the punch-press was about half an inch above her.

"Quinn, get me off this." Her voice was a thread away from hysteria. "Get me off *now!*"

But already he was sliding her downward along the length of the flat surface, and then he was picking her up bodily, cradling her against his chest and striding sure-footedly between the dark hulking shapes of the other machinery.

"I can walk," she began weakly.

"Shut up, angel. I don't give a good goddamn whether you're up to doing a freakin' Highland fling right at this minute. Just let me hold you."

They were at the factory door. Without putting her down, he one-handedly felt along the wall for something, and then hesitated. "I have to switch on the power and go back to check on Asquith," he said quietly. "It'll only take a second, but I have to know that he's dead. If he's not, then I guess we've got to get him help, although it goes against all my instincts."

"I feel the same way." She couldn't repress the shudder that ran through her. "But you're right—if he's only unconscious we'll have to get him to a hospital somehow."

He set her gently on her feet, and then, as if he couldn't help himself, he gathered her to him again. His mouth found hers in the dark and then he was kissing her, almost desperately.

"I thought I'd lost you. I thought you were dead," he murmured against her lips.

"I thought *you* were dead. I'm still not sure you're real." Jan saw again the towering fireball, blazing up into the night sky. She shut her mind to the image. "How did you survive the fire?"

"As soon as you got out of the car I thought I'd better be ready for anything," he said, his breath warm against her hair. "I unlatched my own door and shucked off that heavy leather jacket—" He stopped abruptly. "Hell, that's gone," he said mildly. "I've had that since just after Kuwait." She felt him shrug. "Anyway, when the first round slammed into the car I was out of there like a jackrabbit, and as I hit the ground I kept rolling. I was just getting to my feet and starting to circle the vehicle to get to you when the damn thing blew. The blast must have knocked me out. When I came to a few minutes ago, the first thing I heard was that machine banging away, and I knew that whatever it was, it wasn't good."

"No, it—it wasn't good." She tightened her hold on him. "I knew I was going to die, Quinn. I intended to take Leon down with me."

"I grasped that much in the split second that I had while I was aiming at him. But I'm glad we did it my way this time, angel." His hands framed her face. "He didn't survive my bullet, I'm sure of that. But I'm going to have to make a statement to the authorities about what went down here tonight, and I don't want to give them anything they can use against us. Wait here a minute."

Wait a minute? She would wait a lifetime for him, she thought, as he gave her a swift, hard kiss and turned from her to the electrical box on the wall. A second later the glare of the fluorescents once more flooded the place with a harsh, sickly light, and almost simultaneously the punch-press clanged down on its metal bed.

Quinn's soot-streaked features were shadowed with concern. She gave him a wan smile.

"I'm okay. Go do what you have to do." Her face felt strangely stiff as she spoke, and she put her hand to it. She drew it away and then stared at her fingers, appalled. They were smeared with a mixture of blood and ash.

"You put me in mind of one of those legendary Celtic warrior-women, darlin'—Medb, maybe, or Derdriu." His grin flashed white out of his own grimy face. "You look beautiful to me," he added softly.

He held her gaze for a moment longer and then, setting his jaw and unholstering his gun, he cautiously made his way back to the clattering machine in the corner, and the sprawled figure of the man beside it.

She hadn't gotten the answers from Leon that she'd hoped for, Jan thought, turning her back to the grim task that Quinn was engaged in. On the wall beside the electrical box was another square metal container, this one with a distinctive red cross painted on it. She swung it open, and was gratified to find that it still contained some emergency supplies, a tightly capped bottle of alcohol and a sealed package of surgical gauze among them.

Her face was stinging and the gauze was filthy by the time Quinn joined her. He took her arm.

"No need to call for a medic on him," he said briefly. "Come on, let's get the hell out of this place. I think I know where he hid his car."

He hit the main electrical switch as she went out the door ahead of him, and for the last time, the Bilt-Fine punch-press abruptly fell silent.

"Did he tell you anything about the bombing?"

Quinn's arm went around her shoulder as he hustled her down the concrete-slab walkway that skirted the factory.

"Nothing much. He referred to the messages once, but he was more interested in telling me how I'd brought the authorities down on him. He was dealing in illegal arms."

Beside her he drew in a breath. "So that was the way of it," he said softly. "The bastard didn't just blame you for the death of his little brother, but he also held you responsible for exposing him. No wonder he was obsessed with making your life a living hell."

"He truly hated me," she admitted. "But his hatred and his blame made me see my own actions in a different light, Quinn." She stopped and looked up at him. "I was just as obsessed with punishing myself as Leon was. I accepted that I was capable of killing a man in cold blood, that I'd slipped over the line and become the kind of person that I studied and profiled. I don't think that anymore."

There was still a flickering light coming from the dying flames of Sullivan's sedan, and the moon augmented it enough so that she could see the sudden fierce relief that crossed his features.

"Thank God," he said simply. "I didn't know what else I could do to convince you that you weren't a killer. That's why I lied to you, angel—I was going crazy thinking of you turning yourself in."

"I know." Her eyes met his, and gently she brought her hand to his face. She pressed her palm against his cheek tenderly. "I *know*, Quinn. I shouldn't have blamed you for that. You were doing what I hired you to do— protecting me."

"And instead I nearly let you get killed." His voice

was tinged with anger, and she touched light fingers against his mouth.

"No. *I* nearly got us both killed. You saved my life," she said firmly. "You didn't like this set-up from the first."

"We were both keeping to our roles— I was thinking like a bodyguard, and you were thinking like a cop," he conceded. "Hell, in your shoes I would have wanted to bring the bastard in, too. But what we've got to decide now is how you're going to disappear again. Tarranova and Fitz aren't fools—they're going to start looking into you more closely once they find out what happened here tonight, and they'll make the connection to Jan Childs almost immediately. By the time they come to arrest you, I want you at least a couple of states away, and under a new identity."

They had resumed walking, and as they rounded the corner to the back of the building, she was glad that he wasn't looking at her. He'd misunderstood. He thought she believed herself innocent of any crime, and he was determined to keep her out of custody for as long as it took to discover who really had killed Richard Asquith—and if no other killer was found, he intended to settle her in a new life for good.

"We came in on the regular road. This must have been the factory's service road." Quinn was pointing at a badly overgrown, cracked asphalt lane leading up to a large pair of loading bay doors at the back of the building. "Asquith must have been familiar with this place."

"He said he'd been here before," she admitted distractedly.

"I'm betting his car's not too far away—maybe just past that bend, where the trees are." He looked at her. "Are you up to the walk? You look shaky, sweetheart."

"If you leave me here alone, McGuire, I guarantee I'll get more than the shakes." She looked up at him and mustered a wry smile. "I might even go so far as to have the heebie-jeebies. Let's go."

Under different circumstances, it would have been a nice night for a walk, she thought as they set off down the small road, his arm around her and his rangy stride considerably shortened. The autumn air was crisp enough to remind her that winter wasn't far off, but the heavy wool peacoat kept her warm. Quinn, clad only in his T-shirt and jeans, didn't even seem to notice the chill. He wouldn't understand, she thought despairingly. He'd thought of her as completely innocent from the beginning, and he still did. How was she going to explain to him that *her* basic position hadn't changed either?

She had to turn herself in. But she was going back to Raleigh to do it, and she would surrender herself with the best defense lawyer she could afford at her side. She had one strike against her already, Jan thought—she couldn't remember what had happened on that fateful night when she'd shot Richard Asquith. But she now had enough faith in who she was to realize that she had to have had some compelling reason to do it, and she wanted a fair trial for herself.

Starting all over with Quinn at her side would be the easy choice, but running from justice went against everything she believed in. Even if it wasn't, how fair would it be to saddle the man she loved with the life of a fugitive, for her sake? Somehow she had to make him understand that she had to put this part of her life behind her before she could create a new one with him.

"I *want* to go with you, Quinn," she began with difficulty. "I wouldn't care where we went or how hard it might be in the beginning. It would be enough that we were together. But—''

She stopped. He was staring at her, those silvery eyes dark and unreadable. Suddenly the asphalt under her feet seemed as unstable as shifting sand, and in that instant she was abruptly back at the Bilt-Fine factory again, with something poised and ready to smash her world to bits.

She was the one who'd made a mistake, Jan thought, meeting his gaze in disbelief. But how *could* she have? How could she have misread everything he'd said tonight, everything he'd done, so completely? How could she accept that she knew so little about the man that she'd only imagined everything she'd thought they had between them?

She *didn't* accept it. She didn't and she wouldn't, she told herself grimly.

His arm fell from her shoulders. ''I wouldn't be going with you. I thought you understood,'' he said tightly. ''But I need to know you're safe before I leave.''

''Before you leave.'' She echoed his words flatly. ''And just where are you going once you've packed me onto a bus for points unknown?''

''That's not important right now—'' he began, but she overrode him with sudden anger.

''I'm not Jane Smith anymore, McGuire, so you can't put me off like you did her. I'm not even the Jan Childs that I used to be. I'm a woman who figures she deserves some straight answers from the man she loves—from the man who loves *her*. And you do love me, don't you?'' She planted herself in front of him, her hands on her hips.

He looked momentarily startled. ''Dammit, Jan, this isn't the time or the place—''

''Yes.'' She held his gaze steadily. ''This *is* the time

and the place. Here and now—because according to you that's all we have.''

He started to look away, his jaw tense, but then, almost unwillingly, he looked back at her. Some of the rigidity left his posture.

''I don't have the right to love you.'' There was an edge of harshness to his tone, but it wasn't directed at her. ''I never had the right, and I knew it, but still I—'' The firm lips closed, as if he'd already said too much. He took a deep breath and started to turn away. ''Come on. We'd better find that car and get out of here.''

He'd taken two steps before she found her voice. ''Truth or dare, McGuire,'' she called after him sharply, not moving from where she stood.

He looked over his shoulder at her, his eyes widening. ''What?''

''You heard me. Truth or dare.'' She could feel her courage ebbing away under that opaque gaze, but she continued. ''Your choice.''

Something flashed across his features, and if she hadn't known him better she might have thought it was fear. ''I'm not choosing,'' he said evenly. ''Let's go—''

''Then I'll choose for you,'' she said, her gaze intent. ''Dare.''

A corner of his mouth lifted. ''Dare? And what is it you're daring me to do, angel?''

''I dare you to tell me about the wild geese, Quinn,'' she said calmly. ''Because for some reason, I think that's what this is all about.''

''That's crazy.'' His voice was as hard as she'd ever heard it. ''I told you, it's a damned legend—a myth. How the hell could it have anything to do with you and me?''

''I don't know. But it does, I'm sure of it.'' She tipped

her head to one side appraisingly. "So sure of it that I'll make you a deal, McGuire. You tell me about this—this *myth,* and I'll go away tomorrow like you want me to. If you don't, I'm turning myself in to Jennifer Tarranova tonight."

His gaze narrowed. "I always said you fought dirty, darlin', but this is way below the belt."

"Is it?" She lifted an eyebrow. "I guess that's the difference between us, then, soldier. I'm not bound by some outmoded code of honor. Not when it comes to this. So what's it to be—do you accept my dare or not?"

"There's nothing to tell you." His features seemed carved from stone. "Like I said, it's just a legend."

She'd gambled and lost, Jan thought slowly, looking at him. She hadn't realized how far he'd go to guard his past.

Now she did.

The fire that had been in her a moment ago had gone cold. She hunched her shoulders into the suddenly inadequate warmth of the wool coat. "You win, McGuire," she said tonelessly. "Let's go."

Without waiting for him she set off down the moon-shadowed road, her shoulders set. She'd just given the man her heart, and he'd lobbed it back at her as swiftly as if it had been a live grenade that he expected to explode in his hands. She'd been right, she thought slowly—that *had* been fear she'd seen in his eyes. She recognized it, because it was something she'd seen too often in the mirror herself these last few months, and for the same reason.

Quinn McGuire didn't want her to know who he was. He didn't want her to know what he'd done. No wonder he'd understood so well what she'd been going through.

And that revelation plus a buck would get her a latté,

she told herself tightly. If there was a bus leaving for Raleigh tonight, she intended to be on it. Maybe when there were a couple of hundred miles of highway between them the memories they'd made would start to fade. Maybe she would stop feeling as if she'd been ripped in two.

His quiet voice came from behind her.

"They say that wild geese are the souls of mercenaries who died in battle. The legend is that they're doomed to fly forever, searching in vain for a home they never had."

Turning, she saw him, still standing motionless where she'd left him. He began to walk toward her, but he wasn't looking at her. His gaze was fixed on the moon, bleached and almost full, in the dark sky above.

"I never believed any of it." He shrugged, and smiled humorlessly. "Well, not much, anyway. I'm Irish, so I never dismiss these things completely. But then they started to die, one by one, and I needed to believe in something."

He fell silent. He reached the place where she stood, and stopped walking himself, his hands shoved into the front pockets of his jeans as if finally he was beginning to feel the cold. Jan looked up at him.

"Jack Tanner," she said softly. "Paddy Doyle. And a young man called Haskins."

"I forgot you were a detective, Detective." Quinn looked away from the sky and down at her. "I suppose Sully told you."

"That's all he told me—that three men had died and it had hit you hard." She didn't lower her gaze. "I don't know anything else."

"There were more than three. They just happen to be the ones whose faces I still remember," he said harshly.

"Jack went first, on a day a lot like this one, as I recall. He was a quiet, solid soldier, except that every six months or so he'd go off on a bender. He only got drunk on his wife's birthday and his little boy's birthday, he told me once, because those were the two days that he couldn't stand being sober. I found out that he'd joined up after they'd been killed in a house fire."

"The poor man," Jan breathed, her eyes dark with compassion. "How could anyone ever get over something like that?"

"He found a way," Quinn said briefly. "About six months later he volunteered to check a trail for mines before the rest of the men went through. He stepped on one near the end of the trail and was killed instantly. The night that he died I heard a flock of wild geese fly overhead in the dark, in a country where there were no geese at all."

She didn't believe in myths and legends either, Jan told herself uneasily. But his words had sent a chill down her spine. "Paddy Doyle?" she prompted gently, trying to shake off the feeling of foreboding that was growing in her. "Sullivan said he was a friend."

"Paddy." Even at this grim moment, Quinn's face broke into a reminiscent smile. He shook his head. "He was quite a lad, that boyo. He was black Irish, and unlike me, he definitely had kissed the Blarney Stone, along with just about every female who'd ever caught his eye. He loved women, and they loved him. He was a natural wonder, he was." His smile faded. "His luck ran out one day when a rebel assassin gunned him down. I got the assassin, but Paddy died in my arms a few seconds later. He knew about the legend, too—hell, we all did— and just before he died he told me to look for him the next time the wild geese flew by."

"You heard them again that night," she said. It wasn't a question.

"Yeah, I heard them. It was the height of summer, in some godforsaken desert town, and I heard them as clear as anything. I even thought I could see them, against that huge red desert moon." A corner of his mouth lifted wryly. "I'd gone out and gotten drunk after Paddy's death, though. The next day I told myself it had been the whiskey."

"But you didn't convince yourself, did you?"

He glanced over at her. "No, I couldn't quite convince myself," he said softly.

The worst was yet to come, she thought fearfully. What was it Sullivan had said? *"Quinn feels responsible for all of them. But Haskins's death is the one he'll let himself get killed over."*

Suddenly she wished she hadn't forced him to relive these memories that were obviously tearing him apart. What right did she have? she asked herself angrily. What right did *anyone* have? He'd journeyed to hell a dozen times, and here she was asking him to tell her about the trip. It was insensitive, it was invasive, it was—

It was something she had to do, she thought dully. Because Sully had also said that only by learning about Quinn's past did she have any hope of saving him. She still didn't know from what. But she was about to find out.

"Did you get the man who took down the Haskins boy, too?" Her question seemed to rouse him from his thoughts. He looked at her as if he'd forgotten she was still there.

"No, I didn't," he said calmly. "Not yet."

This was what drove him, she realized slowly. He still had unfinished business. As Sully had said, Quinn felt responsible for the men who'd fought alongside him. He would consider it a debt of honor to avenge their deaths.

She was a woman. She saw vengeance as futile and ultimately destructive, whoever won out. But the man in front of her was ready to throw his life away pursuing it, and suddenly that made her angry.

"You're going back to find him and kill him, aren't you?" she said, crossing her arms and lifting her chin. "You want him to pay for this boy's death, but what if you get killed instead? How many more deaths does it take before this stupid legend is fulfilled, Quinn? And why does it have to be *you* who goes back to avenge him?"

"I'm not going back to find the man who killed Michael Haskins." His voice was toneless. "I don't have to. *I* killed him."

The bleakness in his voice shocked her as much as what he'd just said. She took an involuntary step back. "I don't understand," she whispered, pressing a hand to her mouth. "You—*you* killed him? But Sully said that his death affected you most of all. He said he was afraid you would let yourself get—" She stopped, her eyes widening with comprehension.

"Like I said, I'm definitely going to have a talk with Sully one of these days." There was an edge to Quinn's voice. "Michael Haskins should never have been in the business. Maybe he thought being a mercenary was romantic or something, I don't know. He wanted to be a writer someday. We called him Hemingway."

Everyone feels guilty about the past.... He'd said that to her—was it really only earlier today? Jan thought in brief confusion. Now she knew what he'd been referring to. The death of Michael Haskins was Quinn's heart of darkness—the pain at the very center of his being.

She'd once seen him as haunted. She'd been right.

"You don't have to tell me if you don't want to," she said quietly.

"You're the only person I think I could tell." He frowned. "Even Sullivan doesn't know the whole story. I went to the man who'd hired us for the job we were on, and I told him that Haskins was too inexperienced, that the boy was going to get himself killed—or get one of us killed. It was the only way I could think of to break him of his crazy romantic notions, and send him back home alive. I hadn't been able to talk him into quitting. Anyway, he was paid off and he left, never knowing that I was the one who'd engineered it, and I felt somehow relieved. I guess in a way he reminded me of myself, when I was younger."

He raked a restless hand through his hair and looked away. He was tough and hard, Jan thought sadly—but no one was tough enough or hard enough to take this much pain for so long.

"There's not much more to tell. I didn't know it, but he'd gone and hired himself to the other side. A day later I laid down a line of fire to break through a weak spot in the enemy's position, and when we took the ground later in the afternoon, the first body I stumbled over was Michael Haskins." He rubbed his jawline wearily. "I went through the papers that I found on him, and wrote to his parents. I heard the geese fly over that night and I've heard them practically every night since."

"And what is it they want? Why do you think you hear them?" She held her breath, waiting for his answer.

"Why, they want me to join them, of course." He looked at her in mild surprise. "That's my fate. That's the only way I'll ever atone for the things I've done, angel."

"But you were a *soldier,* Quinn. It was your *job.*"

"He was just a damn fool *kid!*" There was sudden fury in his voice. "Was that my job—to cut down a boy who hardly knew which way to hold his gun? Was it my job to close my eyes to a friend who was falling apart and heading for suicide? Maybe I should tell myself that it was my job to be looking the other way when that goddamn assassin killed Paddy."

He looked at her, and the anger disappeared as swiftly as it had come. "I wish I'd met you before I became the man I am now, but I didn't. I can't give you a future. I can't even tell you that I love you so much that your tears break my heart and your smile binds it up again. I've got nothing left of myself to give you—nothing of value, anyway."

"I'll take whatever it is you do have, McGuire." She gazed at him steadily. "I'm not such a bargain myself, you know."

"Don't ever think that." With a step he bridged the small gap between them. His hands came up to frame her face and his eyes met hers. "You're the one good thing that happened to me. But you're going to have to walk away from me, angel, and when you do, I want you to forget me."

"Why?" Her question came out in an anguished whisper, and her vision blurred. "Why, Quinn? It doesn't have to be that way—we could *make* a future together, you and—"

"I've got a future. I've seen it."

"You've *seen* it?" Again she felt a chill run down her spine, and involuntarily she stepped back from him. He released her, his hands falling to his sides. "What did you see? What's the future you see for yourself, Quinn?"

He didn't answer her, and suddenly the pain was too much to bear. The tears spilling over, she threw herself at him, slamming the palms of her hands against his broad chest. "What did you see, dammit? I want to know!"

He grasped her wrists and pulled her to him, but she felt as if they were already a thousand miles apart. "Tell me, Quinn." With difficulty she brought her voice under control. "You owe me that much, at least."

"I fall in battle. I'm buried in an unmarked grave. And the wild geese come to take me home." His eyes were as dark as the night. "That's what's in my future, angel. And that's why I want you to go."

Chapter Thirteen

"Thanks for everything, Sully—especially for letting me stay here at the office last night." Jan held out her hand to the dark-haired man. He ignored it and gathered her to him in a bone-crushing hug.

"Has he lost his mind entirely?" he said fiercely into her hair. "Lettin' a woman like you walk out of his life—he's a damn fool. I'm guessing he'll come after you as soon as he finds you've really gone."

Gently she withdrew from his embrace. "He won't. He said something about taking on another assignment and shipping out tomorrow night. Maybe you can talk him out of it. I couldn't." She looked up at him. "He told me about the wild geese, Sully. But it seems I'm not the woman who saves him."

"Then nobody can," the detective said flatly. "What if he asks me where you've gone?"

"You can tell him." She shrugged. "Besides, it'll be in the papers soon enough, even here. It's good copy—rogue cop gives herself up and goes for the old amnesia defense." She tried to smile, but her effort didn't succeed.

"That reminds me." He strode to his desk and pulled out a slim file folder. "These were faxed through to me late last night by my guy in Raleigh. They're copies of your notes on the serial killer investigation you were working on just before Asquith was killed. Do not— repeat *not*—ask me how he got his hands on them.''

He grinned wickedly at her and this time she did smile. ''I'll look them over on the bus trip. They might jog something loose in my memory.'' Idly she opened the file and glanced at the first few pages in it. She frowned. ''The Second-Story Strangler. Most of these notes I made before that last blank spot in my memory, so I remember them. I just can't recall who we finally charged with the killings.''

Sullivan shook his head. ''No one. You never found him, apparently, although it's possible the investigation scared him off. The killings stopped around the time you left Raleigh.'' He looked at her quizzically. ''What? Did you remember something?''

''No, not really,'' she said slowly. ''It's only that I was sure this case was closed, even though I don't remember the details. I thought we'd identified the killer.'' She closed the file and shrugged. ''Obviously not.''

''I also got some other information, but it's more or less background material—where you lived when you were a kid, the schools you went to, stuff like that. I asked Al to dig up everything, but that was a few days ago, when your memory was pretty much a complete blank.'' Sullivan nodded at a thicker folder on his desk. ''I guess it's not really relevant now, is it?''

''I remember enough about my childhood to know that if I never get the rest back, I won't lose any sleep over it,'' Jan said dryly. ''But thanks anyway, Sully.'' She looked at her watch. ''I'd better get going if I want to drop by the hospital before my bus leaves.''

''They probably won't let you see the Kozlikov

woman. The latest word is that she's showing some slight improvement, but she's still in critical condition.'' Sullivan's gaze hardened. He opened his office door and followed her into the carpeted hall. ''That bastard Asquith. A fast death was better than he deserved.''

''I only wish I'd gotten more information out of him. I acted impulsively, agreeing to meet him on such short notice and without knowing the layout of the location first. Quinn was pretty pissed off at me.'' She smiled shakily. ''Look after him for me, Sully. He's a good man.''

''He's a stupid man,'' he said shortly. ''But I care about him, too. I'll try to talk him out of this next assignment.''

''He said he'd seen his future.'' She put her hand on his sleeve. ''He—he said he would fall in battle. He said he would be buried in an unmarked grave. He really believes it.''

''And then his soul will rejoin his comrades.'' He closed his eyes for a moment. ''That damned legend.''

''Have you ever heard them, Sully?'' Her fingers tightened on his sleeve. ''Is there any way it's not just a legend—that there's some truth to it?''

Instead of answering her, he put his hand in his pants pocket. He brought it out and opened his palm. In it was a small fan-shaped shell with a perfectly formed hole right in the middle of it.

''I found that years ago. It's never been off my person since.''

''What is it?'' She put out a tentative finger and touched it. It felt silky from years of wear.

''I guess you could call it a talisman. The arrow that flieth by day, the pestilence that walketh in darkness—this reminds me that I'm protected against them. Psalm

91," he added, seeing her confusion. "I mislaid it once. I wouldn't get on the chopper that was taking us out until I found it. Quinn was pretty pissed off at me that day, too." He gave her a quick grin, folded his palm around the small shell, and dropped it back into his pocket. "So you see, you're talking to a superstitious man. But yeah, I thought I heard them once."

It wasn't what she'd hoped he'd say. As they reached the reception area she turned to him. "Promise me one thing, Sully." Her hand on the door, she paused, her gaze shadowed and urgent. "If he ever needs me, call me. I don't know what's going to happen to me, but as long as I still have breath in my body, I swear I'll find a way to get to him. *Promise* me, Sully."

He nodded slowly. "I promise. It's the real thing with you, isn't it?"

"Yes." She looked up at him, her smile crooked. "It's the real thing with me. And it was the real thing with him, too. I think I always knew that…just like I think I always knew it wouldn't change anything in the end."

Sully would keep his word, she thought half an hour later as she exited the subway and walked the few blocks to the hospital. But he would never call her, and both of them knew that. One day he might get a letter, or learn the news from an old friend, and, as Quinn had done the night she'd met him, he would hold a private wake for his friend. But he probably wouldn't inform her, and in a way she was glad.

Quinn would always be in her heart. Fifty years from now, if she closed her eyes, she would be able to see him as clearly as if he were standing in front of her, smiling at her in that way that had always had the power to make her knees go weak. She didn't want to know when death came for him. And she knew she would never let herself look up into an autumn sky to watch a skein of geese fly overhead.

She hastened her pace as she neared the hospital. Her bus left in an hour, and although getting to the terminal only meant hopping back on the Red Line and getting out three stops later, she still had to find out which floor Carla was on.

Probably Sully was right, and she wouldn't be allowed in to see Carla. But she wouldn't have felt easy leaving Boston without at least checking on her condition. Gary blamed her for what had happened to the woman he loved, she knew. Even before the bombing he'd made it clear that he thought she was putting Carla in jeopardy, and at the hospital yesterday he'd furiously dismissed her attempt at comfort.

But he was wrong. The only person to blame for what had happened to Carla was Leon. The Asquith brothers had both been reprehensible men, Jan told herself grimly. Leon, with his obsessive hatred and greed, and Richard, with his penchant for sadism toward women.

The killings stopped around the time you left Raleigh.

Sully's words resounded in her mind, and she stopped dead in the middle of the sidewalk. An annoyed woman sidestepped to avoid running into her, but Jan didn't notice.

She'd been taken aback when Sullivan had told her that the Second-Story Strangler hadn't been caught. For some reason that hadn't seemed right to her, although she had nothing concrete to base her feelings on. But if an arrest hadn't been made, then why had she been so certain that the Strangler case had been closed?

What if you'd thought you had discovered his identity, but you didn't report it? What if the man you suspected was someone wealthy and powerful, a leader of the business community, and you wanted to be absolutely sure of your suspicions before you even wrote his name down in your notes...especially since he was your fiancé?

It fit. She began walking again, her mind racing through the possibilities and her adrenaline surging. Even Leon had admitted that his brother's sexual proclivities were strange and cruel. That fit with the killer's methodology, which didn't involve rape, but did involve beating his victims after binding them up with leather straps. And after Richard's death the Strangler apparently hadn't struck again. If she had confronted Richard with her suspicions and something he'd said had confirmed them, the situation could well have escalated rapidly. She might have drawn her weapon in the line of duty, and then been left with no option but to use it against the man she'd profiled as a serial killer.

And if that was so, no jury in the world would fault her. More importantly, her own conscience would be clear.

"Jane."

Excitedly absorbed in her theory, she looked up just in time to see Gary, standing a few feet away from the entrance to the hospital. He was wearing a cotton shirt with his jacket slung over one arm, and a bunch of hothouse flowers clasped loosely in his other hand, as if he didn't realize he was carrying them. Meeting his glance, Jan felt her heart drop.

His face was tear-streaked, and his mouth was twisted into a wrenching grimace. He looked down at the flowers and let them fall to the sidewalk.

"She—she's dead, Jan. She didn't make it."

"Oh, *no!*" Her hand went to her mouth. "Oh, Gary, I'm so *sorry*."

He'd obviously just learned the terrible news, she thought with aching compassion. He must have come here prepared to visit the woman that he loved, and he was as neatly and carefully dressed as if he was going on a first date. Even his shoes and his belt were buffed and gleaming.

Instead, he'd found that he'd lost his Carla forever. Even as she watched, his head bowed and his shoulders started to shake.

"Oh, Gary..." She took a step toward him, and as the first sobs wracked his frame she wrapped her arms around him, her own throat tightening. "I can't tell you how sorry I am."

People were passing by, but aside from a few sympathetic glances, most of them considerately averted their eyes from Gary's obvious grief. Jan held him to her, knowing that nothing she could say would be of any comfort. He just needed to be close to someone who cared about him, she thought sorrowfully, patting his back as if he was a child in pain. Right now he would be feeling completely alone and bereft...

...the way he had in the past, when that belt that was right now wrapped around his waist, that belt with the gleamingly polished truck emblem on the buckle, had cut into his flesh so cruelly and endlessly....

Beneath her hand she could feel thick ropes of scar tissue, easily discernable through the thin cotton shirt. And as if her mind had needed only this one last jolt, the final missing piece of her memory fell back into place.

She stiffened in shock. Immediately she tried to hide her reaction, but it was too late.

"You remember, don't you?" His voice was right by her ear, and his hold had tightened on her. "I'm holding a gun on you under this jacket, Li'l Bit. My car's in the lot on North Anderson, so let's take a little stroll and go get it.''

"You don't want to hurt me, Gary…*Garnet*."

The two of them were still frozen in a tableau of grief and comfort. No one passing by seemed to notice that anything was wrong.

"You're right. I never wanted to hurt you, not even when you forgot everything we'd once been to each other and set out to destroy *me,* Li'l Bit.'' There was an edge to the whispered voice so close to her ear. "So go ahead and make a run for it. The streets are full of potential victims I can shoot instead, Jan. It's up to you.''

He'd killed six women in cold blood, she thought dully. The Second-Story Strangler wouldn't hesitate to take down as many innocent strangers as he could if she pushed him.

But once he'd been the only friend she'd had—a terrified, vulnerable child like herself. Wasn't there *anything* of that little boy still left in the man?

Slowly and cautiously she drew back from him, just enough to meet his gaze. It was still tear-filled, she saw. "Why, Garnet?" she said softly. *"Why?"*

He blinked the last of the tears away and stared at her. No, she thought, the child was gone. All that was left was the man that he'd become—the man that years of cruelty and abuse had created.

"Because you knew who I was," Garnet Vogel said harshly. *"And you knew what I'd done."*

"YEAH, I know, Sully." Quinn spoke impatiently into the phone. "But I went to the terminal, and she wasn't there. I waited until the Raleigh bus pulled out, but she never showed. What? No, I'm at your office." He fell silent for a moment, and then sighed. "I don't know. Hell, maybe I just wanted to say goodbye properly or something. You're sure she wasn't going to turn herself in to Tarranova? Yeah, I'll do that. I'll call you on your cell phone if I hear anything."

He slammed down the receiver and sat back in Sullivan's black leather chair, his frustrated glance scanning the room unseeingly. He'd been playing twenty questions with Donny Fitzgerald since dawn this morning, and Fitz had insisted he accompany the crime scene unit to the Bilt-Fine factory. The gray sedan had still been smouldering outside the front entrance, and Leon Asquith's body had still been lying in the same spot, but that wasn't what had bothered Quinn. All he could see was Jan's slim, stiff figure, bound to that godless machine, a split second away from death, the way he'd seen it in that instant when he'd taken his shot at Asquith and cut the power.

He'd come so close to losing her. Then he'd turned around and let her go. And he'd do the same again, if he had to.

But he just needed to see her one more time. He hadn't even intended to let her know he'd come to watch her go. The most he'd hoped for was a last glimpse of that shining brown hair, those serious blue eyes, that slim, ramrod-straight figure as she disappeared from his life forever.

He hadn't even had that.

He'd phoned the hospital a few minutes ago, and the nurse on duty had told him that although Kozlikov was now expected to pull through, the only person who'd been in to see her this morning had been her boyfriend.

Sully's indispensible secretary, Moira, had actually been on the phone to Gary Crowe when he'd walked in about half an hour ago, and he'd heard her telling him that Jan was on her way there if he wanted to see her. After hanging up on Crowe, Moira had seen Quinn's raised eyebrows and had explained that Gary had called to leave a message for Jan to meet him, saying something about wanting to apologize for his reaction the previous day.

She hadn't gone to the hospital. She hadn't been on the bus for Raleigh. There was only one other option—she'd changed her mind and decided to turn herself in to the Boston police. He bit back an oath. She was probably already in an interrogation room, being read her rights and most likely waiving them. By nightfall she'd be behind bars, and that had been the one thing he hadn't wanted to happen to her. It looked bad—all the evidence pointed at her. He had faith in the justice system, but not blind faith. There was a strong possibility she'd just signed her own death warrant.

Impatiently he dug in his jeans pocket for the card that Tarranova had given him the night before, and, picking up the phone again, he dialled her pager number. Leaving a curt message, he sat back, hoping that it wouldn't take long for her to return his call and wishing there was something more he could do.

On Sully's paper-strewn desk—the man was a slob, Quinn thought with mild disgust—was a folder, half-hidden under an appointment book that was open to the wrong day. Idly he pulled it toward him, his interest quickening when he saw the name scrawled on the cover in Terry's execrable handwriting. Flipping the folder open, he scanned the first few paragraphs of typewritten notes, feeling a slight disappointment as he realized that instead of new details concerning the killing of Richard

Asquith, as he'd hoped, the report only covered Jan's early life.

There was no real need for him to go through it now, and in a way he felt as if he was prying. But for some reason he felt as if he'd been given a gift, and he kept reading.

After today he would never see her again—except in his mind's eye, and with every breath he took. What harm was there in bolstering his memories of the woman he loved with as much as he could learn about her?

She'd been good at reading. She'd been lousy at geography, apparently, which was odd, considering how often she'd been uprooted by her flighty mother. Georgia. Wyoming. Vermont. Quinn's mouth tightened. Marie Childs had seemingly dragged her little girl all over the country, not caring if she started at two or three new schools during the course of a year, and only wanting to follow whatever man she was obsessed with at the time.

In front of him, Sully's private line rang and Quinn picked it up abstractedly, his eyes still on the page in front of him.

"McGuire? It's Jennifer Tarranova. What's up?"

Her voice was brisk and businesslike, but there wasn't the edge to it that he would have expected if Jan had already talked to her. Quinn dissembled. "Nothing important. But I went back to my apartment after I left you and Fitz, and Jane…"—he'd almost said Jan, he thought in chagrin—"…Jane wasn't there. I wondered if she'd come looking for me at the precinct."

"What am I, a dating service?" On the other end of the line Tarranova snorted. "No, McGuire, I don't know where your lady is. I'm at the hospital, and I've got a bigger headache right now."

It wasn't just briskness he heard in her tone, Quinn realized. It was anger, but it wasn't directed at him.

"What's the matter?" he asked sharply. "I thought the Kozlikov woman was expected to pull through—"

"She is. It's not her I'm worried about." She broke off abruptly, and then he heard her sigh. "Maybe I should alert you and Jane, at that. It's the boyfriend."

"Crowe?" He frowned in confusion.

"Gary Crowe isn't his real name, and apparently he hasn't known Carla all that long, either," Tarranova said. "We did a background check on him, along with anyone else who had access to that apartment before the bombing."

"Are you sure your information's right?" He closed his eyes, remembering again the scene in Jan's apartment when he'd first met Carla and Gary. "Kozlikov said something about them celebrating an anniversary a few days ago."

"If they did, it would have been a two-month anniversary, at most," Tarranova said shortly. "Gary met her at the hospital where she worked. He spun her some story about being there to see a sick friend, although I'm pretty sure that'll turn out to be a lie, just like everything else we thought we knew about him."

"What do you mean?" He felt a sick chill settle in the pit of his stomach. "What else has he lied about?"

"Well, he forgot to mention that he used to be in the army before they discharged him dishonorably, for one thing," Tarranova said. "And he forgot to tell us that he was a demolitions expert for another. I think he set that bomb himself—and that he knew just how to do it so that he wouldn't be injured. What I haven't figured out yet is what he had against Jane. He had to be the person who was stalking her, but it doesn't make sense."

"I don't understand that either," Quinn said harshly. "But we can look for motives later, Detective. I think Gary's got her."

In a few sentences he outlined the situation, only holding back Jan's real identity. No one had to know that yet, he thought grimly. It didn't affect the need to find her as soon as possible.

"I'll put an APB out for him as soon as I get his license plate. *Dammit*—the bastard's been playing us for fools right from the start!" Tarranova's normally quiet tones were heated. "We'll get him, McGuire, don't worry. And when we do, believe me, the gloves will be off with a vengeance. Gary Crowe, or Garnet Vogel, or whatever the hell his name really is, won't be planting any more bombs for ten to twenty years, if I have anything to say about it."

"Garnet Vogel?" The chill in his stomach turned to pure ice.

"Yeah. That's the name he enlisted under, anyway. I'll call you at this number when we get him, McGuire." Her briskness was replaced with distracted sympathy. "She'll be okay, big guy. We'll have a whole police department keeping their eyes peeled for him within minutes."

She rang off, and slowly Quinn replaced the receiver on Sullivan's phone. A whole police force wasn't going to be enough, he thought. But Tarranova was right about the other—Garnet had been one jump ahead of them from the first. He still was. And now he had Jan.

For a moment his brain shut down completely, seized with an unthinking terror that he'd never felt for himself. The bastard had Jan. He was past playing games with her—this time he would kill her. She would die in some terrible way, and all she would know was that the man who had sworn to protect her had left her alone and unguarded—

Coldly he imposed a steely order on his thoughts. Fear wasn't going to save her. Logic might. He had to approach this like a battle, with him a one-man army and Vogel the enemy.

Where would he have taken her? A man who had carefully stalked his victim for weeks, slowly escalating her terror with clues and messages, wouldn't simply drive her to the nearest alley and finish her off. No, he would see her death as the last act of his campaign of fear, and he would choose the location for it very carefully.

Quinn's gaze flew to the file in front of him. They'd once lived together as brother and sister just outside a small town called Ferlan, about an hour north of Boston. He punched the intercom button.

"Moira, can you have one of the guys bring a car around for me? One with a full tank and a phone," he said shortly. "And get through to the clerk's office in a town called Ferlan. I want an address from about twelve years ago."

He hung up and got swiftly to his feet. For a second he just stood, going over a checklist in his mind.

He wasn't armed. He'd had to leave his gun with Fitz this morning, so ballistics could run a confirmation on it, but that couldn't be helped. At least he would know the enemy's location, and perhaps most valuable of all, in the coming confrontation he would have the element of surprise on his side. He couldn't afford to call the authorities in on this and risk losing that element.

It was war, he thought grimly. And he was determined to win, even if it cost him his life.

Chapter Fourteen

"We're home. Come on, Li'l Bit, wake up. We can't sit here all night."

Groggily she opened her eyes. She felt sick and her head hurt, she thought crossly. Why was Garnet making her get up? Had Mama told him to get her ready for school?

He opened the car door and cold air rushed in. With it Jan's mind cleared, and she sat up swiftly. Just as swiftly she bent back down again, retching, although there was nothing in her stomach to bring up.

"I let you sleep for as long as I could, but it took a day or two for your system to get used to the drugs last time, remember?" He sounded concerned. As she leaned out of the car he held her hair back with one hand—not the one that was holding the gun, she thought dizzily. "Or maybe you don't," he added kindly.

"I—I remember, Garnet." Wiping her mouth with the back of her hand, she looked up at him stonily. "I remember everything now. Where are we?"

"At the old place—or what's left of it. Come on, I'll show you." He motioned with the gun, and slowly she got out of the car, holding onto the door frame until her legs felt steady enough to support her. The light was fading from the sky, but it was easy enough to see that they were in a clearing somewhere out in the country.

"The house used to be just over that hill. I had it torn down when I bought the property for back taxes a year ago." Garnet frowned. "This used to be all pine trees, but they were old even when we lived here. They must have come down in a storm one year."

"This is where we used to live?"

Jan looked around her in disbelief. It looked like a war zone, she thought uneasily. The small clearing was covered with rotting trunks and the twisted, broken limbs of the trees that had once stood here. Where the bark had peeled off, the pale wood showed through, like the bleached bones of soldiers who had fallen in some forgotten battle.

"Watch your step. Some of those branches are like pikes, for God's sake." She'd almost slipped, and he grabbed at her arm to keep her from falling. "I got a bad gash one day when I came out here. Hey—remember when we thought we could make glue out of pine pitch, and I got it all over my clothes?"

"No, Garnet. I don't remember that one." He'd brought her here to kill her, Jan thought. But before he did, it seemed as though he wanted to take a trip down memory lane with her. He wasn't sane, of course. No one who had done the things he had could be.

"Dad skinned me that night, for sure. That's what he used to call it, remember? I'm gonna skin you, boy. And he did." Garnet shook his head. "He damn well did. I looked him up a few years ago, you know."

"Why? You always said that when you finally got old enough to leave you never wanted to see him again."

If he wanted to talk, she would let him talk, she thought. She would encourage him. She needed all the time she could get before she tried to get the gun away from him, because right now she still was finding it hard to keep her balance.

"Yeah, but I also said I wished I was big enough to kill him." He gave her a smile. "Well, I grew up and got big enough, so I paid him a visit."

"You killed him." She didn't make it a question. She didn't have to.

"Uh-huh. But first I gave him a skinning, just like he used to do to me, and with the same damn belt." He nodded down at the gleaming buckle at his waist. "I took it with me after I killed him."

"You became him, Garnet—you became *worse* than him," she said impulsively. "The things you did to those women—"

"That wasn't *me*, that was *him!* I tried to tell you that when you wanted to arrest me, but you wouldn't listen—" He broke off abruptly. "Don't make me mad, Jan. I don't want to do anything bad to you." His mood changed again. "Gee, I was so happy when I ran into you in that coffee shop, and we recognized each other. We had a lot of fun those few weeks, didn't we?"

He sounded wistful, and for a second—just for a second—she could hear an echo of the little boy he'd once been, the one who'd crept out of his bed and into hers to hold her when Mama and his father were fighting. She *had* been glad to meet Garnet again, after all those years. Like she'd told Quinn, she had always wondered what had happened to him after their parents had parted. For a while, she had enjoyed having a big brother again.

But then she'd begun to notice things.

At first they were just small discrepancies—he would tell her he'd been out of town the previous few days when she was certain she'd caught a glimpse of him on the street. His disappearances always coincided with the killings of the Second-Story Strangler.

Actually, she'd thought of him when she'd viewed the first victim's body—the woman had been beaten with a belt. The terrible sight had brought back the memory of Garnet's scars. But she hadn't been able to bring herself to believe that the frightened, wounded boy she'd loved like a brother had grown into a man who was capable of such horrors.

A neighbor of the last victim had furnished the police with a vague description of a suspect. It hadn't been anything near proof, but it had been enough for Jan.

The profile she'd postulated of the killer fit her step-brother exactly. Along with his lies and the neighbor's description, it was too much for her to ignore.

But she'd given him a chance to explain himself, hoping against hope that she was wrong. His hurt and indignant denial had allayed her suspicions a little—or perhaps, she admitted to herself now, she had wanted them to be allayed. Garnet would have known, though, that eventually she would start going over the evidence again, and that it was only a matter of time before she put out a warrant for his arrest. Somehow he'd gotten into Richard's house that night, knowing that she was planning to spend the evening with him. When Richard had left the room for a moment Garnet had slipped from his hiding place, brought the butt of his own gun down on her head, and presumably had killed Richard as he'd re-entered the room.

I'd gone straight there from work, Jan thought dully now. *He would have known that I'd have my gun on me, and he used it instead of his own for the murder. He was planning to set me up right from the first. So why did he take me with him?*

She didn't remember much about that nightmarish trip with him after the murder—only that it had gone on for what seemed like days, and that every time she began to come out of her drugged stupor, he would pull the car over and give her another injection. But Boston's notorious construction had provided her with an opportunity to escape.

He'd been stuck in traffic, and he hadn't been able to risk giving her an injection when the drivers nearby might see what was happening. She'd pretended she was still unconscious anyway, and finally she'd gotten up her courage and leapt from the stationary car.

He hadn't dared come after her. His own lane of traffic started moving, and he'd driven off, not wanting to draw attention to himself. In her panic she'd kept running, until the accident that had robbed her of her memory had occurred.

"What were you planning to do with me, Garnet? Why didn't you just leave me to be arrested for Richard's murder?" She looked at him, keeping her eyes unfocused and feeling a slight return of her strength.

"I wanted you to live with me out here, of course." He sounded surprised. "I thought I could build us a house and it would be just like when we were kids again, except without the adults. I knew you wouldn't be able to leave me if everyone thought you were a murderer, too. But then you ran away from me, and I knew it was never going to come true."

He grimaced. "The worst part of all was having to pretend I was crazy about that cow Carla. I had to work fast, so I could already be living with her by the time I persuaded her to tell you about the empty apartment next door. I thought you might get suspicious if I showed up about the same time you did."

"The messages, the attack on Martine? Those were all you?" At his nod she went on. "You set the explosion at the apartment, too?"

"It wasn't hard. I actually had the detonator in my pocket, except I wasn't expecting to get hit myself." He frowned. "That was a mistake. But everything else went according to plan, right down to my anonymous phone call to Leon, telling him where his brother's murderer was hiding out. He came on the next plane, and I made sure Carla saw him at your door."

"So you set him up as well," Jan said with an edge to her voice. "What about the Trinity Tavern, in the washroom?"

"I followed you there before I met Carla at the gym. I suggested we catch a movie that was playing a block away from the tavern and made some excuse to leave my seat soon after it started. I went to the Trinity, did what I had to do, and when I returned I told her I'd had trouble finding our row in the dark." He looked abashed. "I'm sorry about that, Jan, I really am. I didn't mean to hurt you that night—I just wanted to frighten you. The damn rope must have been stronger than it looked. Anyway, the Irishman got to you in time, and that's the main thing."

He'd mentioned Quinn. She hadn't wanted him to, because she'd been trying with all her might not to think of him. But now it was impossible to hold back the memories and the sorrow.

He would probably never know what had happened to her. Maybe he would think that she'd disappeared into a new life, as he'd wanted her to do. She hoped so. It was all she could endure, knowing that she would never see him again, never touch him, never hear that whiskey-

and-cream voice in her ear as they made sweet, sweet love through the night.

She didn't want him to know that she'd died. He'd had too much pain in his life already.

And she was going to die, she knew it. She still was in no shape to take on Garnet, and their little stroll around the property had seemingly come to an end. He'd halted in one of the few areas that wasn't strewn with fallen trees.

"Well, Jan, this is it," he said softly. "This is where it all began, and I guess this is where it ends. I wish it hadn't had to turn out this way."

"I'm sorry, too, Garnet." She met his gaze. "Are you sure it has to?"

It was almost full dusk now. Beyond the patch of soft, loamy earth where they were standing were the bone-like shapes of the fallen trees. Past those was the rest of the woods—the maples and the oaks that had been strong enough to survive the storm that had felled the pines. It didn't feel like home, Jan thought. It didn't feel like it had ever been home. A sudden rush of longing came over her. Home was a pair of strong arms, a gray gaze meeting hers, a smile that could make her heart turn over with love.

She was never going home again.

"You wouldn't believe me when I said it wasn't really me who did those things. You wanted to punish me. You turned against me, Jan." Garnet gave her a push. "Yeah, it has to be this way. Walk about ten feet away and then stop."

She would close her eyes, Jan decided. She would close her eyes when she turned to face him, and instead of this desolate landscape, her last vision would be of a big man leaning over the bottom half of a Dutch door, watching a handful of small birds settling down for the night. Her last vision would be of Quinn. There was really nothing else she wanted to take with her into that final darkness.

She turned, her eyes already closed, and she smiled. She could almost believe he was with her now. She could almost *sense* his presence.

"Goodbye, Jan."

She heard the small click as Garnet took the safety off. She felt the cold November air on her cheek. She knew these would be the last sensations she would experience.

"Vogel!"

Her eyes flew open. The gun in Garnet's hand was aimed straight at her, but his gaze was focused on the big, shadowy figure approaching them from the dark line of trees. It was Quinn, his long stride eating up the distance between them easily.

He'd come to save her. She bit back a hysterical little laugh that had more than a hint of a sob about it. He was on his own two feet, rather than a white charger. His jeans and T-shirt certainly weren't a suit of shining armor, but it seemed she had her *parfit gentil* knight anyway.

He'd come to save her, and he didn't appear to be armed. He was prepared to lay down his life for her.

"I'll make you a deal, Vogel." He was much closer now, and the soft voice wasn't even raised. "Me for her. It'll take her till dawn to get to Ferlan on foot—longer if you shot her full of dope like you did the last time. By then you could be halfway to Mexico or all the way to Canada. They'll never catch you. What do you say?"

"For God's sake, Quinn!" She tried to take a step

forward, and then swayed dizzily, just managing to keep herself from falling. "Do you think I would let you—"

"What makes you think I wouldn't kill you and then her?" Garnet sounded merely curious, but his eyes never left the approaching figure.

"You don't really want to kill her. You just need someone to die here, in this spot. That's the only way you can wash away the memories, isn't it?" Quinn's voice was soothingly understanding. He'd slowed his pace, but still he advanced. "Why don't you take me up on my offer, Vogel? It won't be on the table forever."

"The thing is, I've got the gun." The light was fading fast. It was hard to see Garnet's expression, but he sounded as if he was smiling. "So I don't have to make any deal at all, McGuire. I think I'll pass, if it's all the same to you."

Quinn had been talking to gain time, Jan realized apprehensively. He was only about twenty feet away from Garnet now. Maybe the other man didn't realize it, but she knew Quinn had every intention of tackling him, gun or no gun.

"Okay, McGuire, that's far enough—"

Even before the words were out of Garnet's mouth Quinn sprang. Immediately the other man fired, but already the broad shoulders had hit the dirt in a half-roll that brought Quinn to within a few feet of him. In one fluid motion he rose, and then the two men were grappling for the gun.

"Run, Jan! *Run!*"

His hoarse shout brought her to her senses. She had no idea what it would take to bring him to *his,* she thought furiously, stumbling unsteadily toward them. If Quinn McGuire still thought she was the type to scuttle away and leave him to fate—

The earth swung crazily around her, and she felt herself falling.

''*Jan!*''

She was seeing double. Two Quinns spun around, their expressions identically anguished, as she fell. Two Garnets slipped out from the massive arms that were pinning them. And two hands came up, with two guns, and pulled off two shots that echoed emptily around the dark clearing.

Just before she lost consciousness completely, Jan's vision cleared. She saw Quinn's head snap back, saw the blood obscuring the air around him...

...and then she saw the one and only man she would ever love fall to the ground as the last of the dusk darkened into night.

SHE COULD smell dirt. She could *taste* dirt. Painfully she raised her head and spat. Even that small movement made her feel nauseous, but the dizziness had gone. She opened her eyes. Slowly she got to her knees.

The moon was perfectly full. It hung over the small clearing with enough light to make it easy to see Garnet, although his back was to her and she couldn't make out what he was doing.

Quinn was dead. He had to be dead. She'd seen the shot that had taken him down, and she had no hope at all that he'd survived it. So that was that. Her world had been smashed beyond repair, and she had nothing left to lose. Hunched over like an old woman, Jan got to her feet, and as she did, Garnet moved slightly to one side and she could see what it was he'd been doing.

The pitiless moonlight shone coldly down on a rectangle of freshly turned earth. Garnet had been filling in a grave.

He'd been filling in Quinn's grave.

"I'm going to kill you, Vogel." Her lips were cracked and dry and her throat sounded like it was still clogged with earth. She took an unsteady step forward.

He looked around, startled. Then he laughed, and she knew for certain that the child he'd once been had died a long, long time ago. He put down the shovel he was holding and bent down to pick up the gun at his feet.

"You're as crazy as he was. Li'l Bit, you don't really think you stand a chance here, do you?" His hands hung at his sides, loose and relaxed. In the moonlight she saw him shake his head disbelievingly.

"I *am* as crazy as he was. And my name isn't Li'l Bit, Vogel." She kept walking, planting her feet heavily and carefully, one in front of the other. "My name is Jan Childs. I'm a cop, and you killed the man I love. I'm going to kill you."

"I don't think so, Jan." Carelessly he raised the gun and fired.

A searing heat sliced through her upper arm, and she staggered, once. Then, with immense care, she brought her right foot forward and continued walking toward him.

"I'm a cop. You killed the man I love. I'm going to see you die, Vogel," she said thickly. Her hair was matted with leaves and earth, and it fell into her eyes, but it didn't matter. Nothing mattered.

There was a strange look on Garnet's face. It wasn't fear, not yet. In a minute it would be, Jan thought. He fired again, and this time she almost fell.

He'd gotten a rib, or just grazed one. She felt a sudden warm stickiness on her right side, but she shut her mind to the pain. She drew in a shallow breath, clenched her jaw tightly, and took a step.

"You killed the man I love," she ground out with difficulty. She took another lurching step, and another. "You're going to die, Vogel."

Through the lank and filthy strands of hair she could see him, and now it *was* fear, she thought with satisfaction. His eyes were wide and his mouth was open. His hand was actually shaking as he pulled the trigger again, and then again.

"His name was Quinn McGuire," she whispered hoarsely, feeling the pain blooming at the outside of her thigh and knowing that this time she wasn't going to be able to hold it back. "He was...the man I *loved*. I'll...see you...die, Vogel."

Garnet was staring at her as if he was looking at a ghost—and perhaps he was, Jan thought hazily. Her reason for living had gone, so perhaps the thing staggering toward him was her spirit. She saw the gun drop from his nerveless fingers, and saw him start to back away from her.

"You should be *dead!*" His voice was a frightened hiss. "Why aren't you dead?" He took another swift step backward, his face a mask of terror. "Don't come any closer! Stay away from—"

He stumbled on one of the fallen limbs, and fell backward, still staring at her with wide, horrified eyes. She saw a spasm pass over his features.

Then she saw the sharp limb protruding from his chest.

"Dad?" His voice was a child's whisper. "Dad, please— I didn't mean it. Please don't...don't give me a skinnin'...."

She'd been wrong, Jan thought, her gaze meeting the fearful brown eyes that looked up at her. There was something left of the child who'd once been her refuge, and that child had reappeared now, at the moment of Garnet Vogel's death.

She looked down at him, forcing herself to stay upright with an effort.

"It's okay, Garnet," she rasped painfully. "Go to sleep now. It's all over."

The brown eyes closed and the slim body convulsed once, and then it was true. It *was* all over.

She turned away and started walking awkwardly back to the middle of the clearing. She had the terrible feeling that none of her wounds was mortal, and that seemed like the cruelest blow of all. She stopped, her hand clamped to her burning thigh, and then she heard them.

It was a high, wild sound, and it was coming from the sky far above her. She raised her head and looked up, her blood congealing in her veins. They were in a V-formation, and they were steadily circling downward, toward the clearing.

I fall in battle. I'm buried in an unmarked grave. And the wild geese come to take me home....

An icy rage filled her. *"Damn you—no!"* Her words were a cracked and broken battle cry. "You're not getting him!"

She was at the grave and on her knees, and her fingers were already frantically scrabbling at the loose dirt. He wouldn't have had time to dig deep, she thought insanely. And the earth was intermixed with rotting leaves and small branches—there was a *chance,* wasn't there? *Wasn't* there?

Above her the silken rush of wings grew steadily louder and closer, and she no longer knew if she was really hearing it or whether it was a hallucination. She felt her nails breaking off, down to the quick, and the pain in her shoulder was burning like a white-hot flame, but still she dug, throwing clumps of earth to the side.

"He's the man I love. He's the man I *love,* dammit!" She was sobbing, the tears mingling with the grime on her face. She could feel the warm wetness soaking the entire side of her shirt, could feel the blood seeping from her torn jeans, and her hands were flying, flying, scattering dirt and leaves—

—and then she felt something. More carefully, she brushed the dirt aside, and saw the pale gleam of his hair under her hands. There was a dark, sticky mass obscuring the pewter strands. He was face down.

She felt her heart crack right in two.

"Oh, Quinn," she whispered, her fist to her mouth. "Oh, Quinn—*no.*" Gingerly she touched her fingertips to the stickiness, gently searching for an entry wound. She felt a furrow that seemed to traverse the whole side of his head, but as she probed deeper, she suddenly started to shake.

Was it possible that the bullet hadn't actually entered at all? Was it possible that he was still *alive?*

She'd been digging furiously before, but now she was tossing earth aside like a machine, uncovering the whole length of him in seconds. The world seemed filled with noise and movement—the rushing of the wind gathering speed, the high, eerie cry all around her, and the sense that she was running out of time, running out of time.

There was still some dirt caked onto his clothing, but she ignored that. Grabbing the back of his belt and the shoulder seam of his T-shirt, she hauled him up, feeling the muscles in her arms screaming and popping, and not caring about the now-fiery pain in her side. Suddenly he was over the edge of the grave, and she toppled backward, falling hard on her rump.

She was up again in an instant, and turning him over.

The dark blood from his head wound had trickled forward onto an eyelid. His mouth was closed. The pale hair was begrimed with dirt and his skin was almost white in the moonlight.

And suddenly she came to her senses.

He was dead. He'd told her what his future held, and he'd been right. He'd fallen in battle, fighting for her. He'd been buried in an unmarked grave. And his soul was even now winging upward to search forever for a home he'd never had.

She clenched her fists and looked up at the sky. There was nothing to see, but she was sure she could still hear them, far away and getting farther.

"But he *did* have a home. His home was with *me!*" Her words came out in a keening, anguished wail, and the tears started pouring down her face. "His home was with me, dammit!" she cried, bringing her fists crashing down on his chest. "He was the man that I loved, and his home was with *me!*"

Quinn choked.

Jan froze.

Slowly and painfully he rolled over onto his side, coughing the earth from his mouth. Then he carefully put his weight on one elbow, and looked up at her.

One eye was plastered shut with dried blood. But the other one met her unbelieving gaze.

"You—you're alive," he croaked. "Dear God, I thought surely he'd kill you, too, angel." Realization flashed behind his one good eye, and with an effort he craned his neck and looked over his shoulder.

"He's dead, Quinn. He's dead." It was inadequate, but all of a sudden she couldn't seem to get out the words she wanted to say.

"What the hell is that, angel?" He jerked his head backward at the open grave behind him. "And why the hell am I covered in dirt?"

"Because it came true, Quinn," she whispered shakily. "The geese came to take you home. Except—except I wouldn't let them."

"You wouldn't let them." One corner of his mouth rose painfully in a crooked smile. "My God. The legend said nothing about that, darlin'. The damn legend said nothing about a woman so headstrong and stubborn that she wouldn't let them take me."

"I don't care. It all came true, and every part was fulfilled." Her voice trembled. "So they don't have anymore claim on you, do they?"

He squinted up at the moon, and then back down at her, a sudden fierce joy in his gaze. "No, they don't have a claim anymore. It's just a legend now, and the legend's been told."

He rose slightly on his elbow and leaned toward her. Slowly she closed the distance between them, and felt his arm go around her, holding her to him as if he'd never let her go.

"Which only leaves us with real life," he said softly into her hair. "Do you think you could be happy with one battered, presently unemployed Irishman who's got nothing to give you but every last piece of his heart, angel?"

"I think I could, McGuire," Jan murmured as his mouth found hers. He squeezed her tighter and she gasped.

"What is it, darlin'? Were you hurt?" he asked in quick concern.

"Two clean shots, and I think there might be a bullet

lodged in a lower rib,'' she said, biting her lip. "Quinn, I don't know if I can make it to the car.''

"A bullet lodged in your—'' He swore under his breath, and stood, only swaying slightly. He bent down, helped her to her feet, and then swept her off them, cradling her in his arms.

"No problem entirely, angel,'' he said softly. "I'll take you home.''

...and up in the sky, somewhere behind the moon but not as high as the stars, a flock of wild geese saw Quinn McGuire carry the woman he loved from his last battlefield.

Epilogue

Just inside the high brick wall that surrounded the Belgian convent was a small graveyard, with only weathered stones to mark the final resting places of those who were buried there. By one of them was a huge bunch of bird-of-paradise blooms, incongruously tropical-looking against the bare November landscape. The big man who'd placed them on the ground hunkered down on his heels and raked one hand through his short hair.

"Well, now, Sister, I'm wanting that bill marked paid in full," he said softly. "You stuck me with it out of the blue, and I don't mind telling you, I thought it was pretty damn underhanded of you at the time. But I paid it off a year ago now, so I hope you're satisfied."

The damn wind was making his eyes water, Quinn thought in annoyance. He swiped the back of one hand across them and cleared his throat.

"Anyway, along the way I found myself a crazy woman who wouldn't let me die. Sound like anyone you know, Sister?" In the tan of his face a quick grin flashed, and then he sobered again. "I love her completely," he said quietly. "But what I really came to ask you was if you'd mind if we used your name, Sister. Jan and I talked it over and we both thought we'd like to name our daughter Bertille when she comes, if that's fine with you. I guessed it would be, but you always were a stickler for etiquette, so I thought I'd better get your permission first.''

He was silent for a few minutes. Then he got slowly to his feet, his glance lingering on the headstone. It had nothing but the name she'd taken when she'd joined her order, and her dates of birth and death. It didn't seem enough, Quinn thought. Not nearly enough. But he knew that was all she would have wanted.

''Go with God, Sister,'' he whispered.

He turned away from the quiet graveside and looked up. Suddenly hastening his pace, Quinn walked back to the gates, where the woman who was his whole world was waiting for him.

*Be sure to watch the fireworks explode
when Terrence Sullivan is reunited
with a lost love in*

SULLIVAN'S LAST STAND,

*coming only to Harlequin Intrigue
in September 2001.*

*And now for a sneak preview,
please turn the page.*

Chapter One

He hadn't changed at all in one year. He was still the most gorgeous male she'd ever seen.

She might have known, Bailey thought in resignation, crossing her arms and waiting for him to see her standing in the doorway. She gave an audible snort and had the satisfaction of seeing his eyes fly open as his startled gaze met hers.

"Your firm screwed up, Sullivan."

"My firm screwed—" Abruptly he swung his own legs off the desk as his eyes met hers. "I don't think so, Bailey, honey," he said. "Unless you can prove what you just said."

"Angelica, my adopted sister, was one of the cases I sent your way to have her husband followed."

"She married Aaron Plowright four or five years ago, going from cocktail waitress to billionaire wife in one fell swoop, right? So why did you send her to me? Did she mislay some trifling object like a yacht that she wanted us to locate for her without the hubby finding out?"

"No. She thought hubby had a trifling object that he didn't want her to find out about. Aaron had to go away on an unexpected business trip last weekend, and apparently your—'' She stopped abruptly, her breath suddenly short and her heartbeat speeding up.

"Go on."

He'd stood up and shucked off the suit jacket he'd been wearing. Now he was unbuttoning the cuffs of his shirt and rolling his sleeves back. He glanced over at her.

"What is it?"

How many times had she seen him do that in the past? she thought helplessly. The answer came to her immediately—*three*. Three times in the past he'd stood in front of her and lazily started to undress, and those three times he'd kept going. They'd made love three times together. Well, that wasn't strictly true—they'd spent three nights together and made love time and again. She swallowed with difficulty.

"Nothing. I just want to make sure I don't leave anything out," she said, her tone as professional as she could make it. "Aaron went away on what he said was an emergency business trip, and your operative, Hank Jackson, followed him. Apparently Angelica's suspicions were correct. But Jackson made a judgment call that sucked big time. Jackson gave Angelica the gist of his findings over the phone on Sunday night. Aaron's 'business meeting' was with a gorgeous brunette, and they weren't exactly discussing a merger. According to Jackson, they were in the middle of one—a very personal, very *intimate* merger."

"So what's the big problem?"

"The problem is that Angelica's not the most stable person that you could drop a bombshell like that on, even if she did semi-suspect something. Now she's disappeared, and no one seems to have any idea where she's gone." Her eyes met his and her voice hardened.

"Jackson's your man, Sullivan. I'm holding you responsible for anything that's happened to Angelica."

"If anything's happened to her and *if* Hank behaved unprofessionally, then I'll accept that responsibility," he said curtly. "But maybe you should keep personal out of this yourself, honey. It's not Hank Jackson who blew it as far as you're concerned, is it? It's me. *I'm* the one who screwed up big time. I'm sorry for what happened last year, Bailey. No excuses. I handled things badly."

She stared at him, completely taken off guard. Once she would have given almost anything to hear him say those words. She hadn't been able to forget him completely, but she'd gotten on with her life. His twelve-month late apology shouldn't have the power to rip away the scar tissue of composure it had taken her so long to build up.

But it did. Bailey blinked. "You're wrong, Sullivan. I'm over you completely." Her voice was barely audible. "Want proof?"

She got to her feet and leaned over the desk until she was close enough to him to lightly grasp the pearl-gray silk of his tie. With a swift movement she brought her lips to his.

"Completely. Over. You," she whispered against his mouth.

AND YOU THOUGHT TEXAS WAS BIG!

HARLEQUIN®
INTRIGUE®

continues its most secret, seriously sinister and deadly *confidential* series in the Big Sky state with four more sexy cowboy agents guaranteed to take your breath away!

Men bound by love, loyalty and the law— these specialized government operatives have vowed to keep their missions and identities confidential....

SOMEONE TO PROTECT HER
PATRICIA ROSEMOOR
September 2001

SPECIAL ASSIGNMENT: BABY
DEBRA WEBB
October 2001

LICENSED TO MARRY
CHARLOTTE DOUGLAS
November 2001

SECRET AGENT HEIRESS
JULIE MILLER
December 2001

Available wherever Harlequin books are sold.

HARLEQUIN®
Makes any time special ®

Visit us at www.eHarlequin.com　　　　HIMONTANA

Harlequin truly does make any time special. . . . This year we are celebrating weddings in style!

A
Walk
Down
the Aisle
WEDDING CELEBRATION

To help us celebrate, we want you to tell us how wearing the Harlequin wedding gown will make your wedding day special. As the grand prize, Harlequin will offer one lucky bride the chance to **"Walk Down the Aisle"** in the Harlequin wedding gown!

There's more...

For her honeymoon, she and her groom will spend five nights at the **Hyatt Regency Maui.** As part of this five-night honeymoon at the hotel renowned for its romantic attractions, the couple will enjoy a candlelit dinner for two in Swan Court, a sunset sail on the hotel's catamaran, and duet spa treatments.

A HYATT RESORT AND SPA® Maui • Molokai • Lanai

To enter, please write, in, 250 words or less, how wearing the Harlequin wedding gown will make your wedding day special. The entry will be judged based on its emotionally compelling nature, its originality and creativity, and its sincerity. This contest is open to Canadian and U.S. residents only and to those who are 18 years of age and older. There is no purchase necessary to enter. Void where prohibited. See further contest rules attached. Please send your entry to:

Walk Down the Aisle Contest

In Canada	In U.S.A.
P.O. Box 637	P.O. Box 9076
Fort Erie, Ontario	3010 Walden Ave.
L2A 5X3	Buffalo, NY 14269-9076

You can also enter by visiting www.eHarlequin.com
Win the Harlequin wedding gown and the vacation of a lifetime!
The deadline for entries is October 1, 2001.

HARLEQUIN®
Makes any time special ®

PHWDACONT1

HARLEQUIN WALK DOWN THE AISLE TO MAUI CONTEST 1197
OFFICIAL RULES
NO PURCHASE NECESSARY TO ENTER

1. To enter, follow directions published in the offer to which you are responding. Contest begins April 2, 2001, and ends on October 1, 2001. Method of entry may vary. Mailed entries must be postmarked by October 1, 2001, and received by October 8, 2001.

2. Contest entry may be, at times, presented via the Internet, but will be restricted solely to residents of certain geographic areas that are disclosed on the Web site. To enter via the Internet, if permissible, access the Harlequin Web site (www.eHarlequin.com) and follow the directions displayed online. Online entries must be received by 11:59 p.m. E.S.T. on October 1, 2001.

   In lieu of submitting an entry online, enter by mail by hand-printing (or typing) on an 8½" x 11" plain piece of paper, your name, address (including zip code), Contest number/name and in 250 words or fewer, why winning a Harlequin wedding dress would make your wedding day special. Mail via first-class mail to: Harlequin Walk Down the Aisle Contest 1197, (in the U.S.) P.O. Box 9076, 3010 Walden Avenue, Buffalo, NY 14269-9076, (in Canada) P.O. Box 637, Fort Erie, Ontario L2A 5X3, Canada. Limit one entry per person, household address and e-mail address. Online and/or mailed entries received from persons residing in geographic areas in which Internet entry is not permissible will be disqualified.

3. Contests will be judged by a panel of members of the Harlequin editorial, marketing and public relations staff based on the following criteria:

   - Originality and Creativity—50%
   - Emotionally Compelling—25%
   - Sincerity—25%

   In the event of a tie, duplicate prizes will be awarded. Decisions of the judges are final.

4. All entries become the property of Torstar Corp. and will not be returned. No responsibility is assumed for lost, late, illegible, incomplete, inaccurate, nondelivered or misdirected mail or misdirected e-mail, for technical, hardware or software failures of any kind, lost or unavailable network connections, or failed, incomplete, garbled or delayed computer transmission or any human error which may occur in the receipt or processing of the entries in this Contest.

5. Contest open only to residents of the U.S. (except Puerto Rico) and Canada, who are 18 years of age or older, and is void wherever prohibited by law; all applicable laws and regulations apply. Any litigation within the Province of Quebec respecting the conduct or organization of a publicity contest may be submitted to the Régie des alcools, des courses et des jeux for a ruling. Any litigation respecting the awarding of a prize may be submitted to the Régie des alcools, des courses et des jeux or for the purpose of helping the parties reach a settlement. Employees and immediate family members of Torstar Corp. and D. L. Blair, Inc., their affiliates, subsidiaries and all other agencies, entities and persons connected with the use, marketing or conduct of this Contest are not eligible to enter. Taxes on prizes are the sole responsibility of winners. Acceptance of any prize offered constitutes permission to use winner's name, photograph or other likeness for the purposes of advertising, trade and promotion on behalf of Torstar Corp., its affiliates and subsidiaries without further compensation to the winner, unless prohibited by law.

6. Winners will be determined no later than November 15, 2001, and will be notified by mail. Winners will be required to sign an return an Affidavit of Eligibility form within 15 days after winner notification. Noncompliance within that time period may result in disqualification and an alternative winner may be selected. Winners of trip must execute a Release of Liability prior to ticketi and must possess required travel documents (e.g. passport, photo ID) where applicable. Trip must be completed by November 2002. No substitution of prize permitted by winner. Torstar Corp. and D. L. Blair, Inc., their parents, affiliates, and subsidiaries are not responsible for errors in printing or electronic presentation of Contest, entries and/or game pieces. In the event of printing or other errors which may result in unintended prize values or duplication of prizes, all affected game pieces or entries shall be null and void. If for any reason the Internet portion of the Contest is not capable of running as planned, including infection by computer virus, bugs, tampering, unauthorized intervention, fraud, technical failures, or any other causes beyond the control of Torstar Corp. which corrupt or affect the administration, secrecy, fairness, integrity or proper conduct of the Contest, Torstar Corp. reserves the right, at its sole discretion, to disqualify any individual who tampers with the entry process and to cancel, terminate, modify or suspend the Contest or the Internet portion thereof. In the event of a dispute regarding an online entry, the entry will be deemed submitted by the authorized holder of the e-mail account submitted at the time of entry. Authorized account holder is defined as the natural person who is assigned to an e-mail address by an Internet access provide online service provider or other organization that is responsible for arranging e-mail address for the domain associated with the submitted e-mail address. **Purchase or acceptance of a product offer does not improve your chances of winning**

7. Prizes: (1) Grand Prize—A Harlequin wedding dress (approximate retail value: $3,500) and a 5-night/6-day honeymoon trip Maui, HI, including round-trip air transportation provided by Maui Visitors Bureau from Los Angeles International Airport (winner is responsible for transportation to and from Los Angeles International Airport) and a Harlequin Romance Package, including hotel accomodations (double occupancy) at the Hyatt Regency Maui Resort and Spa, dinner for (2) two at Swan Court, a sunset sail on Kiele V and a spa treatment for the winner (approximate retail value: $4,000); (5) Five runner-up prizes of a $1000 gift certificate to selected retail outlets to be determined by Sponsor (retail value $1000 ea.). Prizes consist of only those items listed as part of the prize. Limit one prize per person. All prizes are valued in U.S. currency.

8. For a list of winners (available after December 17, 2001) send a self-addressed, stamped envelope to: Harlequin Walk Down Aisle Contest 1197 Winners, P.O. Box 4200 Blair, NE 68009-4200 or you may access the www.eHarlequin.com Web site through January 15, 2002.

Contest sponsored by Torstar Corp., P.O. Box 9042, Buffalo, NY 14269-9042, U.S.A.

PHWDACONT2

COMING SOON...

AN EXCITING
OPPORTUNITY TO SAVE
ON THE PURCHASE OF
HARLEQUIN AND
SILHOUETTE BOOKS!

**DETAILS TO FOLLOW
IN OCTOBER 2001!**

YOU WON'T WANT TO MISS IT!

PHQ401

HARLEQUIN®
Makes any time special®

Silhouette®
Where love comes alive™

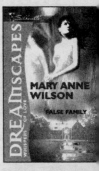

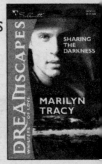